THE BEST AUSTRALIAN STORIES 2015

THE BEST AUSTRALIAN STORIES

2015

EDITED BY AMANDA LOHREY

Published by Black Inc.,
an imprint of Schwartz Publishing Pty Ltd
37–39 Langridge Street
Collingwood VIC 3066, Australia
enquiries@blackincbooks.com
www.blackincbooks.com

ISBN 9781863957786 (pbk)
ISBN 9781925203646 (ebook)

Cover design by Peter Long
Typesetting by Tristan Main

Printed in Australia by Griffin Press. The paper this book is printed on is certified against the Forest Stewardship Council ® Standards. Griffin Press holds FSC chain of custody certification SGS-COC-005088. FSC promotes environmentally responsible, socially beneficial and economically viable management of the world's forests.

Contents

Introduction

Amanda Lohrey

Since 1999 Black Inc. has published an annual anthology of the best short fiction to be found among Australian writing in a given year, or at least the best to have surfaced into visibility. In doing so it has provided an ongoing revelation of the richness and variety that Australian writers bring to the genre of the short story, a form so loose and so generous that almost anything can be attempted within its porous borders. Few rules apply, but if I had to cite one it would be this: by the last line of the story it must have opened out into something larger, and possibly – though not necessarily – more complex than anything we might have imagined or foreseen at the beginning.

When I was a child, my mother would take me to an Easter magic show staged by one of the leading department stores of the day, and my favourite trick was the one where the magician poured seemingly random ingredients into his top hat: flour, milk, eggs in their shells, lolly wrappers, sawdust and talcum powder. Then he would utter the magic formula to produce – a perfectly baked cake. This remains for me analogous to how writers work; they throw a whole lot of items into a melting pot and hope to achieve some kind of alchemy whereby the disparate elements combine into a satisfying form. It's hit or miss and even the best writers sometimes fail.

Whatever the eventual outcome, writers must begin by engaging the reader's interest, and they do this by striving to establish a certain conviction of tone: 'Listen to me, I know things, I have revelations to offer and I will deliver.' Some writers aim at generating a sense of urgency, others for an effect of calm, measured authority. A writer's style may be hectic or leisurely but, either way, conviction of tone is often an initial bluff; in the early drafts of a story writers are rarely in control of the process, and it's as much a journey of discovery for them as it is for the reader. Writer and reader, both, are explorers in the realm of consciousness, with the writer as forward scout, riding back from the frontiers of meaning to offer clues as to the lie of the land.

No two stories in this collection are alike, but in all of them the writer is bringing news. We think we know about Picasso, but John A. Scott revolves the idea of 'Picasso' like a mirror ball, to reveal new facets. We hear the phrase 'globalised citizen' tossed around, but Jo Lennan ('How Is Your Great Life?') creates a detailed portrait of the deracinated state and the ungrounded cultural fluidity of the newly globalised young that is more affecting in its pathos than any official case study. Eleanor Limprecht ('On Ice') suggests another dimension to the 'forgetting' of dementia. Cate Kennedy ('Puppet Show') reinvents Bali. Gay Lynch ('The Abduction of Ganymede') complexifies the notion of the good angel and asks: can there ever be such a thing as a pure motive? Omar Musa writes the subtlest of portraits of political corruption ('Supernova').

While the stories in this collection vary greatly, what they do have in common is an element of danger. At the heart of all stories is a concealed threat, a latent danger that tests our perception of the world, along with our nerve. If there is nothing to fear then there is no reason to read on, but while fear is generative of story it is not enough in itself to create a satisfying reading experience. A story that is wholly paranoid in character cannot render truth, because experience is complex, shot through with light as well as burdened by darkness. The paranoid narrative seeks to exploit our fears for cheap effects (like so much crime-based television), but it leaves a hollow feeling, as nourishing as a cake made of sawdust and ashes. The writers in this collection appealed to me because, in so many different ways, they demonstrate that they have mastered the art of confronting darkness without becoming its captive. Their artistry is a form of enlightenment. Magicians all, they have arrived at their own version of the magic formula, and I like to think the reader will find no sawdust here.

Amanda Lohrey

The Pilgrim's Way

Goldie Goldbloom

1.

Hendel remembers the way his father used to take his hand, before the arrival of the other, fake, son, and he tugs his older sister Grunie's skirt.

'I want to go inside,' Hendel says. 'I'm freezing.'

The Apuan Alps in Tuscany are cold at night, even in May, but Grunie ignores Hendel, who can be demanding and can hog their father's limited attention.

'Stop it,' she says, shaking off his hand. 'I'm listening to Dad's story.'

'Settle down, Hendel,' their father, Avner, says sharply, and then, smiling around at the Italian guests as if nothing has happened, he continues his tale. 'So when the police pulled me over, I told them the kids had chickenpox.'

'*Varicella*,' translates the elderly owner of their villa, Rachel.

The Italians, charmed by this wealthy, charismatic man, laugh. Under cover of darkness, Avner elbows his son, Hendel.

'I'm going to pee my pants,' Hendel whispers to his sister. 'I want my otter.'

But his sister, Grunie, is preoccupied with the way Perel, Avner's newest wife, is massaging her father's beard. She thought Jewish law strictly forbade such displays of eroticism. More than the chill Tuscan air, this gives her goosebumps.

Soon Avner and Perel will say they are tired and have to hit the hay, though her father never tires and the mattresses in the medieval villa they have rented aren't made of hay but are the ordinary kind that squeak and tinkle and make all kinds of noises, all night long. Grunie knows the mattresses talk because Avner and Perel are making love. The first night they were in Italy, Hendel woke up from Perel's screams and Grunie told him that Perel was having a nightmare, the kind Perel sometimes has because of Afghanistan, because of what happened to her there, even though it wasn't that kind of screaming. Hendel had wanted to go and offer his stepmother his stuffed otter but Grunie convinced him it was a terrible idea. She knows fucking is what married people do, and she knows the sounds that go along with it, but she's not really sure of the details. She's simultaneously curious and horrified by her curiosity. Her mother, back in the collapsing Victorian house in New Haven, does not make any noises at night, but then she's lived alone since Avner left to marry wife number two. Perel is wife number three.

'We didn't really have chickenpox,' Grunie says to the group around the table. 'It was just the scars. Left over from a few weeks before.'

She wants the Italians to know her father is a liar. She wants them not to trust him so much, not to laugh at his jokes. She doesn't know why she wants to hurt her father.

Avner, at forty-seven, has ropey runner's legs from marathoning around the streets of New York on weekends. His weedy beard is entirely grey, but he is still capable of enthralling women of any age, including his own daughter. He is far less successful with men, who suspect him, correctly, of having uncontrollable desires.

Avner ruffles Grunie's hair. 'It doesn't matter,' he says. 'It worked. I didn't get a speeding ticket. I still have a perfect driving record.'

Hendel huddles against Grunie. 'Please,' he begs. 'I have to go in. Come with me.' He doesn't want to have to remind her; he's scared of the dark, of the steep, narrow stone staircases between the houses, of the black spotted mastiff that lurks on the upper verandah of their villa, looking, in the dim light, as if it has three heads and six legs.

'I'll take you,' says Perel, who is only too aware of the role expected of stepmothers, even young ones with freshly lacquered nails. She had thought that she would be rescuing these children from a state of divorce-induced quasi-orphan-ness, but it turned out that they didn't need her or even like her most of the time.

'Please, Grunie?' Hendel doesn't even look at Perel's hand with its terrifying purple nails.

'Fine,' Grunie says, wishing Hendel's pyjamas didn't smell of pee, wishing he wasn't touching her at all and wanting to push him off. 'In a minute.'

Across the chestnut farm table lit by flickering candles is an Italian, barely twenty, who is studying architecture in Rome. He's dressed all in tight black, and his long black hair is pulled smoothly back into a ponytail. Grunie met him earlier, when Avner and Perel were having one of their lengthy 'conversations' behind the locked door of their bedroom. She and Hendel had picked their way down to the olive terraces to hunt for Roman coins. That's when she saw him, sitting propped up against one of those stone shrines to a dead saint, drawing in a little book. 'What are you doing?' she'd asked, coming up behind him quietly. He was startled. Grunie's real mother pays for ballet lessons so she can move like this, silently, sensually, but her father disapproves of girls dancing in front of mixed-gender crowds, and each year he attempts, in court, to put a stop to her lessons. At night, however, each of the nights they've been in Italy, Avner and Perel go dancing, and this hypocrisy, more than any of the others, enrages Grunie.

She is a tall, skinny girl and is wearing a floor-length cotton dress left over from the 1960s that she found in her mother's closet, and she bites her nails so badly that there's only a wink of nail left on each finger. She already knows that if she bends, flat-backed, from the waist, to pluck the red poppy growing near the Italian's foot, he will watch her. She has learnt, in this one week with her stepmother, how to swing her body from her hips in a way that, instead of avoiding the attention of men, invites it. Her stepmother Perel has three failed marriages, juicy hips and, no matter what, doesn't want to lose this husband.

It tickles Grunie to think of her father's discomfort when she and Hendel returned from their walk and Hendel blurted,

'Grunie met a boy-oy.' Here, this high in the mountains, the air itself invites her to be someone different to the girl who plays dress-ups with Hendel at home. She is not averse, either, to the attention this elicits from her father, who does not know what to make of this older person who hangs her training bras on the washing lines at the edge of the village and steals her stepmother's lipstick to paint both her and Hendel's faces. Grunie no longer cares if he disapproves of her, because she has discovered that this, too, grants her a dribble of fatherly attention. She has no idea why her mother's steady beam of love is far less fascinating to her than her father's erratic and flickering flame, but she feels for moths, for their craziness, for their obsession with something that could hurt them.

Now she glances across the table and catches the Italian, Massimiliano, looking at her again, and she arches her back in a yawn designed to show off her budding breasts.

Avner wants to slap her, or at the very least send her to her room. What he loves in every other woman, he hates in his daughter. He doesn't, of course, slap her, because he is afraid the Italians will think less of him. He wants Grunie to know she has displeased him with this display, and he waits for her apology. As usual, he is disappointed when she says nothing.

The Italian smiles frankly at Grunie, though he knows she's only a child. He is a citizen of the Vatican City, which has the youngest age of consent – twelve – of any province anywhere in the world. Grunie, he knows, is thirteen. He will dream about Grunie for a week, maybe two, until he returns to the Vatican City and his protector, where he will, once again, become immersed in a life among men. He, however, is no fag. For money, for schooling, he will do anything, but after he graduates he will leave his *padrone* and marry a young woman, a virgin from Stazzema, who will bear him three children before being hit by a Vespa as she tries to cross a street in the Oltrarno, where he will have his architecture firm. He will hear the ambulance but not know it is his wife who has died, ten metres from his office. One of his sons will convert to Judaism and, forty years from now, will counsel Grunie's only son, a patient struggling with being both gay and Orthodox. 'My father,' the therapist will say, 'slept with men, but he was straight. Maybe you are too.' This will be of small comfort when Grunie's son loses his position as the rabbi of a small congregation in Chicago, his house, his wife and his six children as a result of sleeping with this therapist.

'Come on,' Grunie says, taking Hendel's hand. 'I'll go with you now.'

She looks over her shoulder at the Italian man. 'It's so dark,' she says, but Massimiliano does not get the chance to offer to escort them. Avner rises first and says to Hendel, 'I'll take you.'

'Excellent,' Grunie says. 'I'll stay here then.'

'With your mother,' says Avner, staring straight at Massimiliano.

'Stepmother,' replies Grunie. 'My real mother is home in New Haven.'

'I want my otter,' says Hendel as Avner's hand tightens around his wrist.

They walk along a path made from broken clay roofing tiles and climb up a narrow staircase between the houses. None of the houses have windows that overlook this pathway. A statue of a woman holding a dead infant, her free hand over her face, looms from the shadows and Hendel leans his body against his father's. Avner experiences the child's shivers as a weakness. He pushes Hendel's shoulder away from him and feels fatherly doing so. Above them there is a crack and a hiss and the last light bulb in the lane blows out and they are left in darkness. Bats, just barely visible in the purple night, whistle by their heads. Hendel is aware that he is waiting for something to happen. Nearby, a donkey brays and sets off a volley of dog barks.

'She's turning into a *shiksa*,' says Avner, hurriedly hauling Hendel up the last stone stairs where anything could be hiding. Avner, it turns out, is also afraid of the dark.

'Who?' Hendel asks. He suspects his father means Perel, who harbours not-so-secret yearnings for the fast-food cheeseburgers and shellfish of her youth, but Avner surprises him by saying, 'Grunie.'

Hendel is oblivious to everyone's levels of religiosity. The thing he truly cares about is the Latin name for every living thing within a two-kilometre radius. Judaism is, for him, a given, the blackboard on which his life is drawn. He passes, without a pang, the most exquisite Italian restaurants, and runs to devour a vegetable soup prepared by Perel from stock cubes and frozen spinach.

'Grunie's good, Dad,' he says, even though he spends hours every day undermining his sister. He understands, just for a moment, that his father will eventually lose his connection with all of his children because he refuses to see them as individuals, and Hendel wants, with his whole heart, to delay this rejection for Grunie.

'Yes,' Avner says thoughtfully. 'But she has your mother's stubborn streak.'

They can no longer hear the laughter or the crackling of the fire at the party, and now, between the stone walls, the air feels dense and full of the strong, sharp scent of lemons.

'What about you? Don't you have a stubborn streak?' Hendel remembers his father telling him that in order to sell bibles successfully you have to knock on a hundred doors to get a single yes. Avner has, for the past fourteen years, won the national competition for bible salesmen and this trip to Italy is part of a salary package.

'Mine is the good kind of stubborn,' says Avner. 'Your mother's is just the irritating kind.'

'What about Perel?' asks Hendel. 'What kind is hers?'

Avner stops walking to think. 'I don't know,' he says. 'What do you think?

'Hers is the pan-throwing kind,' says Hendel.

'Yes,' says Avner.

'She can't help herself,' Hendel says. 'She's had a bad life. Afghanistan messed with her. She has pressures.'

Avner leans against the cold wall and sighs. After he divorced his first wife, his eldest son, who no longer talks to Avner, said, 'The Talmud says the first time you get married, you get what you pray for. The second time, you get what you deserve.' After a pause, this son added, 'I hope you get what you deserve.'

At the time, Avner had smiled and accepted it as a blessing, but lately he'd been thinking about those words. He'd bailed up one of his older daughters and asked her if she thought he'd been abusive when they all lived together, and when she'd said yes, he'd begun to cry. His latest conquest, Perel, has him afraid to flush the toilet without rolling over each poop and spraying it with Febreze. He is afraid of her PTSD-induced temper, and – for the first time – he understands what it is like to live with someone whose moods can swing so radically.

His son Hendel has more compassion for Perel than he does, understands that war changes people, and he finds this endearing. For once, he looks at his child and likes what he sees: the seriousness, the quirky sense of humour, the generosity.

'She's a piece of work,' says Avner. 'That's for sure.' It's the most he's ever admitted. 'Yes,' says Hendel eagerly, and this time when he leans against his father, Avner allows the closeness. Hendel is nine and he already knows all kinds of things about his father that he shouldn't. Among them this: a well-crafted lie can please his father. And though it's not his custom, his father sometimes tells the truth to please Hendel.

2.

It rains almost every day they are in Italy and their house is so high in the Alps that when Perel looks outside in the morning, it's as if she has gone blind. Clouds surround the villa, pressing damply on the windows, the same grey as the stuccoed stone walls within. Swallows sing invisibly through the rain. Bees emerge from underneath the terracotta roof tiles during a brief lull and one falls when it is struck by a late droplet. It seems right to Perel that it should rain during a free trip.

To keep warm she lies in bed with the electric blanket turned on high, reading a book of poems Avner bought for her in Florence, in the Libreria delle Donne, on Via Fiesolana, also on a rainy day.

'What are those stories about?' Hendel asks, and Perel hands the book to him.

He reads haltingly out loud: 'Let the world's sharpness, like a clasping knife, shut in upon itself and do no harm.'

He asks, 'Why does *morbida* mean soft, and not death?' but since Afghanistan, since the shouts and the cries of the men who arrived at the hospital in many pieces, Perel is not curious about language and is also in a bad mood because she is unable to update her social networking sites and because today, the first of May, is a national holiday in Italy, despite being a Wednesday, and nothing is open.

'I could sleep at home for the same price,' she says. 'And be warm.'

'I'll make you warm, my princess,' says Avner, leaning over the bed to kiss her. Hendel backs away and puts a finger down his throat and makes a gagging noise. The wind rises and comes fluttering from the tiny bathroom, as if a bird is trapped and beating itself against the stones. The bath is festooned with damp bras and stockings and jocks, stirred by the wind, almost alive. Perel generally manages to avoid interacting with Hendel, whom she thinks of as anal and a space cadet. She warns her own child, who is four years old and still malleable, not to go near Hendel. She tells him that Hendel is a weirdo. He appears to be the kind of boy who can look at her and see everything she doesn't want him to know.

Perel conceived her only child while she was in Afghanistan, three years before she met Avner, when she directed a medical clinic in an FOB near Kandahar, through an excess of sympathy for a young guy from Indiana. The soldier wasn't even eighteen. He'd been blown into several large pieces before he could get married, before he could even walk into a bar and get a beer. He'd cried and cried in the emergency tent when he thought he was bleeding to death, saying that his death would kill his mother too, that there was no-one to carry on the family name. He hadn't died just then. It had been later, after Perel got pregnant, that a box containing five hundred Ken dolls wearing fatigues had fallen out of a military helicopter and hit him on the head as he lay outside the hospital, getting some fresh air. Perel's little boy is all that's left of the Indiana man-child-soldier now and she wants the world to be whole for him, beautiful and shiny and fresh in a way that it isn't really but that she wishes it were.

Hendel doesn't know all of this; he just knows that Perel throws frying pans when she smells burning meat and that she is ultra-protective of the spoiled stepbrother. He thinks of Perel as the Evil Stepmother, and spends many evenings telling his mother exaggerated horror stories about Perel's bingeing on macarons from Paris, her obsession with bikini waxing, the irritating side hugs she gives him as he passes.

Their villa is the second last in a line of five, perched on the edge of Monte Spranga, at about five hundred metres above the Mediterranean, which they can see on a clear day.

Most of the village is empty – it's too early for tourists – except for an elderly Englishman, Basil, who makes marble sculptures in the old Etruscan tower, and a young Scotsman,

Rupert, who has been planting the huge terracotta pots with flowers for the season.

Perel hasn't looked twice at Rupert. Once was enough to know that he was exactly the kind of man she finds attractive, the kind of man the Indiana soldier had been before his arms and leg came off, and since she is now travelling with Avner and Avner's two youngest children, since she is a married woman, she avoids Rupert's stares and silently grits her teeth when he whistles underneath her window as he beds geraniums.

When it stops raining, about an hour before nightfall, Perel ventures outside wearing her oldest yoga pants and a thin wife-beater, not wanting to provoke anything, but, sensing Rupert's eyes brushing her bra-less chest, she stiffens. Every time she gets a half glimpse of him he seems to be smirking, and this fills her with shame and frustration. She is sure he sees her as a gold-digger, a woman who wants trips to Italy and pedicures and new cars instead of a satisfying job and a real relationship and children who love her. She wants him to know that she sacrificed her medical career to give someone the last wish of his life. She wants him to know that she is still sending charity to the people of Afghanistan, to their women's clinics. When she sees Rupert looking weedy Avner up and down, she imagines that the gardener somehow knows she is thinking about the Indiana soldier when she comes.

She wants, desperately, to give Rupert the finger, but since she is supposed to be taking Hendel and Grunie to see the pool now that it's stopped raining, she takes their hands instead. Her middle fingers, the ones she wanted to flash at Rupert, feel smothered in the palms of the children.

In the tower, Basil is throwing clay out of the window and yelling. He's tried for years to live up to the reputation of the sculptor who restored the village but has, so far, only made a series of marble cubes that now dot the long grass, looking like dice that have been run over with tanks. Each night, he and Rupert repair to the village of Agliano to eat pizza and drink beer and whine about the bad manners of the Americans. Occasionally they are joined by Lara, the villa's cook, who has been ousted from her job temporarily since the Americans are Jews who keep kosher; who prepare their own food even when they are on holiday, even though their meals smell, to Lara, like cat food. Lara is desired neither by Basil, who has not had the urge in over a decade, nor by Rupert, who desires Perel and has told them so, repeatedly. 'Have you seen her legs?' he asks them, whistling. 'I'd take them fried, on a pizza.'

'Can I go and talk to Rachel and Julia?' Hendel asks Perel as he dodges a piece of flying clay on the way to the pool. He only wants to search the owners' home for his stuffed otter, which has been misplaced since the first day of the trip, but Perel is afraid he will ask the eighty-year-old women, again, if they are married and if they have children and would they adopt a little American boy if only for a week and how would pregnancy work for them since they are two women and they don't produce seed. When the two elderly Italians heard the serious little boy say 'seed' they both blushed. Perel cannot understand why they don't ban Hendel from their villa. Under the circumstances, she would.

3.

When Perel and the children return, after frowning at the mould-clogged pool, an hour before sunset, Hendel asks again if he can go for a real walk. All day he has been mapping the villa. The place is filled with hard edges. Thirteen stone steps down from his father's bedroom to the living room, three more steps down from there to the bathroom with its low ceiling, adequate for Hendel but causing Avner to stoop. A step up to the bath and two steps up to the toilet where even he, nine years old, can hit his head on the heavy chestnut beams if he forgets and stands up quickly.

Beyond the bathroom, another two stone steps down to Hendel and Grunie's room. A leather pillow has been nailed to the lintel, presumably because taller people smack their heads on the stone when they go down into the room. Seventeen stone steps down from the living room to the dining room and another four tiny steps down to the kitchen, which must, in former times, have been the cow byre. Forty-seven steep and uneven stone steps down to the main road, a road that is barely wide enough for human beings. Their car is parked two kilometres down the track, near the entrance to La Via Francigena, the Pilgrim's Way.

Before leaving the United States, Hendel stepped on a nail. He didn't tell anyone until they were on the plane and then only because he couldn't get his shoe back on. His stepmother, Perel, had been a nurse in Afghanistan and Rwanda, places where people did horrifying things to each other, and she told Avner they didn't need to waste a day of their trip stuck in an emergency room, getting billed through the nose for a tetanus shot. She could handle it. So each night she reopened Hendel's wound by poking it with a just-extinguished match. It's the one fortunate thing about all this rain, Perel thinks, because otherwise Avner might have to carry the little hypochondriac all over Florence. I can't believe she is really a nurse, Hendel thinks. She would have been perfect in Auschwitz. Hendel has affected a limp and a series of grimaces so they can't forget his injury. The people Perel worked with in Afghanistan never complained when she performed this procedure with the match on them, in the absence of vaccinations. They brought her presents and kissed her like they meant it.

'Please may I go?' Hendel asks again, and Perel, annoyed at the wasted day, snaps, 'Yes. If you go with your sister.' Perhaps now, with the children out from under her feet and Avner asleep, she can get some colour on the upstairs porch. Before the children are even out the door, she has forgotten about them. Below her, just visible, is Rupert, pulling up wild garlic.

Down at the car park, Hendel steps between two houses and beckons to Grunie. 'It's this way,' he says, though how he knows, she's not sure. The path is very narrow, and at this hour, seven, it's abandoned except for an old man admiring his peonies.

'*Sera,*' he says, straightening.

'*È sera,*' says Hendel, serious as always.

'*Sì.*' The man smiles, though whether at the boy's Italian, or at the child's observation that it is, indeed, evening, it is hard to say.

'*Come si dice?*' asks Hendel, pointing to a purple flower growing out of the stone wall. The old man shrugs. '*Margherita,*' he says.

Hendel repeats the word after him, takes a few more steps and then asks again, '*Come si dice?*' This time it's a tall hedge of rosemary.

'*Rosmarino,*' says the man. He smiles, wishing his own grandsons showed some interest in plant life. Instead, they are off chasing tail in Camaiore. He continues walking with the boy and Grunie trails behind, resentful that she can't understand what they are talking about and angry that no-one forced her to learn a few words in Italian before she came here.

'*Recinto*,' says the man. '*Felci* ... *olivi* ... *clematis* ... *violetta* ... *castagne* ... *papavero* ... *lauro*.' In his twenties Hendel will leave Judaism and study marine biology in San Luis Obispo and Woods Hole. He'll never forget the stuffed otter he lost in Italy or the old man who named the plants for him. He'll call chestnuts *castagne* his whole life.

When the old man pulls down a branch so that Hendel can pick some kind of citrus that looks vaguely like an orange, Hendel won't mention the sharp thorn that drives down under his nail, all the way to the cuticle. It won't feel right to him, to ruin the nameless feeling that has sprung up between him and the Italian. The old man will think, from the boy's tears, that Hendel is strangely moved by his gesture with the fruit, and he'll say words excusing himself that Hendel won't understand and then the Italian will walk back the way they came.

The track, though, is clearly marked with small lime arrows that have been painted on the stone walls, so Hendel and Grunie continue their walk. 'Look,' says Grunie, who is in front. 'The clouds are falling down the mountain.' The path has begun to rise steeply between two high earthen walls, covered in ferns and wild flowers and grass. It is no longer stone underfoot, but a slippery wet clay, ridged with pebbles and branches, and now, instead of being wide enough for a person, the path is only just wide enough for Hendel's sneaker. A large woodpecker flies overhead. It's a bird Hendel knows, but he doesn't call out its Latin name as he usually does, because the hole in his foot is hurting again.

When Hendel had opened the shutters that morning and stood there on one foot, taking in, between the falling clouds, slivers of the spectacular view down to the valley and across to Pedona and the Mediterranean Sea, he'd heard a *chit chit chit*. It was a swallow building a nest in the gutter just above the window. *Hirundo rustica*. Seeing him, the bird hovered at the open window, less than twenty centimetres away from Hendel's face, in a way that he had previously associated with hummingbirds. It cocked its head to look at him with each eye. Opening its beak, it said again, *chit chit*. Then it flew away. In all that time, Hendel had been drinking in the details of the swallow's chest feathers, the delicately spread tail, the talons clenched into its belly, its glossy blue-black head and gleaming white-rimmed eyes. What the bird had decided about him, Hendel didn't know. He couldn't decide anything about himself either. In its strangeness, the bird, *la rondine*, had seemed like a sign, something talking to him from his grown-up life, but Hendel hadn't yet learnt the language. The bird remained a bird.

Now Grunie and Hendel come over a rise and the path widens out a little before entering a wood. Hendel is limping, and because of the faint sounds Hendel makes with each step, Grunie begins to think it may be a real limp. Between the trees it is very dark, and both children think of their mother, at home in New Haven, writing in the bathtub at night, and they wish she were with them. Hendel, because he is fair-minded, tries also to wish that Perel were with them. To the right there is a ravine, perhaps a hundred metres deep, and to the left, a series of crumbling caves cut back into the mountain, each of which exhales dank unhappiness.

'I'm going back,' says Grunie suddenly. She doesn't say, 'This is creepy,' because Hendel is younger than she is and might be scared, but she wants to. When she said goodbye, back in New Haven, her mother whispered in her ear, 'Please watch out for Hendel,' and Grunie takes this responsibility seriously. Her father sometimes dislikes Hendel, and Perel is afraid of him. It's up to Grunie to do all the loving while they are in Italy.

'Okay,' says Hendel, and he turns back, just as it begins to rain again. The visibility drops. Grunie, leading, is no longer sure they are on the path, but she is unwilling to admit to this. She is watching out for Hendel.

After ten minutes of walking in silence though, they find themselves on the steeply descending narrow path they remember. They drop between the high green walls, only this time, instead of walking on slippery clay, there is a cascade of muddy water flooding down the bottom of the gully. Hendel and Grunie stop. There does not appear to be any other way off the mountain, the water in the gully is already knee deep and the rain is heavier. The last rays of the sun illuminate the blades of grass at the tops of the walls and, despite the noise of the water, Grunie can hear Hendel's quick breaths, full of pain from his foot.

'Damn,' she says, before remembering that she is responsible for Hendel's moral education too. 'Darn it.'

Hendel pushes past her, oblivious to her concerns, and puts his sore foot into the stream. 'The water's cold,' he sighs. 'But not too strong.' 'Come back,' Grunie says. Hendel's feet fall into the stream, *plop plop*. Grunie is now alone at the top of the path. She looks up to check whether she can see their villa, or the tower where the madman is throwing clay, or even their mountain but the clouds have closed in again. Looking down, she realises she can no longer see her brother either.

'Hendel?' she calls into the swirling greyness.

'I'm fine,' he calls back. Despite the rushing water and the fog and his pain, he speaks with the same calm, slightly distant voice he always uses. He might as well be saying that they have chicken for dinner. 'Come down. The water is safe.'

She expects Hendel to return for her, but when he doesn't, she puts one foot into the water. Her flimsy sandals are useless now. Inwardly she curses Perel, who would not let her buy Doc Martins. Let Perel, who wanted men like Rupert to look at her, wear strappy sandals. She, Grunie, was a practical sort who needed shit-kicking boots.

She no longer notices the flowers sprouting from the walls of the track. In silence, she picks her way down, one hand on the muddy bank to support herself. The water is thigh high now, pushing hard against the backs of her legs. Small twigs are tangling in a dam behind her when she hears a splash above the din and then a yelp.

'Hendel,' she says softly. She has always imagined that he will die by drowning. As a newborn he could float on his back without any support, and their mother would sometimes leave him for a few seconds, to grab the soap. Now Grunie is frozen, the way she was frozen the first time Perel threw a frying pan at their father. She feels drugged, although she will have no idea what that really means until she travels to Israel in her late teens and smokes pot with some friends. Her reactions are slow and her limbs are numb, whether from the cold water and the rain or from fear, she isn't sure.

'Stand up!' she calls. She tries to run but slips onto one knee, the water curling up over her back and drenching her head. 'Hendel?'

A clap of thunder, almost directly overhead, drowns out any answer he might have given. 'Hendel!' she calls again, running now, slipping and sliding, once completely under the water. The sandals are gone. Her feet are cut. Hendel is a good swimmer, better than her, but he's smaller too. More likely to be clobbered by a branch. She rounds a bend and trips over something, a root or a stone, and sprawls forward, hitting her head against what can only be Hendel's own head, and then she pushes upwards into the air, dragging, with all her puny strength, her brother. Her arm, now, is around his waist. He is retching. She is crying. Her legs have disappeared in all this water and Hendel's whole body shakes once before his eyes roll back in his head and he slumps in a wave against the wall.

Grunie knows she has to stay calm. She's been to Girl Scout camp and can tie fourteen knots. She believes this might be her chance to save a life, but she also believes she might die trying. She thinks she is too young to die; she's never been kissed, not even by Massimiliano, who would, if he got the chance. She's never had a child, written a book, been to Timbuktu. Death seems like something much too small, too simple, on the Pilgrim's Way in the Apuan Alps. She thinks if they die it will be her fault, but if they live she will still be blamed. Grunie clutches Hendel to her and Hendel's pointed little chin digs into her shoulder. His hair smells of wet feathers. Grunie's stomach fills with tears as cold as the rain that is still falling. 'It's okay,' she says, patting him awkwardly, not sure if he is breathing. 'I've got you now.'

When their family is reunited and eating macaroni and cheese by the tiny wood-burning stove, everyone seems to have forgotten Perel's role in the accident. Hendel has had a near-death experience and is going on about cosmic whales, winged otters radiating light and the harmony of all living things. This is all he can talk about now that he has stopped coughing up muddy water. It's all he'll talk about for years to come. People will get sick of hearing about it before he turns thirty.

Everyone has a chance to pat the old Italian man on the back. He, not Grunie, is the hero. Just as she suspected, all the blame has been laid on her, despite the fact that she hauled her brother out of the water. Just because the Italian was the one who reached down from the top of the wall and lifted first Hendel and then

Grunie to safety, and then carried Hendel in his arms the three kilometres to their villa, he gets all the recognition. And Grunie gets the complaints. How could you let him walk in the forest alone? Why did you leave when it was getting dark? Why didn't you ask permission? Grunie knows she could point the finger at Perel but decides to shoulder the blame and keep Perel's secret. The water has changed her, too.

She knows that Perel did not get any colour from her hour of sunshine, but is still smiling. Perel's face, Grunie notices, is glowing, and despite the near-tragedy, her stepmother hums 'La vie en rose' to herself. None of today's drama has touched the place where Perel has gone to in her mind and, for the first time in her adult life, Grunie feels a mature suspicion forming.

The two elderly owners have appeared, bearing elderberry wine and a small panna cotta, 'for the martyr', they say. And other neighbours have arrived too, including a girl from the village below theirs, and twins from the village below that one. None of them speak English and they are unwanted, so they lay their gifts silently on the table and go outside, to the covered porch, to mutter among themselves. Hendel, shrouded in a down quilt, leaves Grunie and floats outside, into the dark.

'*Mi chiamo* Harold,' he lies. 'Michela.' 'Donatella,' say the twins. 'Jack,' says the other boy, and the twins frown at him. Grunie comes outside to protect Hendel. She's hoping the other children have heard her part in the rescue and think well of her, but instead they move away from her and make a gesture with their hands that looks like it might be sign language for I love you except their faces do not say I love you. She guesses, correctly, it really means they are afraid of her, of her bad luck. Hendel is still trying out his basic Italian vocabulary, trying earnestly to connect, and she is beginning to hate him for it.

'Come inside,' she says. 'You'll get sick.'

'You're not my mother,' he says, turning his back on her. He doesn't remember that she pulled him from the water. He only remembers the way she was screaming when the Italian was carrying him, how annoyingly shrill her voice was, how it distracted him from the glowing otters and cosmic whales.

'I'm Mum's representative,' Grunie says. 'Here.'

'No,' Hendel says. 'You're not. Perel is.'

The other children sit still. They don't know what the conversation is about, but they follow the gestures. Grunie has her hand on Hendel's shoulder. He shakes her off. She pushes him. He pulls her hair and screams something in her face.

'Dad!' Grunie yells, because, despite the two new wives, despite Avner's preference for the child that isn't even his, despite his frequent absences and distorted stories and see-through lies, he is still her father, and right now she needs her own rescue.

'It must have been hard, lifting your brother from the water,' a shaky voice comes from the darkest corner of the porch. Julia and her companion, Rachel, lean into the faint light. 'You were very brave, my dear,' Julia says, placing her frail hand on Grunie's. 'We heard all about it.'

'People can lift Volkswagens off their loved ones when they need to,' says Rachel. 'But it's still wonderful. A miracle.'

'Your mother should have been watching you,' says Julia.

'Stepmother,' says Grunie. 'She was resting. On the porch.'

'No,' says Rachel. 'She wasn't. I came up here looking for Rupert. I couldn't find him. I rested for a minute on your porch before going back down the hill and your mother wasn't there.'

'Oh,' says Grunie, and again, inside her, the new Grunie shakes, and droplets of her innocence spray out from her body. 'Where could she have been?'

Hendel is still muttering about the things he saw floating under the water. 'They had cream-coloured wings,' he says. 'In tatters.'

The rain, still falling, trickles into a rain barrel at the edge of the porch. There are goldfish in the barrel and a flowering iris and a fat yellow snail. Grunie thinks that in New Haven small children would drown in these barrels, trying to catch the goldfish, so it wouldn't be allowed. Here, everything is allowed. Even giving her and Hendel small glasses of wine to put them to sleep, which is what their father does now, coming out onto the porch with two jam jars full of ruby liquid.

'Drink,' Avner says. 'It'll put hair on your chest.' He didn't hear Grunie call for him when Hendel pulled her hair, but even if he did, he wouldn't have come out to help her. He believes in the survival of the fittest.

'I don't want hair on my chest,' says Grunie. She saw him through the window, canoodling with Perel. She saw her father ignore her call. She believes that divorce shouldn't exist.

'Your mother has hair on her chest,' Avner says, but even he knows it's because his ex-wife has gone through an early menopause and besides having hair on her chest, has a small reddish moustache too.

'Dad,' says Hendel. 'Will you put me to bed tonight? Not Perel?'

For once, Avner is pleased to be asked. Pleased for the chance to be the most desired parent, even if it's only a choice between him and the lacklustre Perel. Hendel waves a shy goodbye to the other children who think his name is Harold. Avner says goodnight to Julia and Rachel. The old women haven't said a word since he came out onto the porch. Julia's hand still covers Grunie's. Grunie is glad for the warmth, for the notice. But she is worried about her brother, about his fixation on wings. She doesn't know how long he was underwater, or even if he had decided it was easier to swim downstream and she, by falling over him, was the one to nearly drown him. 'Shut up,' Hendel said, when she tried to talk to him about it. 'That's not the important part.' But it was. It was important to her.

Avner doesn't know what to say to Hendel. He doesn't feel guilty, exactly, since he is never the one who is in charge of his children, but he feels something, and he is having a hard time finding a name for it. 'Want me to hold your hand?' he asks, hoping to fill the silence between them. Inside, the house smells faintly of salt, as if the stones are sweating even though they are icy cold. Avner waits for Hendel to take his hand and then, when his son doesn't touch him, he tells himself that Hendel is too old for hand-holding. The strange feeling in him, however, swells. He can taste it, just at the back of his throat, and he tries, again and again, to swallow it down.

'It's lucky that old man was out there,' Avner says, swallowing.

'Yes,' says Hendel, sensing that his father wants something from him. He is curious about the skittering sounds coming from above them, on the roof, but far more concerned with pleasing his father. It's not often he has Avner to himself and today it's happened twice.

'The word for chestnut in Italian is *castagna*,' Hendel says.

'Is it?' says Avner. He is opening cupboards, looking for an extra blanket.

'Thank you for bringing us to Italy,' says Hendel, trying to re-engage his father.

Avner is angry at his son. All along, during the walk up the stairs from the kitchen, he has been angry, he decides. The strange slippery emotion at the back of his throat must be anger.

'What the hell possessed you to go on that walk?' he asks. 'Don't you have a sore foot? Or is that pretend?'

In answer, Hendel sits on the topmost step and peels off his sock. He lifts his foot up for his father to see the hole, now the size of a dime and as deep as the head of a match. It is filled with pus and crusted blood.

'Beautiful,' says Avner, but he sits down next to Hendel and pulls the little boy into his lap. There is a feeling then, which neither has experienced in a long time and barely recognise. They both want the feeling, whatever it is, to last.

Hendel, leaning against his father's hard chest, thinks that it is Perel who drains this feeling from between Avner and him, and so he says, 'Perel told me I could go.' He still hopes his father will divorce the Evil Stepmother and get back together with his quiet, moustachioed mother.

'You could have died,' says Avner. 'Perel would never have let you go. Don't make excuses for your own bad behaviour!' Avner's breath is fast and high. Hendel recognises the signs of his father's impending temper, the tight white lips, the stare jumping out at him like heated razors, and he slips from Avner's lap.

'You don't have to say *Shema* with me,' he says. 'I can put myself to bed.' He had hoped his father would sing the prayer with him and turn on the electric blanket and draw the sheets up to his chin and rub his back until he fell asleep but he knows it all went down the tube the moment he mentioned Perel. Hendel doesn't understand, quite, that in the competition between Perel and him for Avner's love and attention, he is losing. He doesn't yet know that Perel – beautiful, sexy, damaged Perel – is a trophy his father feels he has won, just like this trip to Italy.

Hendel happened as a result of sex, not even particularly satisfying sex, with Avner's first wife (it was an arranged marriage), who is fat now, and manly. Perel was won away from a dozen other suitors because he, Avner, with all his money and his muscles, was a catch. To keep Perel from the kind of men who find her so desirable that they beg her to have their babies, or haul her down among the flower pots, Avner always has to put her first, before his children, before even himself. Hendel won't know this for another six painful years.

Avner feels both rage at Hendel's attempt to blame Perel and some other sensation, more nebulous. He wonders, briefly, why Perel didn't go with the children, and then rejects the thought as being unfaithful. He wants, more than anything, to return to the moment on the stairs when he felt the way he thinks real fathers feel, with their cheeks in their children's hair at bedtime, but he too knows the moment is lost.

The morning after the accident, Grunie opens the shutters before Hendel wakes up from his dreams of spangled humpback whales sliding through the night sky. Grunie puts her hand on his forehead and discovers he has a slight fever. The swallow returns, but only when Grunie leaves the room to tell Avner that Hendel is sick. The swallow looks in at the boy several times as Hendel lies resting after his ordeal. His foot is propped up on the Italian dictionary he'd begged his mother to buy. Hendel doesn't wonder about the bird any more, about its potential for symbolism. He knows there is something wrong with a bird that keeps flying into human space.

In the afternoon he wakes to a sense that someone is in the room with him and he hopes it is his father. He hopes that Avner will try to connect with him again, but when Hendel opens his eyes, he sees the swallow, perched on the open windowsill, tilting its head this way and that. It leaps into the air, makes several tours of the room, and then swoops out of the window. Wow, thinks Hendel. Wow. It likes me. He reaches down to pick at the scab that is forming over the hole in his foot. It stings, but it's a good kind of sting.

When he rolls over to turn on the electric blanket, the swallow returns, and this time it lands on his headboard, right above Hendel's face. As it turns, he gets an elegant view of the bird's anus. One well-aimed squirt would hit him in the eye. But this is a well-behaved swallow. No-one is crapping on Hendel today.

Meanjin

Picasso: A Shorter Life

John A. Scott

1 Smoke

1881 Don Salvador blows cigar smoke into the nostrils of his stillborn nephew, making of him a living soul. Thus, a marvellous being comes into the world – a magus, with the moral inclinations of a corpse. Looking back at his life, everything seems to have happened swiftly – a tumble of betrayals, marriages; infidelities of every kind. Perhaps biography's unforgiving distillation lends to these liaisons the sense of lasting no more than a matter of months. Not so. These attachments are stretched over years. It is crucial here you understand the time scale. The distortions, the inherent cruelty of slowness.

2 Olga

1917 For a man with no interest in music outside of flamenco, who judges dancing as immoral and depraved, it might seem ill-considered to take a ballerina for a wife. Olga Khokhlova comes to Paris with Diaghilev's troupe: one of those dancers he likes to include from a higher social class. The newlyweds take rooms in rue La Boétie, amidst the antique shops and galleries. P^{so} dresses now from Savile Row, in double-breasted tweeds. He slides a gold watch from his pocket. Paints his wife as would a Realist. 'I want to recognise my face,' she insists in cow-accented French, intolerable as his own. She screams, drinks coffee. Both, it seems, obsessively. She bears him a child, Paulo, in whom P^{so} has no interest beyond the age of four. The artist describes his son as 'ordinary' – that most dismissive of character traits – at one stage employing him as his chauffeur. But he drinks. Dying at fifty-four from cirrhosis of the liver, a legacy of drug and alcohol abuse.

3 Marie-Thérèse

1927 Pso (as Andalusian flâneur, out this early afternoon, freeing himself of Olga's screech and clattering), saunters near the Metro OPÉRA to find, among 'the apparition of these faces' labouring upwards to a bitter January air, a seventeen-year-old girl, Greek-nosed, with eyes of blue-grey. He grabs her arm, pulls her from the flow. *I'm Picasso!* he announces, *We are going to do great things together.* Her name is Marie-Thérèse. She has never heard of Picasso; knows nothing of Modern Art, preferring BICYCLING, GYMNASTICS and MOUNTAINEERING. He takes her virginity at a children's camp in Dinard and, finding her sufficiently submissive, installs her in an apartment in rue La Boétie across the road from Olga. His sexual demands are bizarre. Some make her laugh at the thought of them – but he hates her laughter. He prefers to keep her tearful. 'Most of it was sadism,' Marie-Thérèse confirms. 'First rape, then work. Nearly always like that.'

4 Minotaur

1930 Ambroise Vollard, collector, art dealer, commissions from Pso 100 etchings in the neoclassical style. Before too long the Minotaur appears. First, sharing a saucer of champagne with a bearded sculptor, then joining him in bed with his model. Six weeks later Marie-Thérèse tells Pso she is pregnant. The artist is terrified. Is it possible that by the sheer force of his genius one of his creations has impregnated his current lover? Needless to say, the unthinkable comes to pass. A male child, covered with blood-red oils, is born to the young girl and the Spanish artist. Vollard feels in some way responsible for what has happened and mother and child are quickly secreted in his house in Le Tremblay-sur-Mauldre, ten miles from Versailles. For several months the creature remains hairless; what will be horns are barely knuckle-like lumps. The genitals, an inheritance from Pso, are fully formed and would be of prodigious size even for an adult. From the first, Marie-Thérèse deems it satanic. She quickly learns how it shies away from candlelight, rears, swivelling aside with astonishing dexterity. Mercifully, the horned boy dies, *par hazard*, glimpsing its own grotesqueness in a glass – death by self-sight – a condition previously noted in creatures half-bull, half-human. Later, as a consequence, Marie-Thérèse always ensures a candle burns when P^{so} demonstrates an urge for rutting. The candle is an addition which the artist finds exciting – this fragile token of romance to complement buggery.

5 Dora Maar

1936 Then there is the matter of the Jugoslavian photographer. Henriette Theodora Markovich. P^{so} is introduced to her by Éluard. He has seen her just a few days back at the café Deux-Magots. Seen her, black-haired, dark-eyed. Born in Tours, she tells him, the same year as his *Les Demoiselles d'Avignon*. He takes her hand. She is wearing long black gloves embroidered with roses. Stained dark, the lace, at the webbing. He has seen the gloves as well, on that earlier occasion, folded, laid aside. Away from her splayed hand pressed palm-down on the wooden table top. She had been playing a familiar Jugoslavian game. Stabbing rapidly with a knife between her fingers. Blood already flowing from a wound close to the second finger's knuckle. She seemed fascinated by the risk, the sudden pain. He recalls her now a sometime mistress of Bataille. P^{so} enquires as to whether she might present him with a gift of her gloves? That night, that week, sleeplessly, he dreams of her, at her forbidden games. He, peering out from beneath a table, sees her – spectacled, black-ribboned at her neck. Sees her in that bourgeois drawing room with its rugs and its striped wallpaper. Sees her riding on the back of Bataille. What mightn't she do. He falls abandonedly into imaginings – thrusting in the air, his penis wrapped in the silk of that black glove. P^{so}, priapic, rapacious, sees it all from where he sits cross-legged beneath the table. The little Andalusian boy.

6 Commission

1937 As part of a commission to create a mural-sized painting for the Spanish Pavilion at the *Exposition Internationale des Arts et Techniques*, Juan Larrea acquires an appropriately sized studio for Picasso's exclusive use: the giant top-floor attic of 7 rue des

Grands-Augustins, where Balzac had written his 'The Unknown Masterpiece'. Its floor is paved with small red tile hexagons, many of which have been broken in clusters beneath the weight of three centuries worth of ponderous furniture. There is a view (opening up the pair of twelve-paned windows) across geometrical hills of rooftops, chimney stacks; ridges of terraces skittled with chimney pots. Marie-Thérèse remains in Vollard's Tremblay-sur-Mauldre house. During the week P^{so} sleeps at his new studio, still within the range (it comes to him, a tinnitus) of Olga's screams. Meanwhile, a street away in rue Savoie, Dora waits to be summoned.

7 Painful

1937 In his paintings Marie-Thérèse grows fatter, uglier. One night he enters the bedroom to see her seated (half-turned back from the dressing table at his footfall), her face that of a victim of some monstrous stroke, her nose and forehead become one swollen, drooping, doughy, appendage. Over the following days the dismemberment begins – eyes, fingers, nipples, float on a white background. Now every part of her is obliterated. He draws close to his audience: 'It must be painful for a girl to see in a painting that she is on the way out.' Meanwhile, with little more than a month to go before the *exposition*, P^{so} still has no subject for the Spanish Pavilion's empty forty metres.

8 Guernika (1937)

Out from the fields beyond Guernika, barely audible above the relentless bomb-bursts, the fire-roar and the collapse of masonry, comes the sound of mechanical ratatat and the hideous silent chorus of high-pitched bleating. The German aeroplanes are machine-gunning flocks of sheep.

9 The Effect of Fear

1937 Late May, with *Guernica* still a cartoon laid out in black and grey, P^{so} holds a luncheon at the Grands-Augustins studio. The table is set up, centred on the French doors. Seated before him are Giacometti, Ernst, Breton, Roland Penrose and Henry Moore. Late in the afternoon, over the plate of cheeses, P^{so} begins a monologue.

'The woman running from the little cabin on the right,' and he leans back in his chair, 'with one hand held in front of her. Let me tell you,' he says, rising, 'there is something missing there.'

He leaves the room, coming back with a roll of toilet paper which he sticks on the woman's hand.

'There,' he says, addressing the table, 'that leaves no doubt about the commonest effect of fear.' He laughs. And everyone laughs with him.

10 Balls

1937 There is a Dora Maar photograph of P^{so} from the midsummer days spent at Mougins. The artist is seated, legs apart. One can see his balls shifting quietly in the Mediterranean air, as might buoys in the slightest of swells. Clocking against each other. Barely held in check by his swimming costume.

11 A Game of Cards

1937 P^{so} fans open his hand: a king of hearts and four queens. He smiles. But the pleasure is short-lived. At their first sight of him, the Queens begin to weep. Now they sob. Soon it will be clearly heard by those around the table in the smoke-filled room. Now, their miniscule tears fall to the tabletop. He yells at his cards to be quiet. *You are ruining everything*, he bellows. But already it is too late – *Hey, Pablo*, comes the voice of one of the players. *You wouldn't have the Weeping Queens again, would you?* Over time it becomes a stock phrase with which to taunt him: Picasso's got the *Queens* today.

12 Nocturne: Night Fishing in Antibes

1939 Back from Amboise Vollard's funeral, P^{so} finds a new guest at his Antibes studio – Jacqueline Lamba, wife of Breton, and Dora's friend since Art School. The two women spend days together on the beach. Here they are, this August night, promenading, nearly at the quay's edge. Dora with a double-headed ice-cream in her right hand, a bicycle wheeled by her left. There is a grace to them. The grace and serenity of a slow dance (somewhere a blues trumpet is playing, its melody broken, breathless, as though its improviser lay flat upon his back – *le jazz horizontal*). The air is filled with flying insects. Above, a sky blotched with crushed yellowed starlight. Stars of the myopic. Stars as they might appear through the eyes of a weeping woman. Below the stone quay-side, men lean out from a small fishing boat spearing fish attracted by the yellowed acetylene light-flare which deceives them into thinking it a sudden summer's day. When real morning comes, gun emplacements are being set up along the beach.

13 Nude Dressing her Hair

1940 At last he is able to express it. Here, he has captured her, the *essence* of her. Here, as he enters to find Dora naked before the mirror dressing her hair. He paints her that very evening from this memory – snouted, loose-fleshed, splay-footed, massively arsed and thighed. As dog-faced as the skeletal Kasbek, his malnourished Afghan hound. Barely held within the room in which she squats. Her body disgusts him. The thick hair. The darkening moustache. The seepages. The monthly mess with its ammoniac after-stench. He can no longer take the *air* of her into his body. Cannot bear its stinking passage through his nose, the aftertaste of it in his mouth. But what can be done? There is nothing else to do. He beats her repeatedly, often leaving her unconscious on the floor.

14 Goldfish

1943 in Paris, witnesses a particularly bitter winter. Brassaï's goldfish freezes to death in its tank. The studio of Grands-Augustins ices over. The war plays havoc with his artists' supplies. He turns to making figures from cut or torn paper. Using the tip of his cigarette to burn out the features of the face. P^{so} is in love again. A young Art student, younger by forty years, has come to his attention. She reminds him of Rimbaud and he finds the comparison pleasing, a *frisson*, captured by her fine androgyny, this Françoise Gilot.

15 Clippings

1946 Meanwhile, Dora crumbles beneath the ghostweight of Marie-Thérèse. She sits in a darkened room, staring at the naked insides of her fingers, the webbing. The flesh is scarred. Hatched with fine lines. It is how her whole body feels. As though a blade had passed over her every extremity, too close, too close. A thousand cuts. *Fear love,* she sings, *fear love.* Like some modern Ophelia. *Close the window. Open the window. Let the mirror be empty.*

P^{so} has Dora committed. Gives his consent to a program of electric shocks. On 'medical grounds' Doctor Lacan encourages her to convert to Catholicism. P^{so} moves about his audience, noting how he had never been in love with Dora Maar. 'I liked her as though she were a man. I used to say: "You don't attract me, you never have." Well, you can imagine the tears and hysterical scenes that followed!'

As for Marie-Thérèse, she will retain all his letters and, in tiny packages of tissue paper, his finger-nail clippings. It will take her another forty years before she hangs herself.

16 The Last of Dora Maar

1947 She packs two suitcases – one filled largely with grey clothes; the other, various painting materials. She takes a taxi to Gare de Lyon and a train to Avignon, where she is met and driven to a ruined house in the village of Ménerbes. So it is she moves between the Parisian winters and the summers of the Luberon. It is the life of a recluse, her body slowly curving down upon itself like a figure from her photomontages. In 1994 she falls. Dora is bedridden. The shutters of rue Savoie now remain permanently closed. She has a saucepan on which she beats two spoons to call Rosa. She constructs a series of strings with which she can pull necessary objects closer. She will only read books written in, or translated into, English. Three years later she dies alone in her apartment, beneath a large boxwood crucifix and surrounded by the stations of the cross. She has outlived Picasso by twenty-four years. *I am blind,* she writes. *Made from a clutch of earth. But your gaze never leaves me. And your angel keeps me. The soul that still yesterday wept is quiet.* Blood shakes its wings and alights from between the fingers of a glove. *This day,* she whispers, *was a sapphire. Here it is.*

17 Broomstick

1947 Françoise Gilot bears him a child. As usual, it makes him feel young again. He overflows with energy. And then he feels the need to free himself.

'Look at you,' he derides. 'With all your ribs sticking out to be counted. Any other woman would improve after the birth of a baby, but not you. You look like a broom. Do you think brooms appeal to anybody? They don't to me.'

You will recall how, during the war, P^{so} would fashion human figures from torn paper, burning in their features with a cigarette end. Here, now, with war a distancing memory, he returns to this technique. This time we encounter the little man with the dead eyes holding a cigarette to Françoise's cheek. It pits the skin, puckering the flesh around it, a miniscule volcano smouldering on his so-called lover's face.

18 Thinking of Herself

1952 A Spring exhibition of Gilot's paintings is opened at Kahnweiler's. One which garners too much praise – a circumstance intolerable to *le maître*. P^{so} visits the major dealers. Her contract with Kahnweiler is terminated. Everywhere she turns, dealers tell her they cannot show any of her paintings – to do so would be to risk Picasso's displeasure.

Unlike her predecessors, however, she does not consider him a god. By the end of the year Françoise is confiding: 'I despise him. I can't forgive him for turning the person I loved into one I despise. He's become a dirty old man. It is all so grotesque and so ridiculous that I can't even be jealous.'

She informs Picasso that she is going to marry the painter Luc Simon. 'It's monstrous,' he exclaims at the announcement, turning to the audience. 'She thinks only of herself! I'd rather see a woman die, any day, than see her happy with someone else.'

19 A New Afghan

1953 He is seated on a couch. He wears a t-shirt, loose shorts and square-toed sandals. His hands are clasped about his left knee. His legs have lolled apart, sufficient to provide a view (one dare only look for a second) of his famous sack and the monstrous balls that plot within. How he aches to show them to every woman, this bull's endowment. He shows them to his new Afghan, Kabul.

'But I do not have a woman,' he repeats over and over to the long snouted, doe-eyed, creature which seems to embody his misery.

'I am *wounded* without a woman.'

20 Jacqueline

1955 Then suddenly, his wounds are healed. At the Madoura Pottery in Vallauris where he fashions his ceramics, he re-acquaints himself with Jacqueline Roque, a young woman forty-five years his junior. Under her influence he begins a series of canvases and lithographs – variations on the theme of Delacroix's *The Women of Algiers*. The harem women all based on versions of Jacqueline. One February day, three days away from completing the series, he is taken by a sudden silence. The air clears a moment. As if wiped clean. A *coup de torchon*. What is it, this ceasing? It comes to him – a near-constant screaming has fallen away. It is no surprise that late in the afternoon he receives news of Olga's death.

21 Clothes

1957 He's kept them all, for years, these stick-figure's clothes, Françoise's dresses. Clothes belonging to a broomstick. Has kept them in a cupboard under lock and key. How he had come to hate them. And the body they had fitted so perfectly. But now he discerns a use for them – as he had often thought he might – that is, their utter inappropriateness for his new mistress.

'You don't need money for clothes,' he says. 'You need to choose something from the wardrobe.' And he leads her upstairs. Jacqueline can't fit into them. He goes through the mockery of making it possible. Lettings out. Constructing longer hooks. All of which serves to underline her own body's failings. The fabric tears.

22 Cobblestones

1962 It is said, in his years with Jacqueline, Pso produced more works of art than with any other woman. In 1962, for instance, he paints her portrait 72 times; in 1963 he paints her portrait

160 times. But he grows old. He has already swapped his gaping shorts for long flannels, loosely cut. Two years later he undergoes surgery on his prostate. The long held belief that should he cease to work he would die, presses down increasingly upon him. *I paint,* he says, *just as I breathe.* He loses height at an alarming rate. Exhausted, terrified, barely over five feet tall, he works. In Spring of 1968 he begins a suite of what will be 347 etchings – brothel scenes, copulations, observed by various voyeurs, a dwarf, a clown, a jester, a king. A little Andalusian boy. How he has come to loathe his wife! What possessed him to *marry* her! He portrays her as *The Pissing Woman* – the hot yellow water hissing through her flaps, splashing back from the gutter against her thighs. For *her* part, Jacqueline is familiar with P$^{so's}$ own timid performances above the porcelain. The draining-off. The pitiful after-shake. The too-too dark colour of his offering.

Nearby, streets are barricaded with overturned cars. Students are pulling up ancient cobbles for ammunition.

23 Signing

1973 P^{so} clutches a swathe of lithographs to his woolly (pizzle-yellow) chest. 'I can't die now,' he trembles. (Has he wet himself?) '*Now* I must sign my works.' He picks up a coloured pencil. Separates the first of the prints, smooths it out. Scrawls in the corner: *Picasso.* Adds: *Greater than Matisse.* 'What day are we?' he calls to Jacqueline. 'Le 7 Avril.' 'And the year?' '1973.' 'Of course it is,' comes his reply. He adds the date. Draws forth another print: *Picasso. Greater than Manet,* 7.iv. MCMLXXIII. Takes another: *Greater than Velázquez,* 7.iv. MCMLXXIII . . .

24 Smoke

1973 Next day his heart specialist, Pierre Bernal, arrives; two hours before the artist's death. Never a tall man, recent years have shrunk P^{so} to a near homuncular state. A brown wrinkled manikin drowsy in his cot. From the bed he tries to affect a joking manner. But his breath often fails him, and most of what he says cannot be understood. Only after the specialist has gone, does the engrossing begin. The skin, too sparse for the unexpected bloat within, tears apart at what looks to be points of old stitching, as though the *grand-maître* were a monstrous doll from one of Hoffman's tales. Jacqueline waits at the bedside, drifting in and out of momentary sleeps. She is, though, wide awake when death occurs. Don Salvador's cigar smoke is finally expelled through Picasso's nostrils, drifting upwards, back into the still-breathing world. Jacqueline does not leave the bedside. Even when the corpse begins to rot. All of this, with over thirteen years to wait before she shoots herself.

Southerly

2 or 3 Things I Know About You

Claire Corbett

I'm standing in your study, stunned to find it unlocked. Bad teen girl stalker. How could I have got so lucky? Your home so isolated on this hill overlooking the water. I'm almost your neighbour and we never lock our doors either. It's like the country, though ninety minutes from town. But you're a world-famous film director and this weekender, with one of the most beautiful views on earth, stands empty during the week. This is years ago, before CCTV: no sensor lights flood the garden breathing in the dark.

Breathless

I am standing in your study that you told *Cahiers du Cinéma* you built yourself. Gum trees writhe in the night, pale sickle of beach gleams, lighthouse beam winks slower than the racing motor of my heart, which revs higher than your red sportscar. What if someone sees the light I've switched on? Is there a dog? The night is quiet except for the clatter of possums on Colorbond.

Detective

I am standing in your study where I have no business being. Intruding. Looking for your real self. If I'm caught what will they do? The *shame.* To be exposed as every man's terror: the crazy girl who loves too much. I've read every article, seen every film. I could be your daughter but am hopelessly obsessed, more than any character you've created. You haunt my dreams. I search your study. Everything here will bring me closer to you. Finally I will get under that skin, that skein you've woven of art and the marketing of your public self. Your movies, your interviews, the reviews and critiques. I will know you better than any collaborator, fan or scholar.

Goodbye to Language

I am opening the drawers of your desk. Picking up your keepsakes. A leather *wayang kulit* puppet, an ancient tin of corned beef from the North Queensland Meat Export Company, an antique paperweight, glass enclosing purple pansies. In the bottom drawer lies treasure beyond anything I could have imagined. Twenty, thirty handwritten diaries!

Contempt

I'm eighteen, have read all the *Diaries of Anaïs Nin*. Diary-keeping is for dreamy, self-absorbed women. Notoriously, you scorn your scriptwriters: what are you, the famous film director who thinks only in images, the action-hero among artists, doing contemplating your navel in all these notebooks?

A Woman is a Woman

What do I do now? Sit and read your diaries, exposed by the light streaming from your window? I know I am doing wrong but I am excused by love.

In Praise of Love

I cannot stay here. I pull the diaries from the drawer, heap them on the desktop. They are not large; they can be smuggled to my house nearby. *No-one will ever know.* Safer than reading them here and I cannot ignore this windfall. I have to know. I worship you. I am justified.

Masculin/Féminin

Your diaries are stacked on my bed. No-one else is here. The person who shares the house is working on a film in town during the week. I pick up diary after diary, open the volumes, your handwriting neat. Your voice, your soul on the page for no other eyes. Alone in the soft sub-tropic night I commit a traceless wrong, a crime unknown to any but myself. But as I flip through the black books I wonder. The truth is that they're not that interesting. You're not really here. Oh, now *here* is something: your pregnant wife and the pride you feel seeing her heavy and rounded, weighted with your child. At last. A man exulting in his power to change a woman's body, a woman's life, forever. You'd admit it to no-one, not even her. That page the only one that springs to life. That lives in my memory.

A Story of Water
Three days to decide. I could secrete the diaries, the most astonishing keepsake. No other way to own a piece of your soul. But if I return them my sin washes away.

Passion
For a day or two I agonise. Though I'll never be found out, never punished, I will know I've harmed you. Not the power I'm looking for. But I'm afraid to sneak around your garden at night again. I could be caught doing the right thing. Finally, on the last night before you arrive for the weekend I steal back, replace the diaries. You will never know how you've been violated.

I watch one of your films again. And see, finally, you are here. The diaries are no more than the discarded feathers of a bird that flies thousands of miles across the sea. It's the patterns of your flight that show me your soul, looping forever, flashing past at twenty-four frames a second.

Puppet Show

Cate Kennedy

Honeymoon, says the guy inspecting their visas, with a secret little smile. *Honeymoon*, exclaims the limo driver, holding up a sign from the hotel with their names on it – Andrew's the same as ever but hers, with the new surname, confronting her with a small thrilling jolt of realisation. *Mr and Mrs Andrew Dwyer*. Her, now. Her.

Honeymoon, croons the woman at the hotel reception, happy for them, palms clasped together, as if it isn't nearly midnight, as if she's been waiting here just to greet them. She gives a small courteous bow so that Karen finds herself looking at the sharp, perfect part in the woman's jet-black hair and imagining her this morning, in a room far less palatial than this resort reception lounge, raising a graceful hand and running a wooden comb through. Affixing the carved clip, the perfect outfit smoothed ready for a day of upright, straight-backed politeness. Smiling at the happiness and good fortune of others.

'A welcome drink,' says the woman, gesturing to the bamboo lounge suite nearby. They sink gratefully into its cushions as their passports are processed and their bags taken away by two young guys in sarongs.

'We don't tip them,' says Andrew, 'I'm pretty sure we don't tip them, or if we do, it's at the end of our stay, not now.' He has a tone in his voice she heard at the wedding: a stiff, edgy desire to do the right thing, a hint of strained anxiety, a man way out of his comfort zone.

'Don't worry about it now,' she says, smiling, 'it's 11.30, we just need a good night's sleep and we'll get ourselves oriented tomorrow.'

She browses through the bank of brochures on the wall – massages, day tours, handicraft factories, spa treatments. She accepts her drink, marvelling at the carved, twisted decoration of watermelon and pineapple; something laboured over by other graceful hands behind closed doors somewhere, still up fashioning fruit cocktails at 11.30 p.m. for late arrivals. People like us, she thinks, off the plane from Australia. In they trudge out of taxis, with wheeled luggage and red, sweating faces in the sudden humidity. White people with rubber thongs and sports shoes on, and long cargo shorts and brand-name singlets, people with tattoos on their legs and arms, people not wealthy in their own countries but suddenly high-status, demanding, querulous, suspicious, faces as puffy and pale as dough.

Not her and Andrew, though. They are golden. They are on a honeymoon, beaming like royalty. 'Thank you!' they say warmly as they accept their drinks and wait for their room keys. 'Thank you very much!'

I'm going to buy myself one of those dresses, Karen thinks as the beautiful drinks waitress moves away with the empty tray. Dieting for the wedding has made her as slim as she's been since college. With an emotion between relief and disdain, she studies the other passengers arriving from their night flights: overweight, frumpy women with their bra straps visible under their cheap gauzy tops, slumping by the check-in desk. Posture, thinks Karen, a bit hazy with jetlag, it's all about posture, I can see that now.

As yet another staff member escorts them down a manicured path to their villa, unlocking a gate which leads into their own private patio, she lets thoughts of those graceless others fall from her mind. She sees the plunge pool and day bed, the interior visible through glass sliding doors – a huge canopied, carved bed, an artfully draped bednet.

I'm married, thinks Karen. This is it.

'Livin' the dream!' exclaims Andrew with relish, tossing his gnawed bit of pineapple garnish into the garden.

*

Everything delights her: the multi-coloured wheels of fruit sliced on the breakfast buffet, the bathroom with its frangipani flowers arranged on the towels and its resident translucent gecko, the sunny hellos of the girls carrying armfuls of snowy towels up to the day spa. Andrew is relaxed and expansive, his sunglasses pushed up on his head. They have a 'couples massage' on their first morning, lying in a room with a view of impossibly green rice paddies, being scrubbed with ginger and turmeric paste, Andrew rising on an elbow to snap selfie after selfie. Photos for their Facebook wedding page.

Bliss, thinks Karen. Absolute bliss. Sneaking covert glances at Andrew (married!), supine there on the adjacent massage table. He seems much too big for the compact deferential masseuse moving around him, like a gladiator sunning himself, muscles formed by working out and playing football, three mornings a week at the gym. He is a giant here. Hair still barbered from the wedding, tattoos on his biceps. Karen turns her head from him and watches peaceful ducks paddling through the rice paddies. And a human figure, stooped, in the distance. Planting rice, maybe. Such a beautiful photo opportunity, but there is no way she's going to rouse herself from the table to break the hypnotic spell of the moment. There'll be plenty of time for other photos, she thinks.

'We should go out to one of those cultural shows tonight,' she says lazily into the crook of her arms. 'After dinner.'

'Which one do you want to see? There's a few on.'

'The traditional one,' replies Karen. 'The puppet show.'

'Not the Monkey Dance? That's meant to be great.'

'Let's go to the shadow puppets.'

'Whatever you say,' says Andrew, closing his eyes again.

*

She means to enquire at the reception desk, but later, as they wander up a street festooned with sarongs, a man draws breath to speak to them, his face bright and polite. Andrew holds up his hand.

'No,' said Andrew shortly, 'whatever it is, no thanks.'

'Not a tour,' says the man. 'Tickets to cultural event. Wayang Kulit.'

Karen squeezes Andrew's arm. 'That's what I want to see!' she says excitedly. 'That's the one, the shadow puppet . . .' – she hesitates at the word 'show', it doesn't seem quite right – 'the performance!'

'Why don't we just book it through the hotel?'

Karen sees the man's head incline courteously – so polite, these people, listening always with such graciousness – 'Yes, cultural performance of traditional puppets. In village.' He holds out a page illustrated with two spiky elongated figures, poised in theatrical combat.

'In the *village*,' says Karen to Andrew. 'That will be the one. Not the tourist trap one.'

'Yes,' says the man, looking at her. 'Traditional.'

'Come on,' says Karen. 'It looks a lot in rupiah, but seriously, that's only a couple of dollars. We can get a taxi – there's hundreds going up and down the road.'

'Take a taxi, and show them this, yes,' repeats the man. He is wearing quite a natty little hat, Karen notices, made of a folded, tucked piece of batik. Standing on a busy street corner, trying to interest passers-by in a traditional performance in his village.

'OK,' she hears herself saying eagerly. 'We'll have two tickets. For tonight.'

'I was going to say yes,' mutters Andrew. 'You don't have to jump in like that.'

The man nodding, beaming, noting something on a card he hands them, folding their money carefully. Deference, Karen thinks. That's the word she's looking for.

*

The taxi bumps across potholes on the outskirts of the town, pulling up outside a darkened building.

'Isn't this great?' enthuses Karen. 'See, all those guys there in their traditional clothes? And this building must be the village kampong.'

Andrew casts a troubled look at the darkness outside them and leans into the front to address the driver. 'It's safe, right? This is where the, what is it, the puppet show is on?'

'Yes, right inside there. Wayang Kulit. Special building for traditional show.'

Karen feels a pulse of excitement. This is so much better than going with the other guests queuing for the standard show on the hotel's mini-bus; this is the real deal.

'And will you wait here to take us back to the hotel again? When it finishes?'

The driver nods calmly. 'Of course – I wait if you want.'

'That's how poor they are,' whispers Andrew as they approach the dark building, where light seeps through double carved doors. 'They're happy to wait for two hours just to get that return fare. They must spend their whole lives waiting around.'

Karen feels safe next to him, shouldering through the shadows. She sees light hit the high cheekbones of a man waiting there, opening the door for them, ushering them inside, taking their tickets without a word. Stepping through into flickering lamplight, Karen can make out the shapes of expectant people, waiting quietly on folding chairs at the back of the kampong and sitting on mats on the floor. A troupe of gamelan players kneel patiently at their instruments beside a simple raised platform on which a bamboo frame sits, a large white sheet stretched within it.

Karen reaches for her iPhone as they find two chairs tucked down the back, hoping she'll be able to capture some of this atmospheric flickering lantern light in a photo. No flash, obviously, just a discreet photo or bit of footage. But how would a mere photo capture it – the respectful hush, the croaking of frogs outside, the sudden blaring jangle of gamelan? The music seems so exotic and discordant, the gongs lulling her into a kind of trance. And the smells! Smoky scents of teak wood and coconut oil, mosquito coils and the kerosene of the lamps around the stage. An older man solemnly disappears behind the screen and takes his leisurely time settling there and arranging lanterns as the music increases in tempo and volume. Suddenly there are two long-limbed shapes in black silhouette against the screen, the sticks used to manoeuvre their supple limbs and spines just visible. They gesture mysteriously at each other. Karen is lost in it. The gamelan players sit straight-backed and elegant, and every now and then, when one intricately detailed character appears against the screen, its elaborate headdress like a pharaoh's, the audience makes some small collective sound – a murmur or hiss of recognition, or a shared ripple of appreciative laughter. She'll make a photobook of this, she thinks dreamily, taking picture after picture. Or just one of those images printed onto canvas, like a painting, that you could do online.

*

With one final blaring thrum of gamelans, the performance ends and the elderly puppeteer rises slowly to his feet. Karen can see the silhouettes of other audience members start to stretch and rise, and she whispers to Andrew, 'That was fabulous, but I'm dying for a pee. Will you go and make sure our taxi driver is back where we agreed and I'll meet you there in a sec?'

He gives her a wry grin. 'You think you're going to find a toilet here? I bet it's an outhouse down some track, and it'll be pitch black. Can't you hold on until you get back to the resort?'

'No, I really have to go. Look, it's through there.' She points to a side door, gives him a quick kiss on the cheek, and slips out. Her mind is still full of flickering light, acrid scents and jangling gongs, the puppets' elongated, jointed arms, gesturing through some elaborate traditional story, the mechanics of which – to be honest – were lost on her. She follows a winding path of concrete slabs, lit by lamps, following a trail of small arrows hammered into the ground. Down here, she is sure, she will encounter a rudimentary latrine of some sort: whatever the village has managed to build for its visitors. She rounds a corner and feels a quick slip of astonishment at the sight of a tiled, fluorescently lit block of women's toilet stalls. Set there in the darkness, it's as incongruous as a landed UFO. Flushing toilets too! With handbasins!

Afterwards she hurries back, still blinking in amazement, to search for Andrew in the compound's courtyard. Other paths curve before her, and behind the buildings she is aware of floodlights and noise, the revving of big engines. Through the flung-open doors of the building, a group of men are clearing away the rows of folding chairs, lit now by a single electrical globe suspended in the centre of the room.

Karen rounds a corner and stops, taken aback. A long row of enormous air-conditioned buses stand idling, their interior lights revealing rows of plush upholstered seats.

The place is thronged. Tourists move in small groups from bus to bus, looking for the one they have come in, clutching tickets and climbing aboard. Karen sees families with dawdling tired children, the thin fair hair of the girls twisted into rows of braids. Older tourists, too, with large cameras slung around their necks. Many of the buses are long-distance luxury coaches, she notices now, come all the way from the beach resorts. A trip into the mountains to see a cultural show. Maybe two in one evening. Probably all off, now, to the Monkey Dance. And manoeuvring their way around the giant idling coaches, trying to edge their way out of the parking bays, are the tour company minibuses. Karen, searching the crowd for Andrew, recognises one from their own resort, and she's certain the young man driving it is the one who greets them at the front desk each morning – yes, he's waving now, beckoning.

Karen smiles weakly back – what an idiot she was, kidding herself about this – and continues to thread her way through the crowd, dazzled by high-beam lights, dodging vehicles. It's impossible to imagine these monstrous shining vehicles bumping up that potholed dirt track and through the same narrow gates they arrived through, and yet here they are somehow, and the family compound, she sees, is actually a parking lot, and each massive sleek coach is filled with white faces looking out dully through the tinted windows or scrolling through images on their own phones and cameras, talking but not smiling, busy with the next thing on their agenda.

How strange these people look, Karen thinks with a jolt of disorientation, their eyes passing over her so uniformly flat and incurious. And the reason her scanning eyes can't yet spot her husband, she realises, is because everyone here is dressed very much the same, the men in their long shorts and singlets, the women in their rayon batik print dresses, bought that day, on the same street she and Andrew had walked. Where is he?

The coaches thrum and jerk, hydraulic doors shuddering as they wheeze open to admit more people who stand still, querulous and suspicious, repeating their resort names again and again to the nodding drivers. Karen fights down panic – they're leaving, she's left behind, ridiculous! – and finally catches sight of Andrew, waiting for her next to the same small, grimy orange taxi they'd come in.

'Where did you get to?' he says, slipping his arm around her waist. 'I was just starting to worry about you. Thinking maybe you'd lost your way back.' She feels the hot weight of his arm, its thick ropes of flexing muscle.

'Are you kidding?' she answers. 'How could I have got lost? The place is packed. We could have even got a direct shuttle back to the resort – there's one here, I just saw it.'

'Well, I'm still glad we organised our own taxi,' says Andrew stolidly. 'Supporting the local economy.'

'You like the show?' says the driver to Karen. She gives him her honeymoon smile.

'Oh, yes. I loved it. Thank you.'

'It was great to see something traditional,' adds Andrew loyally, although Karen knows he's found the thing way too long and incomprehensible. 'With the music and everything.'

'Yes,' says the driver. 'Wayang Kulit, traditional.'

As he speaks she glances over at the departing motorbikes, roaring nimbly out of the lot with two or three people on each one. The pillion passengers are in traditional dress, the girls still stunningly straight-backed, holding their beautifully coiffed black hair in place as the bikes accelerate. The gamelan players. They're not solemn now, they're laughing, each one stunning as a fashion model, perched on the back of the motorbikes, holding on casually with one hand, tilting their faces into the fresh night air.

'They go back now,' says the driver, following her eyes. 'Back to their village.'

She watches them as they roar off into the darkness, her heart unaccountably aching.

*

'Hard to believe we have to go back to reality tomorrow, isn't it?' Andrew says on their final morning over breakfast. He yawns. 'Back to work for me on Tuesday.'

Karen sees the living room of their house suddenly: the wedding presents set on every surface, flagged with post-it notes, waiting for her thankyou cards. 'We should go to the market today,' she says, 'and buy gifts for people. Have you got the energy?'

Why wouldn't he have the energy, eating three huge meals a day, being waited on hand and foot, swimming lazily in the pool, his fit, perfectly nourished body sprawled at ease now in a cushioned chair? Why wouldn't she, massaged to boneless bliss, a wallet full of spending money, relaxed, pampered, married? She pushes away this feeling, and spears a piece of pineapple. Still carved. Someone must do this every morning, as their job.

'Handicrafts,' she says brightly. 'That's what we need for gifts.'

It feels like a foray into battle, the market. A labyrinth. Slim hands reaching to touch her arm, low insistent voices asking her to name a price, faces seeking eye contact. Women holding up lengths of beautiful fabric to her body, wrapping her in sarongs. Murmuring, always polite, the sound like bees, deepening and rising in volume as soon as you pause, as soon as you betray an interest.

'No thanks,' Andrew keeps saying, growing more brusque and resolute as the onslaught continues. 'No, we're just looking.'

Carved painted cats and windchimes. Incense in woven canisters. Lurid acrylic paintings of Buddha. Cellophane-packed hairclips of clustered plastic frangipani flowers. Silk dresses of every conceivable pattern and colour.

And a whole floor of the market dedicated to offerings – tiny cakes and eggs and flower arrangements, heaped coloured balls of rice. Not for eating, for placing on shrines, dozens of times every day. Cakes and rice eaten only by street dogs, or left to rot when the incense burns down, replaced with fresh ones. It is overwhelming, Karen thinks. It is unstoppable. She's dizzy now. The heat, the smells, the assault of it. Too much of everything.

They buy ginger soap and coconut oil shampoo, incense and vanilla pods. Andrew buys a stack of Bintang t-shirts for the guys at his work, haggling until Karen feels uncomfortable; suddenly he's an expert in intimidation.

'That's a good price to you, is it?' he says. 'Well, it's not what I call a good price. Not at all.' Stern, like an intolerant boss. Like a headmaster. Her towering, bulky husband, meaty hand pressing on a stack of cotton t-shirts, leaning down over the vendor. And the man's face closed, struggling to his feet, his wife faltering behind him.

Andrew, she thinks. Stop. It's so cheap. It's too cheap. And Andrew, sliding the stack into a plastic bag when she protests over beating them down, saying baby, it's a buyer's market like you wouldn't believe. Moving off between the narrow aisles, an expressionless Goliath.

Nauseous now as well as dizzy. The sickly scent of the tropical flowers. Hammocks and kites and dreamcatchers; they are in the handicrafts section now. And Karen sees the stall selling *wayang kulit* puppets. They are the real thing, some made of card and some of something more durable, like hard, cured leather. The elongated painted eyes on their grimacing faces look away from her, the cut-out costumes spilling over their shoulders intricate as lace doilies. Andrew catches her eye and grins indulgently.

'How much for these three?' he says to the stallholder, pointing at some puppets strung up over their heads.

'What are you doing?' says Karen.

'I'm buying you some of these. You loved that performance, didn't you? They'd look great on a wall somewhere at home, don't you think?'

Andrew, wealthy here, assured, a consumer comfort zone he's enjoying. She squeezes his hand. 'Thanks. I mean it.'

'Which ones do you want?'

'Well, I don't know the stories ... they're all different and important characters I think ...'

'These three,' says Andrew again, pointing. 'They look like kind of a set.'

And the stallholder carefully unhooks the puppets with their delicate articulated arms and torsos, shows her how fluidly and expressively they can move, and they strike a deal.

'A present,' says Andrew, grinning like Daddy Warbucks as he pays, 'for my wife.'

The stallholder musters an expression of delight. 'Your first time to Bali?' he says, and when they assent, he cries '*Honeymoon!*'

*

Then the return limo transfer from the resort to the airport, back into the grimy tropical heat of Denpasar, the driver hefting their overstuffed zippered cases into the trunk with a grunt of effort, a man used to lifting the booty of tourists, a man who does it every day. Karen staring out the window at this traffic-clogged highway, vehicles of all descriptions ferrying more and more in and out. I'll give him my money, she thinks. The wad of rupiah she has left in her money belt, grimy with being counted out by fretful, hardworking fingers, money folded and refolded, earned so hard. She'll give him the cash, not make a big deal out of it, just tuck it discretely into his hand when they get out and Andrew is getting the bags.

They pull up at International Departures. Karen has the money in her hand, ready, waiting for Andrew to get out and haul their cases from the boot, so they can start the trudge into the terminal and into the queues full of other sunburnt, sweating white people, all with huge, stuffed suitcases, waiting to check in. A terminal which will be cold with expensive chilled air after the muggy, tarmac-smelling heat of outside. She waits. But Andrew stays sitting. She stares at him, curled notes of a poor currency in her fist by her side.

'Aren't you getting out?' she says and Andrew shakes his head.

'That's his job,' he says, a patient, slightly annoyed edge to his voice. 'That's what he's paid to do. It's part of our transfer.'

Karen hesitates a second, seeing her husband's stubbornly folded arms, the ease with which he's sprawled, waiting for the driver to open his door. Then she pushes open her own door and moves around to the back of the car where the driver is hauling out the bags.

'Sorry,' she says, too brightly, 'they're so heavy! Let me give you a hand!'

But the man stiffens, and she has the sudden, stricken thought that Andrew is right: she's doing it all wrong, she's probably insulting him now. And sure enough, the driver's discomfort is visible as he lugs out her suitcase. Andrew is suddenly out of the car in a flash, looming at his other side, giving her a pissed-off glance and saying 'sorry about that'. Apologising for her.

Karen hesitates, smelling hot tarmac and rubber, fecund rot, jet fuel, the sunscreen sliding off her with her own sweat. Just into that terminal, and into the air conditioning, and through check-in and customs, shunted along into where they belong, passport holders only beyond this point, the guiding lines painted on the floor taking them back to where they come from. Processed. Honeymoon over.

Karen grips the handle of her own case and jerks it up onto the kerb, and the folded wad of money falls from her hand as she does so, fluttering to the ground like rags. The driver watches her crouch hurriedly to claw the notes up off the ground while Andrew is distracted by his own case, and as she rises clumsily to press them into his palm she thinks, well, now his humiliation is probably complete.

'Thankyou!' she blurts, 'thankyou! Terima kasih, good night!' Then into the terminal, x-rayed, stamped, buckled into economy for the long flight home.

*

In Australia, they pass through customs in fluoro-lit early morning, and shuffle with sleepwalkers' obedience into the 'Something to Declare' line, because Karen is concerned about the vanilla and raffia passing quarantine. She unzips her case for the official.

'Here,' she says, pointing, 'this is the organic material.'

'The vanilla's fine,' says the woman. 'What about seeds? Animal products? Anything made of hide?'

'No,' says Andrew firmly.

And Karen hesitates, feeling him tense beside her.

How familiar he looks to her here, back on home turf, still taking up so much space as he stands planted squarely before this official, refusing to be drawn. Her husband. They're married. This is it. She takes in his Bintang t-shirt; his sunburnt forehead; the shuttered, bored sullenness of his expression, as predictable and closed as the faces of the tourists on the bus, paying for their ration of cultural tradition and done with it the moment it was finished.

'Wait,' she says. And she's reaching under the stiff layers of waxed batik with its gorgeous geometrical designs, beneath the compressed stack of cheap t-shirts, beneath the crackling cellophane-wrapped soaps and cats and hairclips – all their loot – for the thin delicate surface of the puppets.

'You got some of those shadow puppets?' says the customs officer, unsurprised. 'Well, yeah – I'm afraid they have to be confiscated. They're untreated buffalo hide.'

Andrew shifts his weight, incredulous.

'What about shoes and that?' he says. 'They're all untanned leather too. All the …' – he makes a wide gesture at the queues of other tourists shuffling through the 'Nothing to Declare' lines – '… all the *crap* these guys have bought, the sandals and jewellery and whatnot? Why aren't they declaring it?'

Up goes his arm, blocky and angry, then falls back to rest in a curled, combative fist on his hip. Karen hears the bullocky, aggrieved tone of implied injustice in her husband's voice as he rocks back on his big sunburnt feet. What do they use, she wonders, to destroy the things they seize – a big incinerator, maybe? Or a large tub of acid? God, that must be jetlag talking, she thinks, catching herself. As if they'd use acid! Burning – that would be better.

She doesn't want to look at Andrew, or witness this display. She pushes her hand through the suitcase now, sure of where she's carefully stowed the three figures. Runs a finger full of regret over the painted hide surface of the first one, tooled with such care and exquisite detail. Imagines the lamplight shining through the intricate lace of these holes, the character rearing up to its full dignified height, chin lifted, wrists tilted, narrowed eyes lined with scarlet, full of power and grace. The puppets' sticks click together uselessly as she tugs them free, their arms and legs splaying, askew, awkward now they're in her hands.

'Take them,' she says flatly, pushing them across the counter. 'Please, just take them away.'

Review of Australian Fiction

The Three Treasures

Melissa Beit

Some things happen without any warning or deliberation. *Wu Wei.* Action without action.

Jase finds me up in the corner of the west paddock, re-stringing a section of fence. I watch him stalking his way up the line, his shaggy mop of hair like an African marigold just past its heyday.

'George Carlyle,' he greets me, grinning. 'You guys are hard to find.'

He watches me remove the elbow-length leather gloves and push my sunglasses up. In spite of these tokens of protection, I've just given myself a long, complicated scratch on my shin from the violent scrolling of barbed wire back into its inert coil, the shape it apparently wants to hold forever. That's an interesting thought, and if my schoolmate hadn't just shown up, I would probably have sat down and dwelt on it at length.

I'm so pleased to see him that I hold out my hand to shake his, and watch Jase cover up his embarrassment by turning the handshake into a complex series of rapper moves, ending with a loose man-hug. I figure we have maybe twenty-five minutes until my father comes back from town, and in that time I have to sweep the driveway, put the spuds on and set the table. I can't stop smiling.

Jase helps me put my tools into the bucket and we run down to the house with the shadows from the trees licking our backs.

'Where's your old man?' Jase asks, and I glance at him, trying to gauge if he's running a gauntlet by showing up here. Other kids had done that for some months after The Mrs Hatten Incident.

'He's in town,' I say, opening the front door. 'He'll be home soon.'

'Wow,' says Jase, following me into the kitchen, apparently disinterested in that piece of news. 'Your house is really tidy.'

I've never been to Jase's house, but I've seen his mum pick him up from school in a green station wagon. She looks neat enough.

'I guess.'

I choose two large potatoes out of the box in the pantry and scrub them clean in the sink. The water on my hands is neither cool nor warm and the potatoes' eyes are plugged with red dirt, which runs like paint over my hands. On my way to the oven I prick the potato skins with my fingernails to stop them from exploding. Jase is slouching in the doorway to the living room, taking everything in. I still can't stop smiling.

'Do you want some water?' I ask him. There isn't anything else. We're out of milk and my dad never buys juice, soft-drink or alcohol. Which is fine by me.

'Nah,' says Jase. He picks up a tape measure from the dining room table, turns it over in his hand and puts it back down again. 'Your house is so *masculine*.'

I get two plates out of the dresser, two knives and two forks. I set them on the table, then arrange salt and pepper, two glasses and the water bottle in the middle. Then I go to the sideboard and get two red cloth serviettes and fold them beside the plates. Jase raises his eyebrows.

*

'What are these?' my dad said, the first night. He didn't look at me.

'Serviettes,' I said, aware I was walking a fine line. When I'd found the tablecloth and matching serviettes in the hall cupboard, I'd briefly considered spreading the red cloth on the table, collecting wildflowers to go in a jam jar.

'What's wrong with paper towels?'

I could have said, paper towels are disposable, a reflection of our throwaway society, these ones are pretty, but instead I said,

'We'll save money if we don't use paper towels every meal.'

My father picked up his fork and speared a chunk of meat. 'Well, you're washing them,' he said.

*

'How's that new English teacher?' Jase says, as he watches me sweep the drive. He offered to help but when I told him we only owned one broom he went and sprawled on the front steps.

'Which new teacher?' I say, but I turn my body away because I know who he's talking about.

'Miss Grantham,' he says, as though her name is a caramel he wants to suck. 'She's hot.'

Is she hot? She doesn't look hot to me, she looks soft. Her hair is brown, pulled back into a loose ponytail, more and more wisps escaping throughout the day until sometime around 2 p.m. her hairband gives up altogether and springs away, releasing the rest of her hair in a glossy curtain. Her face is freckled, her cheeks as round as a child's. Everything about her looks soft, her long skirts and shawls, her small freckled hands, her neat sandalled feet. She looks, I think now, still turned away and sweeping in large efficient strokes, like a mother should look.

'I don't imagine there're many Taoists at Clarence State High,' she said to me in her soft, low voice, the day she returned my essay on the Three Treasures. She pronounced it properly, so that the *t* sounded more like a *d*. And I sat there beaming at her like the Buddha, imagining those hands smoothing my hair back and plumping my pillow.

When she moved off, Clunker said, 'I could eat her for breakfast.'

*

'I have her on Wednesday afternoons,' I say to Jase.

'I'd like to have her every afternoon,' he says.

He's lying, and I wonder why.

*

Rugby union is a Richard Carlyle Approved Activity (an RCAA), one of very few, so I've played every winter for the last six years. Does rugby contravene the principles of Taoism? Probably, but I've found that I can channel the violence on the field around me into something like a dance. I play better rugby now that I've stopped trying to force my way forwards.

'Fuck, George, you never get dirty,' Clunker, a forward, complained to me once. His massive chest smoothed out some parts of his jersey, ruched others. 'But you kick like a fucking ballistic missile.' He slammed me across the shoulders in what I took to be a gesture of camaraderie.

'Jason Reilly's a faggot,' Clunker said a few weeks ago when we were standing in the canteen queue. 'Look at him, little poofter.' Across the asphalt, Jase was dancing with some of the girls from our year, exaggerating all his hip movements and shaking out his red bush of hair, singing in falsetto, until eventually the girls had had enough and pushed him away good-naturedly. 'Fuck he can surf though,' said Clunker, rotating a finger in his ear hole.

I laughed out loud. I keep doing that lately, even though I try not to.

*

Spattering gravel warns us. By the time the sedan pulls into the garage I've finished the sweeping and Jase has sprung to attention, tucked his shirt in and done something to tame his hair. I have butterflies in my stomach.

When my dad unfolds himself from the car and walks over to us, unsmiling, Jase extends his hand like a bank manager. No rapper moves now. 'Mr Carlyle,' he says. 'My name's Jason Reilly. I'm at school with George.'

My dad looks at Jase's hand like it's a dead invertebrate, no surprises there, but then puts his own hand out and shakes it, once.

'Did you get that fence fixed?' he says to my chest, wiping his hand on his trousers.

'Yes, sir.'

'Dinner on?'

'Yes, sir.'

'Bring in the shopping.' He turns away and stumps into the

house without making eye contact with either of us. I have a personal theory that my father hates himself so much he can't bear to see his own reflection in other people's eyes. He re-emerges at the doorway and addresses the clothesline behind us. 'Put that broom away.'

'Man,' breathes Jase in awe. 'He is one hundred percent 1950s.' He ruffles his hair back out of place. 'You call him sir?'

'I have to go in now,' I say.

There is not a single tree on our entire holding. Not even a shrub. Just concrete, lawn and pasture, all bullied into neatness. But the bush closes in around us like a big messy hug, and at this time of day, when the sun has already left the land but still strokes the highest limbs of the trees, I feel like the dot inside the yin–yang symbol, the chaos within the order. The farm only started to make sense to me when I saw it in juxtaposition with the bush. Sunny side, shady side. Hard, soft. Taoism has saved my life.

'Can I come back?' asks Jase, collecting his bike from the side of the house. His helmet squashes his hair down but it protests out the sides.

'Yes,' I say. My father hadn't told him to leave, which I take to be a good sign. Then I remember the slow wipe down the trouser leg. I smile to take the sting out of my words. 'But not too often.'

*

I eat each night to the screech and ring of cutlery. Most of our meals are mute affairs.

'The school gave me a laptop today.'

There's a very long silence while my father cuts his rissole into small pieces, all the same size. 'You will not use it.'

I wait to see what will happen. All the things I could say (they gave them out to everyone in my class, we have to learn how to use them, we have to *use* them, this is the twenty-first fucking century) are, one by one, sent out of my mouth on a breath, without ever being spoken. I place a piece of potato on my tongue with immense care, and spend the next moments considering the texture of the skin compared with the mealy body, the brown and white taste of it. The first of the Three Treasures is compassion.

'Yes, sir,' I say at last.

My father's relief is palpable. He wipes his mouth on the red serviette, visibly stained, and then stares at it for a while, as though in confusion.

'Who was that boy?'

Which boy? I almost ask. I don't think of Jase as a boy, or a girl for that matter, or even a human being. Just as himself, Jase. 'Jason Reilly.' I stop myself from smiling, just in time. 'He's in my grade.'

'Does he play footy?'

I don't even consider lying. 'No.'

'What did he want?'

My father exists within the uncomfortable belief that other people act only out of greed and need. He has no friends. None of his co-workers down at the depot ever come here, although they wave at me on the street, and clip me over the earhole after a good rugby match.

The possible retorts crowd my mouth and I wait until they've wandered off, single file, before saying, 'He's my friend.'

My empty mouth feels dry all of a sudden, because I can already hear him saying the terrible words, in the same way he's just dismissed the laptop, lying in my schoolbag across the hall, filled with unfulfillable potential.

You will not see him. He cannot come here.

It's some time before I realise that my father has aligned his knife and fork and risen from the table without speaking.

*

My father spent several years in prison, before I was born. I'm not sure what crime he committed, but I think it was one of the felonies that get you a ride in the electric chair in some American states: armed robbery, murder, rape. I know nothing about his childhood, or his family of origin, whether he was an only child, or if I have aunts or uncles or cousins or grandparents somewhere on the planet. My mother ran off when I was four, with a man my father worked with at the depot. I don't remember anything about her, not even what she looked like, but once, when I was in the supermarket with my father, we walked down the laundry aisle and I smelled her. I kept going back to that aisle and trying to pin down the exact bottle or box that her smell had emanated from, but it was elusive, like the scent coming out of a lomandra flower, that disappears when your nose is right up against the spikes, but nearly knocks you over the moment you turn away. Eventually my father tired of my absconding and smacked me, hard, although I was almost nine years old.

I tower a foot or so over his head these days and since I've become a closet Taoist we've moved past the yelling→cheek→smacking→defiance→hitting cycle, I believe, but my stomach still roils whenever my father is displeased with me.

*

Mrs Hatten was my teacher in year six. When I made some comment in Health about the origin of babies and the class dissolved in hilarity, Mrs Hatten thinned her lips and asked to see me after school. When all the other kids had gone she gave me a book to put in my schoolbag: *Where did I come from?* I read it when I got home from school, sitting on my bed, and I remember finding it fascinating, and not in any way disgusting or rude or dirty. But those were the words my father used when he found the book where I'd left it on my bedside table, and those were the words he shouted at Mrs Hatten the next day, so that the whole school heard, even though they were in an empty classroom with the door closed. Mrs Hatten shouted too. She shouted, if George comes to school with any more bruises, I'm calling DOCS. That made my dad stop shouting and leave.

'I'm sorry,' I said, that night at the dinner table. I still wasn't sure what I'd done wrong, but I wanted my father to stop looking frightened. Even inexplicable anger was better than the terror I'd seen in his face since his blue with Mrs Hatten.

I remember that he picked up his knife and fork as usual but then held them like drumsticks for a long time, an Energiser bunny all out of batteries. Then he dropped his cutlery and put his hands to his face. I still remember the way his shoulders shook.

When I found the book about Taoism in the school library, I made sure I never brought it home. I keep it in my locker and read it in the lunch hour or in between classes.

*

At 10 p.m. my father switches the light off in the shed, and comes back to the house. He shuts off the lights in the kitchen, locks the front door, enters the hallway and stops outside my room. I lift my head. He knocks.

'Come in,' I say. I mark my place in the chemistry textbook and turn to face him.

He looks out my dark window and clears his throat. 'That laptop,' he says.

'Yes, sir?'

'What would you be using it for?'

'Assignments mostly. Typing out assignments. I have computing once a week, I'd use it then too, in class.'

My father frowns at the window, possibly at his own reflection. 'You couldn't use it to look up porn or something?'

'No, sir,' I say gently. 'We have no internet here. And I'm not interested in porn.' It's the truth, so I make sure it sounds like it. The second of the Treasures is moderation, which porn ain't, from what I've seen of it.

My father digs deep in his trouser pockets as though looking for change. His discomfort is catching. Then he looks at me. 'Because, you know, I wouldn't want you finding out where babies come from or anything like that.'

My father has made a joke. His first ever joke.

I smile. 'No, sir.'

He nods and turns, stops at the door. 'I'll have to think about it, the laptop.'

'Yes, sir.'

'Goodnight, son,' he says.

I love you, Dad, I don't say. 'Goodnight, sir.'

*

'You know they have machines to do that these days,' says Jase watching me sweep, twirling a football in his hands. My father is out but he'll be home in an hour. 'They're called *blowers*. My mum rang up this lawn mowing company once and asked for a mow and blow. I nearly pissed myself.' The north-easterly has scattered gum leaves all over the driveway, even though the nearest tree stands a hundred metres away. I love that. 'Where's your mum?' Jase asks.

'Gone. Where's your dad?'

'Dead. Hey! I see what you mean. We could set them up, my mum and your dad, make our own Brady Bunch.'

The thought of my father making anything as commonplace and convivial as a blended family is laughable. But I don't feel like laughing. My throat is thick and tight, so the next words are forced out of it, against any will of my own.

'I don't want to be your brother.' I make myself meet his eyes, even though it's as painful as looking straight at the sun.

He plays with the ball in his hands, rolling it, patting it into the air, and then drops it on the ground and lets it roll away. He looks out across the farm with a 180-degree glance that lasts for several seconds and ends up on my face. 'I see,' he says, and there's no mockery in his eyes. He does see.

He walks over and takes the broom out of my hands. My arms fall to my sides as though they've been deboned. He lifts one of my hands and places it on his chest, over his heart.

The third Treasure is humility, not putting oneself first in the world, but sometimes things happen without any warning or deliberation.

Still Life

Little Toki

Colin Oehring

1.

I should have known better than to demand my father stop the car. We were on day one of a projected three-week trip and my father's much-reiterated aim was to check in at the Zululand Safari Lodge before dark. But we'd been on the road for three long, uninterrupted hours and I was tired and twelve and willing to seize upon any opportunity to stop, to spend money.

Roadside stands were a common enough sight on the highways and byways of South Africa and there was nothing to suggest that this one – set up on the otherwise empty stretch of highway between Mtubatuba and Shikishela – was anything special. But I was drawn to it, irresistibly.

Normally my father would sigh at my avidity: he might moan or discreetly roll his eyes heavenward, or cast a look of weary allegiance towards my mother. But in the end he would always give in. This time, though, he shot boldly past the stand. And without a word. I sulked. I cried. I made an exhibition of myself.

I remember the jingle playing on the radio, 'we love braaivleis, rugby, sunny skies and Chevrolet, braaivleis, rugby, sunny skies and Chevrolet ...' as my parents began to argue, as there rose from me a crescendo of complaint, a demented throbbing chorus that grew louder and more intense until at last my father gave out a strange cry and hit the brakes hard, bringing the big Chevrolet to a skidding halt.

For a time no-one spoke. Then my mother began to cry. I felt torn between wanting to flee and wanting to make things better, for already I was feeling guilty. But the lure of the stand was strong and I got out of the car and walked back along the hot road in the direction of the makeshift table set up in front of the parked kombivan.

In the passenger seat sat a white man with long stringy blond hair, smoking a cigarette, one tanned arm hanging from the window. Behind the table, on which were arrayed trinkets and brooches, pendants and beads and figurines, some beaded jewellery, a couple of little boxes, a clumsily fashioned giraffe, nothing to interest me, stood a black man of about thirty-five. I didn't like his scarred face, nor his insincere smile.

I was about to head back to the car when I saw, tucked half out of sight, two little wooden legs. I reached out and discovered that they belonged to a little dark stick creature. I stared, captivated, breathing deeply in and deeply out, before taking him up into my hands.

The Tokolosche is a familiar figure in South African folklore, a small hairy creature – rarely if ever up to any good – and about whom I had first learnt from Iris, our Zulu maid. Iris liked of an afternoon to gather up all the shoes in the house and to sit cross-legged in our courtyard polishing one after the other while relating to me African folk tales that purported, in their final sentence, to explain how things had come to be how they were: And so that is how the hippo lost all his fur!

What I liked to hear about were the Tokolosche. These creatures terrified Iris and she told me that her husband had placed their bed up on paint tins to prevent them from 'joining her' at night. She cautioned me always to sleep on my back, and blushed when I asked why.

At school, Garth de Mierwe told me that the Tokolosche was a sex maniac and endowed with a penis so long it had to be slung over its shoulder.

There was no sign of a penis here but of course this little Toki was only a wooden approximation crafted of stick and a greasy sort of twine, a cheaply, crudely fashioned thing with little patches of fur, like a cheap nylon, glued to his little legs, his arms, and on his head. His plastic eyes, not the least bit lifelike, were glued haphazardly, crude white paste leaking out of the side of its left eye like the crust of sleep. Sharp teeth cut bluntly from white cloth. And a little red smudge of tongue.

I held it up to the black man who smiled knowingly and took the figure from me. My mother was standing beside me now and it was to her that he made his pitch. Speaking in fluent English he claimed that the figure protected its owner against evil spirits, that it brought good fortune, prosperity and excellent health, guaranteed. I turned to my mother, who reluctantly asked the man how much it was. He told her. And my heart sank. Even I could see that this little Toki was overpriced. And yet she smiled a little smile, and paid.

2.

It was after eight, and dark, by the time we turned off the third and final exit and drove up the dirt road to the Safari Lodge. A young black woman showed us to our huts by torchlight and once settled I examined my little Toki.

He was a fragile thing and although I wanted to keep him close I worried that if I took him to bed I might, by rolling about, destroy him. There was a small stand beside my bed, with two drawers. In the top one I found a Gideon's Bible. I took it out, dropped it into the bottom drawer and slid Toki in the top drawer.

I slept until six, when I was woken by a single brisk knock on the door. I sat up and watched as a young black man came into my room, bearing a wooden tray upon which sat a tea pot and a single cup. He smiled broadly at me and placed the tray on a small stand at the end of my bed. After checking that Toki was safely in his place I fell back to sleep for another two hours, wondering when at last I woke to full daylight whether the young black man had been an apparition. But there it was, the tea tray, perched on the table at the end of my bed.

3.

We saw, on our first day at the lodge, antelope and impala, wart-hog and giraffe. None distracted me long from the thought of my little Toki waiting for me in his drawer. And as soon as we returned I rushed back to my hut to check that he was where I'd left him.

And there he was, looking, I thought, in his wooden, expressionless way, pleased to see me. I set him beside me on my pillow and began to talk. I told him about my parents, and about our house in Durban, and about Iris, and how at night you could see from our backyard, glittering beyond the sugar plantations, the lights of the township she lived in. And when I told him about the time my uncle, on a hunting trip to Tanzania, had shot an elderly leopard out of a tree, I could almost hear him laugh.

That first day set the pattern for the following week – a pattern to which, day by day, I increasingly did not, or was not able to, conform. For I soon started to weaken, to sicken, in fact, to the point where, on the fourth day, a doctor had to be called in.

But first I must explain what happened on our second night.

4.

We'd gone that day on yet another game drive, further afield this time, beyond the confines of the Safari Park and into Umfolozi National Park, where lions and rhinos and elephants and leopards freely roamed. I went to bed early and had started telling Toki about my day when my father came in and asked me who I was talking to. I pretended not to know what he was talking about.

I fell quickly asleep, forgetting entirely to say goodnight to Toki. Perhaps it was this oversight – this omission – that led to what happened next. I woke sometime in the early morning to a scratching sound. It was coming from the drawer. Carefully I opened it and there erupted a great shriek. It was a sound like that of an animal caught in a trap, and it echoed alarmingly around the hut. I slammed the drawer shut. It took me a moment to realise that the shrieking in fact was my own.

My father was the first on the scene. I pulled myself together. I told him that I'd had a bad dream, that he should go back to bed, that I was fine, absolutely fine. And when I was once more alone I slowly, and with thundering heart, opened the drawer again.

Apart from his eyes, which had taken on a new sheen, a new depth, which had come to luminous life, the thing that struck me most forcibly about Toki's transformation was the way he was breathing: rapidly, as a terrified animal might. For some reason I thought of a crouching frog, breathing in and out great belly-fuls of air – but of course he looked nothing like a frog. He was far too hairy, for one thing. No longer a bundle of sticks and glue and nylon fur he was now completely covered with a black glossy pelt. It looked silky to the touch, almost but not quite oily.

I could see by his swivelling, fear-filled eyes that he was more terrified than I; even so it took me several minutes before I reached out to touch him. He made a little squeaking sound and scampered further back into the corner of the drawer, breathing even more rapidly. I put my finger to my lips and shushed him. It was clear that he understood. He continued to cower, but quietly.

The Tokolosches I'd heard about were trickster figures, brim full of devilish confidence, and possessed of sexual mania. This little creature, which shuddered under my softest touch, whose little heart beat and trembled, when eventually he let me stroke him, inspired in me tremendous love. I no longer felt myself in any kind of danger.

After he had settled somewhat I reached into the drawer and ever so gently levered my hand underneath him – he felt strange and moist: had he wet himself, I wondered, in his terror? – and very slowly I lifted him up. I held him for a time in the palm of my hand and once his breathing had settled I placed him very lightly on my pillow.

I can't say how long I lay there, looking at him, while he, sitting on my pillow, inches from my face, looked back at me with his rich dark shining eyes. I soon discovered that my voice, far from alarming him, appeared to calm him. I murmured at first sweet nothings, which he quickly appeared to grow bored with, and so I told him instead about our visit to St Lucia two days earlier, and about the way the ranger banged on the side of the boat each time we went round a bend in the river so as not to startle the hippos. I talked just to keep talking. And when after a time he seemed to grow tired – his eyes narrowing, his chin dipping – I put him back inside the drawer.

I lay awake for a long time, though I must eventually have dozed off because at six-thirty I was once again startled by the knock at the door and the delivery of my tea tray.

5.

The first thing Toki demanded, when eventually he spoke, was food.

I will do my best to explain what it was like, listening to the little beast speak. It began as a kind of intuition – by this I mean that I had a vague sense of what he was thinking or hoping to say. These intuitions gradually began to formalise themselves into words, into complete sentences – not out loud, you understand, but as a kind of silvery whisper in my mind – and soon we were able to conduct entire conversations. No subject, no idea, however abstract, seemed beyond his grasp.

Toki was clear in expressing his needs and desires and it made perfect sense to me that having taken on a living shape he now required sustenance, nourishment. The only trouble was that his appetite grew and grew. At first he made do with the occasional snack – a few gummi bears, some crisps, the chocolate mint from the pillow – but it seemed that the more he ate the greater his appetite became. I began smuggling leftovers from breakfast and lunch and dinner into the hut for him, which soon became a risky business. In the end, though, when I became too weak to leave the hut, Toki simply polished off everything that was brought to me on a tray. This confused the clinical picture. Why, my parents wanted to know, if I was eating so much did I appear to be wasting away? The less I ate, the more he needed to. By the third day I had no appetite at all – and when my parents forced me to eat, I could not keep it down.

In the morning I sat just outside the hut on a folding chair watching the zebras graze and the other guests traipse to the pool and back, white towels slung over their shoulders. I overheard my mother and father arguing about me. How sullen I'd become, how remote! My father said that I was heading towards adolescence and that this sort of behaviour was to be expected; but my mother made the point that I hadn't been like this a week ago.

I grew anxious. How long before they made the connection? After an hour or so I went back to bed and cleaned out Toki's drawer. Perhaps I should explain here, for the curious or practical-minded, that once he started eating he also started shitting. This too made perfect sense. He was now a living thing and I suppose that what goes in must come out. I spread out in the bottom of Toki's drawer some two-day-old newspaper and this I replaced twice a day. Even when my whole body ached, when fever swept through me, when I was too ill and weak to reach for my glass of water, I scrupulously cleaned out the whiffy little pellets he left in a corner. I hated the thought of Toki sitting in his own shit.

That afternoon I managed to walk the 500 metres to the watering hole and there I sat watching as first the warthog and then twenty minutes later the nyala drank their fill. By the time I walked back to the hut, the sheets had been changed and there was a new chocolate mint on the pillow. I unwrapped it and gave it to Toki; he ate it eagerly. I rolled the green foil into a little ball and flicked it high into the air. Toki and I watched it rise. Toki and I watched as it fell down near my feet.

6.

It was on the third night that I received my first ever blow job. My parents had booked a night game drive and by this point it was obvious that I was far too unwell to come along. They didn't like to leave me alone, they said, but this was precisely what I longed for, to be left alone, or rather to be left alone with Toki, and so I insisted that that they go.

Little Toki was an expert cocksucker – he managed to keep his sharp little fangs well out of the way, and seemed to have no gag reflex. You might argue that I was still young and that size wasn't likely to be much of an issue, and in a sense you'd be right; but bear in mind that Toki, for all his growth, was himself only a small beast – smaller than an infant – and the way he took my little prick all the way down to the shaft, his cold wet nose pressed into my sparsely haired crotch, is surely to be applauded.

I wasn't ejaculating in those far-off days, but I did reach what I'd now call a dry orgasm: a tingling sensation in the tip of my cock built to climactic shiver, which then ran through my balls and even up into my stomach. Little Toki, his tongue flickering at the corners of his mouth, crawled down my leg, nestling comfortably against my right ankle and here, for the rest of this our second-last night together, he slept soundly.

7.

It was on the fourth day that the doctor was summoned. The Zululand Safari Lodge did not have one to call its own but they did have an arrangement with a larger hotel in nearby Ubizane. Dr Traugott was a sandy haired man with great big freckled hands, small yellow teeth and a chattering mouth.

Even now I can feel the cold chill of his stethoscope on my

bare chest and on my back, and smell his warm, sour and not entirely unpleasant breath. Examination over, he asked my parents whether he could have a few moments alone with me. I saw their hesitation but they did as he asked.

Once they were gone from the hut he sat down on the bed beside me, fished about in his coat and retrieved a pipe that, after elaborate preparations, he lit. I thought this a strange thing for a doctor to do during an examination, even in those days. I watched as he puffed. His pale eyes had taken on a misty vacant look but when he turned to look at me they had cleared to a new lucidity. He asked me whether I'd been seeing strange things.

A part of me wanted to point to the drawer where Toki sat, to be rid of my secret. But I did not reply.

'What about strange dreams?' I was silent. That was when he asked, 'Are you eating the food they bring you – or are you disposing of it?' I nodded.

'Which? Disposing?' I nodded again. After some more questioning – and I was honest in my answers, though without ever giving Toki away – the doctor called my parents back in. The problem, he told them, was not within his competence. They asked, what sort of problem was it, then? It was a spiritual matter, said the doctor – the German word he used was *seelisch*.

'I'd like the boy to see my colleague,' said the doctor. 'Dr Mngabu is his name. He's what we call a *sangoma*.'

'A witch doctor, you mean.' This from my father.

'Dr Mngabu is a traditional healer,' replied Dr Traugott, coolly. 'He lives and practises in a nearby village.'

'Will he come here?' asked my mother. 'No. We will have to go see him. Tomorrow.' Thereupon ensued much uproar, much debate. But eventually an agreement was reached: my father would accompany me and Dr Traugott.

8.

I feel a little embarrassed setting down what happened next. Suffice it to say that sometime between midnight and breakfast I felt a long Toki cock sliding up inside me. My arsehole when I woke on that fifth morning was raw and bruised and burning and I finally understood what Iris warned about all those years earlier. There was even some spotting on the sheets and I remember thinking what a good thing it was that we weren't home: it would have been a challenge there to hide the laundry from my mother. Here at the lodge the sheets were changed each day as if by magic and I knew that by the time I'd returned from my visit to the witch doctor the sheets would be fresh and tight and crisp. And if I didn't return – well, then it wouldn't matter, would it.

9.

I wish I could describe the journey from the lodge to the village but for most of the trip I was stretched out across the back seat, the plush velour against my hot cheek, my eyes closed. At one point I turned onto my back but all I could see were snatches of vast sky and the odd power line. We turned onto a rocky track, unsuited to the long wheelbase and soft suspension of the Chevvie, and then the car stopped. Staggering out of the back seat, I could see what appeared to be a small village, a few scattered beehive huts. We were greeted by a youthful woman bedecked in beads who kissed the doctor on both cheeks and lightly touched the top of my head before directing us to the second hut on the left. My father wished me luck, shook my hand. The doctor bent low and explained, his hot sour breath tickling my ear, that I must upon entering the hut lick the *sangoma*'s hand. I did not argue, so glazed and dazed and emptied out was I.

My impression of the inside of the hut was a blurred and queasy thing; I felt uneasy. I remember that cow-tail fly whisks hung on the walls; that there were a great number of glass jars; and that herbs lay drying on what looked like tea towels on the ground. It was dark and warm and there hung in the air a resiny smell.

The witch doctor, who crouched in front of a wall of glass jars, was wrapped in a cloak of leopard skin. Tied about his waist was a pouch made from the dried-out bladder of a goat. He extended his hand, palm up, and leaning over, I licked it. The *sangoma* nodded, gestured for me to sit straight, and stared at me for a long time. Then he began to ask, all in gestures you understand, for not a word passed between us, a series of questions.

Once I had answered gesture with gesture, as honestly as I was able, he began to burn what smelled like sage in a small ceramic pot, adding to this various dried herbs and who knew what else from the glass jars arrayed behind him.

When he gestured for me to get undressed, I felt no scruple. Nor did I feel fear when he took from his pouch a razor blade. The small incision he made, just above my right temple, was painless. But when he dipped his right index finger into the medicine, the *muti* he had made, and began to massage the potion into the cut, I winced. It stung and it throbbed. He repeated this procedure at my left temple, at the point where my collar bone met my shoulder, and – turning me gently about – on each cheek of my bum. Then he indicated for me to get dressed.

I sat before him and watched as he began throwing an assortment of bones and coloured pebbles onto a mat. This he stared at for a time, before smiling broadly, apparently pleased with what he saw. He gave me a very small pebble to swallow and this I did baulk at, but he persisted and I gave in. The last thing I remember is that he began making crosses in the air above me and in front of me, to the left of me and to the right of me ...

It was night when I came to, and cold. The witch doctor was gone. There was a gas lamp in the corner, and by its flickering light I could see the anxious face of my father peering over me. The doctor, who stood beside him, wore a satisfied look, a little complacent. I was feeling much better that night as we drove back to the lodge: still weak and frail but somehow in possession of myself. It would have been impossible to navigate the way without the directions of Dr Traugott. I sat upright this time and as we drove through the not-so-dark night – for it was the night of the super moon – I saw illuminated by its pale light no end of wonders.

Back at the lodge, I went straight to my hut. The bed was made as I knew it would be. And there was the mint chocolate on the pillow. I sat there for a moment on the edge of the bed, and began unwrapping the chocolate. I bit into it and watched with pleasure as the lurid green filling began to ooze out. I caught it just in time with my quick tongue. I chewed, swallowed, and placed the remaining chocolate in my mouth. Only then did I pull open the drawer and peering in saw all that was left of Toki – a few sticks, a twist of twine, and a smear of stinky mud.

Meanjin

The Abduction of Ganymede

Gay Lynch

> The male human is beautiful when his cheeks are still smooth, his body hairless, his head full-maned, his eyes clear, his manner shy and his belly flat.
>
> Germaine Greer, *The Boy*

You rest your arm on the balustrade of the stairs leading to the railway concourse while checking your phone app for the platform number and departure time of the train to Freo. You hear the tapping of rubber shoes on the black filigreed metal steps, a whoosh of air that flaps like clothing or wings and smells of perspiration and fried food. Someone cannons into you from behind. As you fall, you half turn, to see a thin boy using his arm like a paddle in turbulent waters to shore you up against the rail. You gasp at his face. At the piece of red leather tied around his hairless neck; at the tatty lace scarf veering to one side during the collision. At his beauty.

His full lips tremble, his eyes dart across your face and away as if in terror of a commuter in a silk shirt calling a transit guard. Or the police. Panic travels across his soft childish face. You want to press your thumb against the cleft in his tilted chin, like the god who placed it there.

When he sees you swaying in the right direction, he retracts his arm and pulls his too-small, dirty-green jacket across his chest, sweeps his fingers through shaggy fronds of yellow hair as a girl his age might do, shakes a bracelet of threaded plastic seeds down his arm to his wrist. He looks about thirteen.

Next he splays two uncertain fingers in a V against his lips and gasps as if he's been hurt before and he thinks you, not he, effected this collision, exposing him to danger. You feel his indecisive breath on your neck, before he leaps past you onto the platform. As he rounds a newsstand he swings back to look at you, his face pink and parchment-gold against the green of his collar, like an angel boy in the morning light.

Curving your hand round the flesh at your side, you draw in a sharp painful breath, registering an abrasion that may stain the only article of clothing remaining after a week of all-day conference-going and long boozy dinners. In fact, you had been wearing the shirt the previous night when, in the pursuit of knowledge and under the influence of Benedictine, you had kissed a postdoc not much younger than you in a taxi on its way to Miss Maud's Swedish Hotel. Such irony that his semen had not so much flown like tap-water but damned up when he passed out – before you had chanced to read his three-line bio.

The swell of morning commuters nudges you forward, gathers you up and you surge along with them. Before you reach the row of carriages and step up into the third, you glance at the signed route: City West; West Leederville; Subiaco; Daglish; Shenton Park; Karrakata; Loch Street; Claremont; Swanbourne; Grant Street, Cottlesloe; Mosman; North Fremantle; Fremantle (18.7 km). You like trains – their tetchy engines, their hissing doors, the steep drop beneath the carriages to the rails, signalling your strange fear of jumping, not of falling. You push past a girl with earphones threaded through her spiky absinthe-coloured hair, playing a game on her phone and past a middle-aged man reading a Manga comic, to take the only empty seat, on a bench that runs between the luggage corral and the door.

At first you don't notice the beautiful boy, clutching at vertical yellow poles to counteract the weight of his backpack; creeping past you like a Manna crab, heading towards the far wall of the carriage as if pursued by demons; sliding down the wall at the end of the carriage; hunkering down over his cracked running shoes. He doesn't appear to notice you at all as he twirls the end of his lacy scarf. Well good.

You open Germaine Greer's *The Boy* to a page of text, feeling like a paedophile. Then glance around to make sure that no-one observes you flicking past Proem with its disturbing elongated illustration, to a page comprising only text. 'Adolescence is not a moment but a process. A male child becomes a boy when it starts but may not yet be a man when it finishes,' Greer asserts. Surely it is different, as close to actra-fraternal as you can get, for an art academic to view a photograph showing a boy's penis, compared to the way a voyeur might: dreaming of power? After all, you are about to meet a researcher in the field of Neoplatonic readings of the male nude – in more neutral circumstances. After the meeting you'll go with him to a gallery that serves decent food and coffee, to renegotiate your criticism of his paper.

The boy on the floor begins to weep in a soft quiet way, using his sleeve to cover his face, but you can tell. Should you say something? It's probably nothing to do with the small bump he gave you on the stairs. He cannot realise how vulnerable he looks, how much he invites undesirable attention. You sit up straighter, try to flick him a rueful smile as if to say 'you're alright … I'm alright … Cheer up,' but he doesn't appear to notice you at all. Not now or until he mowed you down. You cross your bare legs. Apart from the small abrasion and a fright, you have come to no harm. Sunshine warms the back of your neck through the window.

At the next stop, more passengers exit than climb aboard. The boy remains crunched over his bag on the floor refusing eye contact. Why does he not pull himself together and take a seat? But he is not your responsibility, any more than the poststructuralist who fell asleep in your bed last night.

*

At Subiaco Station, two bare-chested youths of sixteen or so wait on the platform scrunching their white t-shirts in front of them. You know nothing more about Subiaco than last week's television footage of transit guards beating unconscious pumped-up spectators from the nearby stadium. You see no resemblance between these two youths and AFL initiates. One drags behind the other in a khaki military-style jacket with epaulettes. One looks sleepy, the other nervy. Their torsos are pale and lean; their thigh muscles show little definition beneath denim jeans sagging at half-mast. Rocking against each other as they leap into the carriage, they manage to stay upright, their searchlight eyes tracking back and forth across the aisle, seeking anyone blocking their access, before they subside on the seat opposite you.

In the warmth of the carriage, the smaller one with a thin, pointy face – ratty would be too unkind for he is pretty in an unvarnished way – slumps on the seat, one arm draped across the rise of his belly, long slim fingers dangling, head nodding on his skinny chest. He elbows his mate in the ribs. 'Kasimir. Kasi.'

The other starts, an aggrieved look on his face. 'What the fuck?' He dabs at a smear of blood from a mouth pleated with anxiety and wrings water out of his shirt onto the upholstery.

They confer.

'I don't give a fuck, Ethan,' he says.

You can't follow their conversation about not getting enough, and when it went in, and fantasy, but you know they aren't talking about Harry Potter. That they're off their faces on something. You glance uneasily around the carriage trying not to meet their eyes, still shielding the illustrations in Greer's book with your hand.

The taller one, Kasi, stares directly at you. Holds your gaze in an aggressive way. You close the book. He has handsome Slavic features: strong dark eyebrows that meet across his long nose, deep-set brown eyes, a wide mouth and a fine curly hair sprouting at his throat. He has pushed decent imitation designer sunglasses into his dark hair.

Next, he stares across the space to *your* boy and points him out to his mate.

Prickles run down your spine.

'If he looks at me that way again,' says Ethan, sitting up, 'I'll ram his head through the window.' He throws a brace of savage looks across the carriage. His bloodshot eyes roll before he subsides on the seat again.

Kasi replies, in a pleasant-enough tone, beating his oddly sensuous, long eyelashes. 'Not before you tell him. Then, we'll put him through the glass.'

You feel an urgent need to get away from both of them but, simultaneously, you want to manoeuvre yourself between them and the angel on the floor. You can't sit and watch someone beat up a prepubescent kid.

Meanwhile, the beautiful boy refuses to lift his concentration from the patterns on the floor but his tears have stopped. Two wise but ineffectual moves.

You place your hands on your book and lean forward. You intend asking Kasi questions about the suburbs through which you're passing, establishing yourself in a light and animated tone as a harmless tourist. Which you are.

He grunts and turns to face you.

'Can you tell me about Claremont? From here, I can see a lot of trees. Are there places to moor your boat by the river?' you ask.

'It's a rich suburb,' he says 'Next to Peppermint Grove. Where wankers live, often just the two of them with fourteen bedrooms and ten bathrooms. Stinking rich.'

'Mining money?'

'May. . .be.'

'What about Swanbourne? Would you like to live there?'

'How do you know I don't?' he replies, dragging his eyes away from the boy on the floor, to glare at you.

'Do you?' You smile, hoping to amend your mistake.

'Watch this space.'

Station signs flash by. The Manga man alights at Cottesloe. Kasi begins to confide his backstory or at least one he thinks you will find appealing. He comes from Melbourne, didn't like school, but Perth is okay. He sounds articulate. You decide he has a mother and a father who at some point showed an interest in him. You keep trying verbally to hold him at bay. Ask him questions that lead away from the school's failure to keep him. What does he like doing best? Does he like music?

You get nothing back. He shrugs. Then recommends that you go to the Maritime Museum at Freo for the shipwrecks, and to be sure and eat at Fisherman's Wharf.

You nod and while you think of more questions, you point out the unsettling sight of a black hawk, buffeted by wind, flying backwards past the train window.

He barely turns his head. Suddenly, apropos of nothing, he stands up – how can this happen while conversing with someone once adept at social discourse? – *and* with no further warning but a reflex fondling of his balls, launches himself across the carriage.

Your heart lurches.

The beautiful boy looks up from examining the minute striations on the palms of his hands: life lines, ancient scars. You think, after all, he can't be more than twelve.

But his potential aggressor has your full attention. His hair is unfashionably spiked and glitters with some kind of stale fruity gel that you smell as he passes. He wants you to watch. Perhaps to intervene and stop him. You, rupturing his performance will delight him. It will cause a scene. He will draw out the moment before he acts. You know this and you *will* not rattle his cage.

Kasi drops on his haunches to whisper into the boy's ear. Through his spiky hair you notice scars like evidence of lightning strikes on the back of his scalp. Hairdressers should be compelled to notify authorities. The boy turns his head to the window, doesn't speak. His skin shines with perspiration. The older boy weighs up his seeming passivity. Perhaps he is warning the kid to keep away from his friend Ethan – knows his work – wants to save him from chemical violence.

You glance uneasily around the carriage. You think of the shape of a body in a shattered window, on a train travelling at speed. The damage to the boy's beautiful skin when flung by angry young gods.

Kasi retreats to his seat and begins flexing his skinny arms. They look quite white in the sunlight, with their smattering of black moles.

You resume your burble with less confidence. He pretends an avuncular politeness beyond his years – the little shit has made his point and you should treat him with respect – relaxed, leaning back in his seat, left ankle crossed across his right knee. So erratic. Earlier, you could not help but like the positive aspects of his personality. His intelligence. His certain acceptance that an educated fellow-commuter will play this game with him. Could he mean well, after all? Your ignorance about Perth pleases him, you know this, as he points out landmarks, tells you he will help you find the Fremantle Arts Centre, once the Claremont Mental Hospital, when you arrive.

Intermittently the boy on the floor lifts his head and sniffs the air around him like quarry or like someone selling something. The train carriage has lost any hope of being a neutral space. In either case, who among the passengers, deep in books, tapping on keyboards, chatting on their phones, massaging leather bags, will defend him? None, you surmise and he knows it although people often surprise you in crises. What looks like suturing thread but is probably acrylic cotton holds parts of his worn, green coat together. In his disguised agitation he has snapped a section apart revealing only the golden curves of his immature chest. He tugs the lapels together and attempts the difficult feat of disappearing into the floor.

Get off at the next stop, you send by telekinesis. *Don't stand up until the last possible moment. Then run.*

*

The train brakes at Mosman and a grey-skirted schoolgirl jumps on, taking the seat beside you. Instead of wearing her ribboned straw hat she holds it against her blue blazer; no doubt a hangable offence. You *will* her to be quiet.

Kasi appears immediately drawn to her and deftly restarts your conversation in an effort to show his best side. Now that is charitable.

An ostensibly respectable adult talking to the boy upsets the girl's radar and she gives him eye contact. She should not. She should keep her head down.

He becomes excited again, leaning forward from his bench seat, baring his rickety teeth in our general direction. You imagine his mind discarding and ticking points that he thinks will interest the schoolgirl. Nothing too personal. He tells you again which road you should take when you disembark at Freo. He asks *her* if she likes to study.

The schoolgirl has scraped her hair back from her forehead and pinned service badges on her lapels; she is an advertisement for the values education offered at her expensive school. She wants to help and she begins to chip in on your tourist conversation with the boy. You are gracious and try to steer the conversation away from him but it is too late.

Her voice is sweet, refined and pleasant. Friendly.

He is not unattractive with his wide crooked smile, his eagerness to engage. But unpredictable.

He speaks more slowly. Moves smoothly into an anecdote about his stay in a Melbourne hospital. There was nothing physically wrong with him, he says. They'd locked him up and pumped him full of drugs for nothing. He'd had to do a heap of tests. More details slide into place. Although he doesn't say so, it is clear he has been detained for three weeks by mental health provisions.

The schoolgirl seems curiously unaware of his sense of thwarted entitlement, or is scrupulously polite. 'I quite like tests,' the girl says. Perhaps she acts deliberately obtuse. Is she passive aggressive?

Momentarily, he switches his attention back to the boy on the floor, who places his head in his hands. Kasi reminds you of your dog, toying with two mice . . . letting one limp away a certain distance but keeping an eye on it as he bats the second one with his paw.

'Well done,' he says, his attention returning to the schoolgirl. 'To do so well at exams. I hope you like university. Not for me. I couldn't concentrate at school. I was smart and everything but . . .'

You turn your head away to the window. You want to take the girl's hand and apologise. *Don't talk to him. Really. I misled you.*

To your great relief, the girl rises and reaches for the strap, leaving you to focus on the cherub-faced boy on the floor. He is dragging small change from his jacket pocket, cupping his hand to count the coins, perhaps to see if he has a sufficient number to buy food or a bottle of water.

Kasi and the schoolgirl continue chatting until the next stop where she gets off.

He stares at her legs as she alights. 'Nice girl.' He waves to her. 'I can take you to the Maritime Museum if you want,' he says inviting you back into the conversation.

'Oh, thank you,' you say.

He points it out in the distance, layered wings of silvery-white on the point, rather like the Sydney Opera House.

'I should find both places, I think.' How will you shake him off? 'Perhaps you could give me directions.'

'Really nice girl.'

'Sweet.'

'She was a bit suspicious of me,' he adds.

'I don't think so.'

'Yes, she was.'

'Well, you can't blame her in a way.'

He prickles up.

You lost his trust.

'Do you mean my tattoo?'

You shake your head. It is small, as far as tattoos go; you hadn't noticed it on his scrawny shoulder.

He clenches his fists. 'What do you mean?'

'Well, some boys don't have a good track-record with girls. Not everyone is kind and polite like you.'

'Yeah. That's right.'

'She has to keep herself safe,' you say.

He nods. His friend sprawls looking half-alive, throws out a fruity cough that makes him nurse his chest with one hand.

You look away, scan the carriage for fascinating details. The boy on the floor remains motionless. Perhaps he is frozen, in terror. Resignation.

Before the last stop you try to ease out of the conversation, watch the beautiful boy stand up and move to the middle door to exit at Fremantle. Two passengers queue behind him, preparing to alight. When the train screeches to a stop Kasimir and Ethan swing out of their seats and into the aisle – in no great hurry but close enough to reach around and touch him – once more gripping their damp, scrunched tee shirts against their crotches, as they shoulder their way up behind him. Ethan sniffs and coughs into his tee shirt. You stand, fingers searching your tote bag for your phone. Who should you call? The postdoc? He shouldn't be far away? A transit guard? Haven't seen one. One hand on the strap you edge forward.

They swing away on the balls of their feet following the boy, who has his head down trying to weave around disembarking passengers as he trudges forward through the railway turnstile. He hides behind a curtain of hair that has flopped into his face.

Before they reach the roadside, Kasi lunges forward to hiss something in the boy's ear and takes hold of his arm. And as if to dismiss *you,* he spins around so that you are face to face again and calls out, 'turn right here and follow the next street to the water.'

You nod and thank him. Even from a distance, you hear his mate grumbling, only compos enough to fling hostile looks about him.

The first blow falls. In your struggle to reach the boy you drop Greer's book. 'Stop it,' you cry. 'He's my nephew.' You call on your inchoate friendship. 'Please. Kasi…mir.'

He releases him, punishing his arm with one last thump, and turns towards you as if you've betrayed him. 'Why didn't you say so, you dumb bitch?'

His friend shambles forward, stepping over a bedraggled black bird facedown in the gutter, a stream of blood trickling from beneath its beak. Poor kite.

You seize your newly adopted nephew, slinging your arm around his slight shoulders. He tries to shrug you off. You decide to reschedule your date with the young academic until you've clarified your thinking about Rembrandt's transmogrification of Michelangelo's famous drawing of a beautiful boy. You tug the boy through the graceful 100-year-old station archway, into the twenty-first century, towards the esplanade and a feed of fish and chips. Glancing back, you see them, Kasimir and Ethan, giving you the finger before turning in the opposite direction.

Breaking Beauty

On Ice

Eleanor Limprecht

Deb knocked on the door of Room 17 and tried the handle. It was locked. She pulled the set of keys from her lanyard. Patients weren't meant to lock their doors but Mrs Ciszek forgot, as she forgot many things. If the head nurse listened to Deb they would have disabled the locks by now. She found the right key, turned it and pushed down the handle, breathing in the corridor scent of bleach with the ammonia tinge of adult nappies beneath. Mrs Ciszek's room smelled like the lavender soap – Yardley's – that reminded Deb of her own Nan.

'Mrs Ciszek, it's Deb. Wake up, time to take your pills.' She rolled the meds cart inside and flicked the light-switch on the wall beside her. The fluorescent tubes buzzed and flickered, lazy, like they needed to be woken as well. She walked over to the window to open the blinds and glanced over at the figure in Mrs Ciszek's bed.

Oh shit, not this again.

The blankets were moving and shifting, two white-haired heads lay side by side on the plastic-lined pillow.

Mrs Ciszek propped herself up on one elbow, spry for a woman of her age. She looked down at herself and pulled the sheet across her wrinkled, flattened breasts. Her hair was a halo of frizz, her eyes blinked. She reached to the bedside table for her specs and put them on. 'It's not what it looks like, Rob,' she said. 'He needed a place to sleep.'

'Don't worry, I'm not your husband,' Deb said. She grabbed the dressing gown from behind the door and brought it to her. 'But Mrs Ciszek, we can't do this anymore. It's not allowed.'

The figure beside Mrs Ciszek rolled away from them, still asleep, taking the blankets with him. He exposed a back covered with fine, downy hair in a trail to the crack of his arse. How the two of them could fit – much less sleep – in one of those single beds was a miracle in itself. Deb wanted to handle this on her own, but knew she'd lose her job if they found out. She picked up the handset beside the bed and dialled the nurses' station. 'It's Deb,' she said, covering the mouthpiece, like Mrs Ciszek wasn't going to hear her. 'I'm in Room 17. We have a situation. Yep. Like before.'

While they waited for the head nurse Deb helped Mrs Ciszek into her dressing gown and gave her a little white cup of pills, another cup of water, and watched to make sure that she swallowed both.

'Say aaah,' she said.

'La la laaaa,' Mrs Ciszek said, and Deb smiled. It was their little joke. Every morning. Other nurses hated the dementia ward but Deb thought it was okay. Sure, they forgot everything, sure it was like living in *Groundhog Day*, but they woke up like babies: blinking their eyes at the brand new world. One, Mr Aslam (Room 27) devoured his toast and jam each morning as though it were a miracle. As though a crappy slice of Tip Top, a smear of margarine and a glob of strawberry jam was as good as it got. She didn't mind at all.

Deb could hear the squeak of Jill's white leather shoes coming down the long corridor. 'You know,' she said, 'you really shouldn't let Mr Abrahams into your bed.'

'Where are we meant to do it?' Mrs Ciszek said, 'On the floor?'

*

That was Luke's favourite line when she told him the story. They were sitting in front of the TV, watching *The Voice*, eating pad Thai and red beef curry from plastic takeaway containers slick with oil. She picked up the takeaway from Thai It Up on her way home. Luke put the mute button on, even though one of the contestants he liked was singing – the one with no legs who zoomed onto stage in a motorised wheelchair.

'Are you shitting me?' he said. 'She asked you that? Are they getting it on in there? These people are like, what, ninety? A hundred years old?'

'I think Mrs Ciszek is in her eighties, Mr Abrahams is younger – he might be in his seventies. He's in good shape for a seventy-year-old guy.' Deb grinned. Luke thought her work was boring, once he figured out that she wasn't going to bring him home any veterinary-strength horse tranquilisers or Viagra he wasn't interested. But he kept the show muted, put his beer on the floor and jumped off the couch.

'That shit's crazy,' he said. 'Does she even know who he is? Mate, I need to hook up with some Alzheimer's chicks. They'll be like – *ooh, fuck me*, then they'll forget, and two minutes later, they'll be like – *oooh fuck me*, all over again.'

Luke was standing on the carpet, blocking her view, thrusting his pelvis back and forth as he acted out the scene. Deb laughed, but she put down her plastic fork.

'Yeah, that's just what it's like. Just what dementia is like. It's like porn, Luke, like non-stop geriatric porn.'

'Really?'

'No, you dickhead. I feel sorry for them. But it's weird as well, it's like they're lovebirds. Young teenagers who are really into each other but don't know how to act or how to talk.'

Luke sat back down and punched the remote to turn off the mute button. 'Did you see what Kylie is wearing?' he said, 'Where does she find this shit?'

Deb scraped the last bite of pad Thai into her mouth, leaving nothing but squeezed out lemon in the plastic container. 'Do you want to know the saddest part?'

Luke didn't look at her, just raised an eyebrow.

'Mrs Ciszek is still married. Her husband still comes to visit her once or twice a week, and sometimes she even remembers him. This morning she thought I was him. She started coming up with excuses, as if she knows what she's doing is wrong. Jill said we need to tell her husband about the situation with Mr Abrahams.'

'Wow, that's fucked,' Luke said, taking another swig from his beer, not taking his eyes off the screen. 'Wait till I tell the guys at work this one. Demented old ladies, huh? Who'd have guessed it.'

*

There was a police officer at their staff meeting the next morning. She kept her hat beside her on the table as she spoke about what constitutes assault and what constitutes consent, how the police determine whether someone is even capable of giving consent. She tapped her fingernails on the top of the table as she spoke. Deb sat on her hands to keep from biting her nails. Her stomach felt queasy. She'd gone to bed after dinner, after cleaning the kitchen and making Luke his lunch to take to work the next day. She felt a heaviness; a lethargy that she couldn't trace to one particular thing. Luke stayed up late, his eyes flicking between the screen of his phone and the TV.

'The issue is,' the director of the nursing home was speaking now, a pale woman with pearls the size of eyeballs hanging around her neck, 'the issue when both parties have dementia is that it is difficult to determine whether consent has been given. They might have forgotten. The aged care bodies realise that this is an issue and are drafting some guidelines for dementia patients and sexual behaviour, but at the moment we have nothing but our own sense of right and wrong to guide us. Jill, do you want to speak to this? As the head nurse on the dementia floor, do you think that this is a consensual situation?'

Jill took off her wire-rimmed spectacles and made a show of folding them beside her notebook before speaking. Deb knew her supervisor was loving this moment: being the expert. She tented her fingers and started in on the stages of dementia that Mrs Ciszek and Mr Abrahams were in, their vital stats, family situations. Deb wanted to scream. Everything they were saying, none of it touched on the most crucial part. The two patients – brain-riddled as they both were – wanted to be together. They sought one another out. They made one another happy. Something in this bleak place gave them joy.

They wrapped up deciding that Jill would speak to Mr Ciszek, and they would set up individual counselling sessions for Mrs

Ciszek and Mr Abrahams. 'We can't keep them apart in communal areas,' the director said, 'but we're going to make sure they are not alone in their rooms together. There are a whole raft of OH&S issues as well as ethical and moral, not to mention possible criminal, implications here. As a temporary measure, we are going to move Mr Abrahams to a different floor. That way we can mitigate the situation.'

The meeting wrapped up and the participants all shuffled their papers, clicked their pens, drained their mugs. The police officer replaced her hat and Deb saw a small wave of relief pass over her features. That was done. Jill came over and put her hand on Deb's shoulder. Deb could smell the coffee on her breath. 'I'd appreciate if you could alert Mrs Ciszek to the situation this morning, tell her that Mr Abrahams is moving, just don't tell her where.'

Deb shook her head. 'Why do we have to keep them apart? I think she's going to be really upset, Jill.'

Jill closed her eyes and Deb could see where she had applied her taupe eye shadow unevenly that morning, more on the left eyelid than the right. She opened her eyes.

'Were you just listening?' she said. 'Earth to Deb! You know why we have to separate them.'

Deb nodded and washed out her mug in the sink, scrubbed her hands and left to begin her shift. She filled the meds cart and pushed it down the hall, her mouth dry. She left Mrs Ciszek's room for last.

*

Her phone vibrated in her pocket while she was giving Miss White insulin. She went to the toilet to put the needle into the sharps bin and checked the screen. It was from Luke, a text.

Goin to the pub after work, it's Dan's bday.

She swore under her breath. He had forgotten that her auntie was coming round for dinner. She was visiting from Canberra. Deb peeled off her latex gloves. Maybe he didn't forget. Around her family Luke got nervous and talked about himself too much. On her birthday he'd been drunk and started telling the story about how his mum used to lock him in the outside dunny when he pissed her off. One time she forgot about him and he was out there all night, he'd unravelled the toilet roll on the cold concrete floor and fallen asleep on it. He was ten. Luke laughed at this but no one else did. He grew quiet and put his arm around Deb, taking a swig of his beer.

'Who's up for another round?'

Luke's mum moved to Thailand when he turned seventeen. They visited her on their first trip overseas together – a few months after they started dating. Deb was nineteen; Luke was twenty-three. His mum had skin like leather from the sun and long fingernails with designs that changed weekly. Palm trees, leopard print, rainbows. They were often wrapped around a can of Tiger beer, or the arm of one of the middle-aged, sunburnt and balding tourists she met at the bar. The men never stayed around long, she confided to Deb one night. 'They all come here for a young Thai girl with a tight pussy, not an old lady like me. I don't know why I stay. Can't imagine going back.'

Deb actually felt sorry for her then, in spite of everything. But she also wanted to get out of there, away from the smells of burning rubbish and fish sauce and tiger balm; away from Luke's mum. Luke was sweet about it: he changed the flights so they could leave early. He let her drag him away.

Deb pushed her cart to Room 17. She knocked and swung the door open. Mrs Ciszek sat on her vinyl-covered armchair. The telly was on high volume with one of those American talk shows – *The View* – where highly groomed women gather and peck at the news like a pack of crows.

'Good morning Mrs Ciszek,' Deb shouted. She walked over, grabbed the remote and turned the telly off. Mrs Ciszek looked at her and her face lit up. 'Good morning!' she said. 'You look tired, dear.'

Deb pulled up a chair beside the vinyl armchair. 'I'm okay, how about you? How are you feeling?'

'Good, good,' Mrs Ciszek said. She leaned over towards Deb as though to tell her a secret. 'I might go ice skating today.'

Deb smiled. 'I don't think so, it's 30 degrees outside. Did you used to ice skate, when you were a girl?'

'I grew up in Mazury, Poland,' Mrs Ciszek said, 'where the lakes freeze every winter. On ice I go very, very fast.'

'Is that where you met Rob?' Deb asks. 'In Poland? Or did you meet him here?'

Mrs Ciszek looks at her, tilting her head. 'Who?'

'Your husband. Mr Ciszek.'

She shrugged. Deb passed her the white paper cup of pills. The cup of water.

'Say ahhhh.'

'La la laaaa.'

Deb took the cups and stood to carry them to the bin. She sat back down and put her hand on Mrs Ciszek's arm. There was the buzz of the air conditioner and disembodied voices from the TV from the next room.

'Do you know who Mr Abrahams is?'

Mrs Ciszek looked confused.

Deb tried again: 'Abe?'

She smiled. 'Yes.' Deb felt a shiver of something – joy? – pass through Mrs Ciszek's small, shrivelled body. She wanted to rip a chunk out of her own thumbnail.

'The head nurse, Jill, is moving Abe to another floor. You can't keep going off into one another's rooms, sleeping together. It's dangerous, in your state. And I'm afraid it's just not allowed.'

Mrs Ciszek looked at her. Her mouth hung open, and Deb could see the place where her false teeth ended and her real teeth began. She blinked, her eyes watering.

'Why would you keep us apart?'

Deb thought about Luke. About how, after sex, he always turned his back to her. He didn't like to be touched while he fell asleep.

'Mrs Ciszek, you're still married to Rob. You forget this; you have dementia, so it's complicated. We're trying to come up with a better solution. But for now, please don't be upset. Just for a while, you can see Abe in the dining hall, in the common rooms, but you can't go off alone into one another's rooms.'

Mrs Ciszek worked her jaw. She pulled up her dressing gown, which had fallen off one of her shoulders, showing a thick, beige bra strap. Deb had no idea whether she understood anything. She felt that familiar lethargy again. She wasn't suited for any of this. None of her training prepared her for this task.

'Why not your husband? Why not Rob?' Deb said, as much to herself as to Mrs Ciszek, not expecting the old woman to respond.

She stood, her keys jangling as she did, and walked towards the cart. She pushed it to the door. She almost didn't hear Mrs Ciszek's response, which came just before the TV was switched back on, a creak before an onslaught of sound.

*

Deb sat at home in front of the TV, flicking through channels. A figure skater popped up on the screen – clad in tan tights and a sparkling leotard – spinning and leaping through the air. It was the Winter Olympics and this skater from Romania wore heavy makeup and a fierce look in her eyes as she leapt and scraped, glided and lowered, rose across the ice. Deb had never been on ice, but watching this small figure skater she could imagine how Mrs Ciszek must have felt. The wind rushing past her ears, the cold air on her cheeks.

She went into the kitchen. She had rung her auntie earlier, cancelling dinner, saying she was tired. Auntie said she understood but Deb heard the tightness in her voice. It wasn't often that she came to visit. Deb ate three Weet-Bix for dinner and made a cup of peppermint tea. She took it to bed, flipping through a magazine of Luke's, a copy of *Tracks* where all the guys wore wetsuits and all the girls were taking theirs off. She woke in the middle of the night again, the screen flickering in the next room.

Luke was home. He was on the couch, asleep. The remote had fallen to the floor and she switched the TV off, put the throw over him and watched him cough and turn in his sleep. As he coughed she could smell what he'd taken in: stale cigarettes, rum and Coke, a late-night kebab. His face was creased from the corduroy of the couch, marked with narrow red stripes.

Deb grabbed her keys and walked out into the still night. There were hardly any stars, and the air was jasmine-heavy and humid, as though it might rain. She started her car and backed out of the driveway, drove out of the cul-de-sac and down the street. She didn't know where she was going, she just had to go, to steer something in a direction she chose.

She thought of Mrs Ciszek's words, as she had opened the door to walk out of Room 17 that morning.

After she had asked – 'Why not your husband? Why not Rob?'

'I don't know him, so how can I love him?' Mrs Ciszek had asked, not turning in her chair to watch Deb go.

'Maybe I forget. Maybe I never did.'

Kill Your Darlings

The Level Playing Field

Julie Koh

On the Level Playing Field, the eternal game is afoot.

No-one can remember the exact date the match began, but most people agree it was at four o'clock in the afternoon, Coordinated Universal Time, when the crowd started to roar.

The cheering began as a supermodel and the Chairman of the Board of the Level Playing Field strode out onto the grass. They carried an LV travel case between them.

'Welcome to the levellest playing field in existence,' the Chairman said, leaning into the microphone. 'On the Level Playing Field, everyone plays by the same rules.'

The crowd continued to roar. Bulbs flashed from the sidelines.

The model and the Chairman opened the case, revealing a shining golden trophy to the world.

'This trophy is a symbol of boundless opportunity and freedom,' said the Chairman, his words echoing throughout the stadium. 'On the Level Playing Field, each player pursues his own interest for the good of all. The Level Playing Field is a showcase of the pure artistry of each man.'

Close-ups of the competitors appeared on the big screens around the stadium, showing them jumping up and down in the tunnel, then running onto the Field. The cameras tracked past their faces as they stood in lines on the grass, singing their individual anthems simultaneously.

The players' shirts were plastered with logos. Ads in every language – for fast food, light beers, electronics and credit cards – flicked up on rotation on the perimeter advertising displays.

The players were fired up. They shook their thighs and rolled their heads from side to side.

The referee spoke into his mic and signalled that it was time for kick-off.

*

This is what my friend Paul tells me about the Level Playing Field. He says the game has been going on for so long that people in the crowd have gotten married in the stands, reproduced, and taught their offspring how to roar too.

Just the thought of the Level Playing Field makes my eyes shine.

Paul and I are installation slash performance artists. We work as a duo called Duo. Our most recent artwork was a movement piece involving a troupe of dancers dressed up as pigs dressed up as swans. The only problem is that no-one likes our art, so we don't have any money. Paul says we don't have a market for our work because we're ahead of our time. People just don't get us yet, he says.

'How do you know?' I always ask him. 'What if it's because we're *behind* our time?'

We're really struggling. I threw out my toothbrush the other day then realised I couldn't afford another. Paul reckons that we could maybe find a way to get to the Level Playing Field and compete. Maybe then we would earn enough money to live, and even send some cash back to our families.

Paul's friend knows a guy who's doing recruitment for the Level Playing Field. We arrange to meet him.

'Essentially, you'll be contractors,' the guy says. 'No-one in the crowd is interested in doing this sort of work.'

The guy tells us there'll definitely be opportunities for us to progress up the chain and ultimately play on the Level Playing Field.

Paul gets out his fountain pen and signs his contract with a flourish. I borrow the pen and scratch in my name where the little red and yellow sticky tab arrow says to sign.

*

On the day we're due to travel to the Level Playing Field, Paul turns up in hot pink overalls and a tweed flat cap.

'We're going all the way on the LPF,' he says, 'and we're gonna do it in style.'

The recruiter ticks us off a list and herds us into a shipping container.

I ask if this is normal but he doesn't reply and disappears.

We talk to the other guys already crouched in the container, smoking cigarettes. They're all artists too. Everyone has had the same bright idea about playing on the Level Playing Field.

I complain to Paul about the heat and how it's hard to breathe in here.

'Disregard it!' Paul says. 'The artist must disregard every limitation!'

*

We arrive at the Field in the backs of trucks. A Manager in a suit walks out to meet us. He gets us to jump out in single file and directs us down a manhole.

We climb down into the sewers and tunnel networks below the stadium, where the Manager tells us we're going to live.

I look around. There are thousands of people already living here. It's hard to believe there'll be enough room on the Field for all of us to compete.

The Manager tells us that the rent for the sewers will come straight out of our pay. He says we have to stay invisible and underground during the day when the match is being played.

'Your presence makes the crowd uncomfortable,' he says. 'Apparently, you've all got haunted stares.'

'How rude!' says Paul. 'I'm not haunted, and I certainly don't stare.'

The Manager puts us to work in the tunnels.

We sit underground in long rows, sewing the uniforms of the players and weaving their knee-high socks. All the uniforms we make start off identical but then we pass them down the line so they can be embroidered with different logos before being folded and inserted into clear plastic packets and sent up to the Field.

In the sewer creche, children stitch fluoro yellow sneakers by hand, and thread fluoro yellow laces onto them. The sneakers are sent up with the uniforms, so they can be worn by the players and ball boys.

While we are sewing, we hear the crowd go wild. A player has run to the sideline and has kneeled to tie up the fluoro yellow shoelace of the youngest ball boy. The crowd approves.

The Level Playing Field takes care of all.

*

The Manager tells us that to keep the stadium in tiptop condition, we need to maintain and upgrade it on a continuous basis.

We're only allowed to do this work at night. We listen until the crowd is gone, and emerge from the manhole, blinking under the stadium lights.

To keep the Field level, we trim the blades of the grass with scissors. We form a line on our hands and knees at one end of the Field, and work our way over to the other side.

We test the perimeter ads and the big screens to check they're in good working order. We sweep and hose the stands and keep working on the stadium roof, which is still incomplete.

*

We work every waking hour, seven days a week, but we barely earn any money. The Manager says we're in the process of paying our debt to the Board of the Level Playing Field for bringing us to the Field in the first place. He says this is written in our individually negotiated contracts. None of us has a copy.

In our section of the sewer, an oil painter keels over from overwork and malnutrition. We try to revive him, to no avail. His debt hasn't been paid, so his sixteen-year-old son is brought in to replace him.

The painter's death was inevitable – there's barely any food underground to sustain us.

Paul pokes me a lot and laughs about how hungry we are.

'I can see your ribs,' he says. 'Get some pork belly in you, pronto!'

He's the sort of guy who cracks jokes when he's sad.

*

We figure out ways to get food. At night, we gorge ourselves on half-eaten hot dogs and abandoned cups of chips from the stands. During the day, at half-time, we wait for the players to sit down and eat lunch at a long table on the sidelines. Paul and I stretch out our fingers to see what crumbs we can catch through the drain underneath the table.

It's still not enough, and I despair that we're never going to progress to positions at ground level.

'Disregard it all!' says Paul. 'The artist overcomes! The artist must die rather than surrender!'

'I'm not ready to disregard,' I say.

*

The Board has made the completion of the stadium roof a priority, and allows those artists working on the roof to come out during the daytime to put on the finishing touches.

One day, an abstract sculptor loses his footing and drops to his death onto the Field. No-one hears his scream above the roar of the crowd. The players dodge his body. Two graffiti artists run out and carry him off so that play can proceed uninterrupted.

Above and below ground, artists continue to die. The sixteen-year-old who has been brought in to replace his father has a heart attack.

We make makeshift coffins for the dead but the Board deems them unnecessary. The Manager arranges for the bodies to be dumped back down the manhole. The Board feels this is appropriate so that we can deal with our dead in whatever heathen way we like.

The problem is, there's nowhere for us to bury the bodies. We don't know what to do with them. They're starting to smell.

*

I try to convince Paul that we really have to stop disregarding the reality of the situation.

'You're right,' he says.

He pulls out his fountain pen and we start a petition demanding better working conditions, or release from our contracts. The Manager, however, tells us that the Board will only allow us to present the petition once we have one million signatures. We don't even have a million artists living underground.

It takes so long to complete the petition that, underneath the Level Playing Field, whole generations of artists reproduce, die and are reborn before the petition can be presented to the Board. Paul and I have already been through one life cycle and are nine years old again by the time the Chairman grants us an audience.

We are taken to the Chairman's vast boardroom, where he's sitting at the head of a long table.

'Well,' he says, leaning back in his chair. 'We've considered your petition at length. After much deliberation, we are able to offer you the opportunity to protest the Level Playing Field in an assigned area outside the stadium. We understand that you do not have the means to organise a protest, so if you would like to be allotted funding, you must first submit a grant application. A panel will assess your proposals on the basis of merit.'

'We're not going to sit here for another three generations waiting for you to read our grant application,' says Paul.

'Vicious ingrates!' says the Chairman, folding his arms. 'The Level Playing Field is good to us all. The Level Playing Field enables each and every one of us to manifest our own chandelier and swing from it. If you can't manifest your own chandelier, don't take it out on us. Don't spit on our hard-earned money.'

'Fuck this shit,' says Paul as we're taken back underground. 'Disregard it all! Let's be artists again.'

'We don't have any funding,' I say.

'I've been thinking about one final piece,' says Paul, adjusting his tweed cap. 'We can call it *Funeral I*. Then we'll be done with the Level Playing Field.'

After the meeting, the Manager tells us we have to whip up a rain cover for the Field because there's a ninety per cent chance of torrential rain overnight.

'Hey,' says the Manager, grabbing my shoulder. 'You've been letting the stadium get shabby during this whole petition saga. I better see a crapload of work done by start of play tomorrow.'

We work like crazy overnight on the roof and the grass. When we're done, we make a rain cover and drag it out over the Field.

*

In the morning, the crowd returns.

The commentators talk about the overnight rain, and the cameras zoom in to show officials walking onto the Field to remove the rain cover. The cover is translucent, and stitched together like patchwork. One camera does an extreme close-up, revealing fine hairs on the surface. The cover is made of specially treated human skin.

Officials rush to drag the cover off camera, unveiling a field made of human hair, grouped in patches of black, blond, brunette and red. On the big screens, a camera casts its gaze over the stadium roof, which has been completed using human bones.

The crowd gags. Their beer tastes like sweat; their soft drinks taste like tears.

They rush to the toilets to throw up. Standing under each toilet is a video artist collecting the puke in buckets.

The big screens show the players waiting in the tunnel. They're refusing to put on their new shoes, which have spikes made from sharpened human nails.

'I'm ready,' I say to Paul.

I carry his head onto the Field and place it in the centre, ready for kick-off.

Captial Misfits

How Is Your Great Life?

Jo Lennan

At college, Arjun Mishra had the room across from Ana's. Then a devout boy with a liking for overalls, he had possessed an unfailing sense of what was 'fishy' or 'fancy', these being the words he used to express his disapproval. At their university, which catered to foreigners in Tokyo, they were both scholarship kids among wealthier students. Yet three years after graduation, when she telephoned her old friend, he was living the high life in ritzy Azabu. He worked in IT for a Japanese bank and rented an apartment whose rent, he was proud to say, was more than Priya Vajpayee's whole monthly pay-packet (Priya having been, at college, the student marked out for success).

It was a humid night in July, just past ten o'clock. 'So Ana,' Arjun boomed. 'How is your great life?' An hour and a half later, she fronted up to his building – a steel plate gave its name as the Imperial Satellite – and, entering, took the lift up to the eighth floor. In jeans and a t-shirt and with freshly combed-back hair, he opened the door with a blast from the air conditioning unit. Letting her in, he gave her a key and a thick fold of yen 'for groceries or whatever'.

What could she do but take the money? She had no apartment and no job. She had fallen out with Shigeko, her flatmate and friend. She was waiting to receive a renewed Japanese visa, without which she could not find gainful employment. She didn't really want to go on hostessing, which was how she had made her living since her final year at college. She had never had a problem with what she did for work, but in recent dates with clients she had felt her smile grow wan and feeble, like a bulb about to blow. Worse, the greater her disaffection, the more some clients pursued her, perhaps attracted by what they took for an air of melancholy.

At least Arjun was too tactful to ask her awkward questions; it made it easier that he was brusque and businesslike. Pushing his hair back with his hand, he ran her through his week: on Tuesdays he fasted, on Wednesday nights he met friends for dinner, and on Fridays he went out to a strip club in Roppongi. Or that was what he had done last Friday, he added. Before that, he kept Friday evenings for cleaning and ironing. Now he was thinking of hiring a maid, a Filipina woman who would wash and iron his clothes and vacuum the apartment's fifteen tatami squares.

To Ana's immense relief, he didn't try to entertain her. He offered her the bed but she took the foldout futon, which she packed away each morning along with her possessions. She saw him when he was home late of an evening. At these times he poured red wine, cranked the air con up to full and settled on the couch in an expansive mood. He often spoke about his work and his colleagues at the bank. 'This is consumer banking,' he told her with a shrug. 'It's not a huge amount of money, a few million a branch. The technology is ancient. We're talking 1998, 1999. I was in high school then. When the system goes down, most times it's the temperature. Sometimes the branches don't have dedicated server rooms. The idiots don't realise, they put their coffee cups on the servers, turn off the AC when they leave. These machines are like grandfathers. In the heat they fall asleep. *Oof.*'

He would also ask her opinion on all manner of things, like whether it would hurt 'a great deal' if he waxed his chest. Eventually, though, his comments would turn to Fatima, the Iranian beauty he had fallen for in college. He still spoke of her with wonder, and seemed compelled to go over times he had spent with her.

'Once she came to see me on my break at work,' he recounted one night. 'The job was what we called grooming, which is brushing away cement. It was seven floors up. We worked without safety chains. I was the lowest of the workers, earning 600 yen an hour and plucking chunks of cement from my nostrils every day. My skin was dust, my voice hoarse. On a fifteen-minute break, I met Fatima in a park. I've never seen you like this, she said, her eyes brimming with sorrow. Oh Ana, if you could have seen those big doe eyes of hers!'

He shook his head. 'The jobs I worked! A summer labouring at a farm. A job in a factory crushing plastic in a furnace. My hair would change colour with the plastic in the air. The others left me their time cards and had me punch them out. Come on, they said. *Mou yamerou!* Let's go. But I would stay crushing that plastic until five p.m. exactly.'

Ana was shocked. She knew Arjun had worked through college; she had done the same. Yet she never would have guessed at the conditions he described. On campus he was always clean and crisply dressed. He was the student their lecturer for Asia Pacific Trade, the jovial Professor Gupta, would single out to ask, 'And how is your great life?'

But this, Arjun explained, was why he took such pleasure, coming home each night, in hearing his black Bellini shoes strike the lobby's marble tiles. He was pleased that his couch was upholstered in fine-grained leather, and that his curtains were resistant to sunlight and heat. He was buying his parents a new house in India (it had four spacious bedrooms and brass door handles throughout). He would also wire another ten thousand US dollars, which was a sort of apology for not going home for Diwali, the main holiday of the year. He couldn't leave just now, he said, with how things were at work. Still, he toyed with the idea of going to the States. It was a dream of his to work there and start a sushi chain. Then again, he said to Ana, what if Fatima tried to call him, as perhaps she would one day?

Most of his calls, though, were from colleagues or his mother. 'But Manu – she calls me Manu – how is your health, she asks.' Sitting back against white leather, he swigged his wine and grimaced. 'I'm tired of answering this question.'

*

In Tokyo that July, a series of typhoons threatened. Ana had never acclimatised to summers in Japan; in Tallinn, where she was from, there was nothing like this humidity. It made cowlicks in her hair, it made her top stick to her back, and worst of all it made her feel stupid and sluggish. It was hard to reach anyone among her old group of friends, most of whom now worked in 'office flower' jobs, menial roles that meant long hours and low-level harassment. She whiled away the hours at the nearby Segafredo, and listened idly to the talk of diplomats and bankers. After a long, lacklustre decade, Tokyo was booming again, they said. It was a sign of the times that the hospital up the road was building a new unit for cocaine overdoses. 'But it's only another kind of bankruptcy in disguise,' she heard an American declare. 'Pouring money into Tokyo while the rest of the country is stagnating . . .'

A waiter was tipping a pail of water on the footpath to cool the air. One table over, a man read Nanami Shiono's *Stories of the Romans*. The sky was a soft, close grey; there never seemed to be a sun. Checking her phone – it was near six – she saw a text from Shigeko: 'I hope you are not ungry.' Did she mean hungry or angry? Angry, probably. Ana didn't answer but just then the phone rang.

'So you'll be okay?' said Arjun. 'With the eel guy, I mean?'

'Takuya? He's fine.'

She was still seeing a few clients, Takuya among them. Generous as Arjun was, she had to make some money. And Takuya, who made his living advising restaurants, liked to dine in the company of European women. That night he was taking her to eat *hamo*, a type of eel you could only get during the summer months.

Takuya was one of Shigeko's circle, like many of Ana's clients. The first such introduction had come soon after she had moved in to the comfortable, large apartment not far from the college campus. Ana had answered Shigeko's notice on a board: 'Single Japanese woman seeks English-speaking flatmate.' She turned out to be in her early thirties, with a pale oval face, prominent teeth and demure clothes. She did not ask for a lot of rent, although she did require key money of eighty thousand yen, up front. When Ana moved in, Shigeko made her feel welcome by inviting her along to drinks and dinners out. The first of these dinners was with a policeman named Akimoto. He was kind and unassuming, though Ana wasn't sure why he would take them both to dinner. If he was dating Shigeko, why would he want Ana there? Perhaps it was just kindness to a student on a budget. Anyway, she ate the meal and swapped pleasantries. Afterward, Shigeko gave her a slim white envelope containing twenty thousand yen. A gift from Akimoto – 'for textbooks', she said. Ana tried to refuse the money, but Shigeko pressed it on her, smiling and saying, 'Take it, it's a gift, what's wrong with keeping it?'

Now, just after six, Ana sat at the café, toying with her iced coffee straw. Takuya showed up not long after wearing a blue basketball vest. His greeting came out oddly – 'Thank you for your cooperation' – but that was just his English. He always spoke to her in English, never in Japanese. As they walked toward Roppongi, he talked about business. 'The Japanese food industry is very difficult now,' he said. 'I have to persuade foreign investors to look at Japanese businesses. Profitability is down. You have to work hard to make money.'

Takuya's steps were long and loping; Ana hurried to keep up. They passed the deep green glades of Arisugawa Park, the private hospital and expensive apartments where heady-smelling jasmine flowed from iron-lace balconies. When they reached Roppongi Hills, a newish entertainment quarter, there was at least a tepid breeze waving the pond-grass in the courtyard. Early for their restaurant booking, they rode the elevator up to the viewing deck. Ana knew she was supposed to marvel at the view, to make out like she hadn't lived in Tokyo for years. But when they stepped out of the lift, she was genuinely staggered. The city stretched out in the dusk, a pastel metropolis. Dragonfly-like helicopters were sweeping the pink haze, and the roads were arteries of neon, pulsing and converging. As Takuya led her to the glass, she was filled with a sharp dismay. This was a vertigo not of height but a huge and lateral whirling. How completely the city effaced the earth, she thought. Then she recalled the earthquakes that were a constant in Japan, which showed the ground beneath the lights retained a violent will. She thought of Priya Vajpayee, whose company had been hit – a big tremor had taken out their semi-conductor factory – and felt a perverse relief at the land's defiance.

At the restaurant, she ate the eel, which was suitably exquisite. All the while Takuya spoke in his stilted English, saying of the wasabi, 'Please do have some horseradish.' At one point he declared, 'I'm proud of Japanese food. But not of Japanese guy. Japanese guy is shy and ambiguous.' Ana nodded politely; she was back on autopilot. Still she felt somehow offended by the vest he wore; a few sizes too big, it gaped under his arms. Thankfully he released her when they finished eating; he got involved in talking business with the proprietor. Outside, she looked for taxis. Then without warning someone grabbed her. It was a bouncer for the club next door. He gripped her shoulder and, as if playing a game, a game where you guessed the origins of passing women, shouted, 'You! Ukrainian!' and let out a harsh laugh. Wrenching free, she hailed a cab. It slid to a halt, wonderfully black. Its driver wore white gloves. God, she thought as they pulled away. She had seen the bouncer's face, his grin as hard as his grip had been.

*

The next night, she phoned her parents while taking a walk. Her father, who picked up, asked about the weather, then said in his gravelly voice, 'That's one thing I don't miss, Tokyo summers. And your mother's asthma.'

He had retired three years ago from his import-export job. Working for a company that dealt in commercial ovens and catering equipment, he was posted to Tokyo when Ana was in high school. He settled their family in a poky house in Chiba. Ana and her two brothers soon made new friends and thrived, but their mother felt out of place and socially isolated. At the end of the three-year posting, the family had moved back home, while Ana stayed on for college.

'Hold on. Your mother is saying something. She asks if you have a boyfriend.'

'She always asks if I have a boyfriend.'

'She worries you'll settle down and stay in Tokyo. She also worries Estonia will be re-conquered by Danes.'

'And you, are you worried?'

'I am a fatalist, Ana. You'll do as you will.'

When she got off the call, she found she had reached the park. The air was velvety and soft, and she stopped to sit on a bench. She thought of boyfriends she'd had. Real boyfriends, not clients.

She thought of Daisuke too, though he hadn't been her boyfriend, only a friend. He knew what it was like to live in another country. He had done a high school exchange to Adelaide, Australia and endured racist jibes from neighbourhood boys. Yet this experience hadn't soured him on the West. As an adult, he preferred coffee to green tea, and he read philosophers like Montesquieu and Bentham.

Daisuke – where was he now? Probably still in Tokyo, working for some company. In college, he'd been impressed by *Made In Japan*, a book by Akio Morita, the founder of Sony Corporation. An account of Japan's rise in the postwar period, it made him want to work to better his country. He also decided, as he told Ana, it would probably be best if he married a Japanese woman because of all the strictures of Japanese society. 'It would be too difficult for her,' he said, referring to a hypothetical non-Japanese wife. 'It's even difficult for us Japanese.'

Some time after that, she had stopped seeing Daisuke. Not because of his marriage plans, but because she didn't want him to know she was hostessing. It was a part of her life that she kept separate from college – a world of nice restaurants and bars, of Shigeko and her friends, of drinking parties that went on until the men were shiny-faced and had trouble sitting upright. At college she had boyfriends who were students like her. She slept with some of them, but the sex was awkward, experimental, like she was mimicking a desire she did not really feel.

Once she thought she was pregnant. She had gone to a clinic. She knew there were tests you bought in a box, sticks you were meant to pee on, but she wanted to be sure, she wanted to see a doctor. At the clinic she was directed to undress in a room and sit in a chair with moulded stirrups for her legs. Their purpose became apparent when the assistant pressed a button and the chair tipped back and lifted her legs apart. A paper curtain was positioned to screen everything past her navel, so she was unable to see the doctor who approached. He put his gloved hands on her stomach, pressing here and there, then poked two fingers in her vagina and felt about inside her. Afterward, when she had dressed, the assistant gave her to understand that she wasn't pregnant. She rode the bus home not knowing what to think or feel, but later the same day her period started, as if triggered by relief.

Now, in the park, Ana walked on a little. She was not afraid. She liked the dark. She liked the textures of the trees, the way the warm air seemed to swim. Deeper in the gardens, the small lake wobbled with dim reflections, and in the trees she heard cicadas. She thought back to the time she had gone to a summer festival with Daisuke and then, on returning, lay watching TV and drinking a bottle of white wine. She remembered the night clearly: a golf tournament was on, Tiger Woods was playing and from the trees behind the house came the bleating of cicadas. She knew nothing about golf but was content to lie there watching. Then Daisuke, a little drunk, had said something unexpected. 'You're so free,' he told her, turning from the screen.

'No I'm not,' she said.

'It's because you're talented.'

The remark perplexed her. She did not feel talented. She did not know what he meant, but he didn't elaborate. And nothing happened between them, though she would have liked it to. Nothing happened that night or ever. She regretted this, now that she thought about it. To think that after that exchange they had just lain there side by side, drinking wine and saying nothing, watching golfers hit golf balls on a golf course somewhere.

*

'Do you like men?' Priya asked as they drove to the mountain spa. She swivelled to look at Ana, who was sitting in the back. Priya's likeable colleague Ken was driving them in his car. By 'men' Priya meant noodles, but her tone was deliberately teasing. 'I love them,' she went on. 'Especially cool *men*, in the summer.'

Priya flirted from long habit even though she was now engaged. When they got to the spa and went through to the women's section, leaving Ken to go the men's, Priya's voice lost its sparkle, becoming flatter, merely pleasant. As they soaked in the outside pool she spoke about Sanjeev, her fiancé. They had fallen in love while travelling in Europe – which was the storyline, as she said, of many Indian films. But then he had gone to Princeton and she had come to Tokyo. They had gradually grown distant, and she had dated Japanese men. After graduation and several failed relationships, she had gone home to ask her parents to start looking for a match. Deeply bemused, they had reasoned with her, 'Dear Priya, how do you expect us to find anyone better than Sanjeev?'

'I admitted they were right,' she told Ana with a laugh, basking in the glow of her fiancé's success.

Afterwards they found Ken reading a newspaper on a bench. He wore the hotel's plastic slippers and his hair, with the styling wax washed out, had gone silky and flat. They had to dash to the Nissan because of the pouring rain. They drove back through the wet, stopping off once at a service area for Ken to buy a can of coffee from a dispensing machine. Nearby, a stumbling drunk was startled to see Ana. '*Ara!*' he said, staring. '*Ningyo ka na to omotta*. I thought it was a doll!'

'You know what he said?' Ken asked.

'Yeah,' Ana said and they both laughed sheepishly. When Ken dropped her back at Arjun's, she kissed each of his clean bright cheeks, causing him to blush.

Early the next morning, Ana met Takuya again. They walked through the fish market on their way to a sushi bar for breakfast, and Takuya pointed out the best specimens on offer. Ana walked quickly, especially past the shellfish, which were so mauve, so vagina-like, they might give Takuya ideas. But he was busy explaining a new rule in the market, that visitors had to keep a certain distance from the fish. 'There was an incident,' he said, wearing a disappointed look. 'There were some foreigners. They tried to hug the tuna.'

At the tiny sushi diner, the chef put the sashimi portions directly on the bar, which he wiped with a cloth between one round and the next. They ate several types of fish and some hacked-off squid, which was so recently alive that the pieces were still moving, puckering in protest on their beds of rice.

'By the way,' said Takuya as they left. He walked with his basketballer's gait, his feet splayed oddly wide as if to corner Ana. 'Miura-san sent a message,' he said, meaning Shigeko, whose surname was Miura. 'She mentions her regards. Actually, she is feeling sad that you do not see her.'

Clearly he knew about their disagreement. Shigeko had been annoyed when Ana refused a client, and won the argument by kicking her out. Ana could still picture Shigeko's face that evening, her smile fixed and brittle, her eyes strangely bright.

'It makes it difficult for her,' Takuya went on. 'Because, as you know, the role of a hostess is to bring happiness to people.'

'Is it,' she said flatly, annoyed by the lecture.

He smiled indulgently, spread his hands and said, 'You should meet her. It's not too late. You can say sorry.'

'I'm not sorry.'

Taken aback, Takuya fell silent.

'Thanks for breakfast,' she said, then left him to his day. It was still early in the morning and she walked aimlessly at first, at length finding herself on Omotesando Dori, a fancy shopping street. She was looking in the Prada window when Arjun telephoned.

'How was your date with eel-hands? Or is it eel-dick? Whatever it is you call him.'

Ana laughed. 'Okay.'

'Are you going out tonight?'

'No. Unless you want me to be out.'

'Are you sure, Ana? You're not bringing some boy home?'

'No.' She snorted. 'I'll see you at the apartment.'

*

That night and the coming nights, a typhoon swerved in close, dousing Tokyo with heavy rains. They went out anyway, defying the weather. One night Arjun invited Nitin, a friend of his, to dinner. Nitin was not from college and Ana had never met him, which made her suspect Arjun of trying to set her up. If this was the idea, it didn't work out. Having organised the evening, Arjun quickly became annoyed, starting with Nitin's choice of a budget Italian restaurant. 'Really, this is the place you pick?' It looked basic but okay, with plastic tablecloths.

Nitin rolled his eyes at Ana. He was delicately built and had a fine aquiline nose. He worked in capital markets, where (so Arjun said) the guys took home the biggest pay-packets in town. This was why it rankled Arjun that he ate so cheaply. Nitin, for his part, enjoyed needling Arjun. 'Arjun, why don't you try the house bolognese?' he said. 'Oh, you don't eat beef? Oh, and why would that be, Arjun?'

'Because, you know why. My family—'

'I don't know why.'

'Because I still adhere to some precepts.'

'You do?' Nitin faked surprise. He was like a cat with a stuffed toy, wanting to tease and tear. 'Which precepts are those again? When we go out clubbing?'

Ana waded in. 'Everyone draws a line for himself – or herself.'

'How true, Ana.' He grinned, and she feared what he might say next, but he merely asked a waiter to take their dinner order. Two bolognese, one parmigiana and, yes, the garlic bread to start. Then he resumed the conversation, saying, 'How very true, Ana. I draw my own line. It moves as I do.'

Arjun's mood was foul through dinner. Later, when they had parted from Nitin and were walking home, he said he would take her out again to make up for the night. They would go somewhere fancy, a converted brewery on the harbour, a place he really loved.

True to his word, he made a booking there next evening and met her beforehand at the closest station. She spotted him striding across the tiles in the high cavernous hall. 'I love the space of it,' he said, waving a hand at the height above. 'Space for thinking big. I come here a lot.' He had also been reading a lot, he added as they walked to the restaurant. He rattled off authors – Richard Branson, Bill Clinton. 'A little Shakespeare too. I've been educating myself. I've had the luxury of leisure.'

They reached the brewery and were seated at a table that was spread with a white cloth and laid with gleaming silver. Soberly, Arjun asked if she had noticed a change in him. It was true he looked different, as though his face was smoother, the set of his jaw more confident, but she couldn't put her finger on what exactly the change had been. 'I had my tooth fixed, see,' he said, baring his teeth at her. 'I can now afford to care about such shallow things.'

Behind them on the harbour, the rain was coming down heavily. It was the night when the typhoon was almost upon them, and it was there at the restaurant table Arjun told Ana what really happened with Fatima. 'Her parents sent her to meet a man, a family friend in Tokyo. He was old, she came back and told them. Old and short. But they chatted online, all smiles. All flattery, you know? I had to go away for a while; I was working out of town. When I got back she called me. She was married, she announced. To the older guy, just like that.'

The lights of the harbour struggled bravely through the weather. Arjun told his story – how he had returned to India, hiring four computing experts to teach him one on one. Rising early and working out, then taking his first classes. Eating the lunch his worried mother prepared for him. Stopping for a nap and then studying again. For three months he had worked like this.

'Ana, do you know, my parents had told me once that they'd rather I marry an Indian. But they said I was free to choose. I could bring home a Japanese girl, a Chinese girl, any girl as my wife. They said they would still be happy. They said, we will all be friends.'

'Ana, Fatima called me once. She was drunk. She slurred her speech. It was three months into the marriage. She said, he is sleeping with prostitutes. He thinks he can do what he wants. I've caught him countless times but he doesn't care. I've made a mistake, she said. I'm getting a divorce. I'll call you tomorrow. Yet the next day no call came. I called her parents, they hung up. I talked to her brother, I said I could fly to see them. No, he told me. Don't. He said she never considered me. He said his family was broad-minded, they would have considered a foreigner if she had talked to them, if that was what she'd wanted.'

Holding his fork like a small trident in his fist, Arjun stared unseeingly at the rain-smeared lights.

'Forget her,' Ana said.

'But there were times – I know she felt it. And if she could feel it then, she could feel it always. I could – I told myself – I could inculcate that love. After I saw that, I thought, okay, I'll wait.'

Then he described when he had last seen her, or rather the last two times, both soon after she married. After carefully composing her final college dissertation, he had met her away from prying eyes on a windswept Yokohama beach, handing over the finished essay in electronic and hard copies. He had seen her at graduation; she was there in a silver dress. On her arm was a man she introduced to people as her cousin. All the cameras, Arjun said, sought her in that crowd, searching for her beauty, her white moon of a face.

*

The typhoon had been predicted to hit Tokyo that night. But, as often happened, it swooped away at the last hour, thanks to a quirk of topography that favoured the capital. Next morning when Ana woke, it was to the clearest day she had seen in the city. The air was dry and hot, drawing everyone outdoors. The park was full of pregnant women, children and their maids. This was also the day when Ana's visa came by mail, in an official envelope she tore at hastily. There it was in black and white, her permission to work. She promptly celebrated by doing something she never did: sightseeing. Taking the train to Asakusa, she visited the temple and neighbourhood laneways where old people moved with tiny, precise steps. She ended the tour with an iced tea in a snack bar. She drank it looking onto the storefront opposite, at a spinning mannequin that, 'Sale' sign notwithstanding, cocked its knee and posed with new-season confidence.

That night she and Arjun fried gyoza in a pan. They ate the dumplings on the couch while talking of old times. 'Do you remember, Ana, when that friend of yours came to visit? You had her in my room. I came home to find her in my bed, this plump girl snuggled in the duvet, her big boob coming out a little. She woke up and said sorry. I said, no, no, don't worry, I'm about to get in with you.'

Arjun laughed. 'I did not say that. I was very well behaved, very polite. In those days I was bright and young, not eating meat or drinking.' Recklessly he added, 'Now I'm a tiger.'

Switching the TV on, they watched some CNN footage of floods in Romania, which prompted Arjun to mention a Romanian girl he'd met. She was working at the strip club he had visited that one time. 'She was exhausted, you know? I keep thinking about her. I feel so sad for her.'

It suddenly struck Ana that he was talking about her. It was for her he felt sad, equating her with the tired stripper. 'Arjun,' she told him firmly, muting the TV. 'I was a hostess.' On the screen, torrential rivers wrecked bridges and embankments. 'Are you listening to me? I was a hostess, not a stripper, not a prostitute. It isn't the same thing, which is what I told Shigeko.'

'I know, I know. I'm an ass.' He grinned, hugely relieved. Then his phone rang and he boomed, 'Priya-san, hello. And how is your great life? Oh, *ex*-cellent news.'

Priya had emailed photos of the ring and her fiancé. Viewing the files on his laptop afterwards, Arjun said, 'They're nice pictures. Actually, they look idiotic, smiling away like that. He seems so amazed. You know she said no to him so long. Then he made it in the States. He has a green card, has the package.' He frowned and prodded the last dumpling. 'Do you think it makes a difference, the material things, I mean?'

She now grasped his dilemma, which was that he needed both a 'yes' and a 'no' answer. Pining for Fatima, he wished his wealth would bring her back, while at the same time his idealistic self – the youth in overalls Ana had known in college – hoped it would not work, hoped love could not be bought.

'Sometimes,' she conceded. 'But I think more often not.'

He went out on the balcony and looked up at the sky. His phone rang with a work call. 'Kiran,' he said in answer. And, coming in, he opened his laptop and started speaking Hindi. A server had gone down; connecting remotely, he tried to bring it back up. It was by then almost midnight but he called all of his team. In an aside, he told Ana, 'If I'm not sleeping or having sex, neither will they.'

Leaving him to it, she stretched out on her futon. As he went on working she heard the odd word: 'Server! Ping! *Nankaimo. Tiga, tiga,* okay.' In between work calls, she heard him speaking to his parents. Yes, he told his mother, I'll book to come back for Diwali. Then it was back to his strange muddle of Hindi, English and Japanese. Ana went to sleep thinking of plans for the next day. She would go back to the shops on Omotesando Dori and with her hair in a chignon ask for a sales job. She would use her best Japanese, especially the honorific form that was used by shop girls as it was by hostesses. She would go store to store until someone said yes.

'*Nankaimo, nankaimo,*' Arjun was saying. She drifted off, comforted as if by a bedside story, one of servers like grandfathers in a subtropical summer. She did not know what time it was when he fixed the problem; it was as if he would be there always, tapping at his laptop. Then it was morning and he had gone to work already, and she rose to fold the futon neatly away.

Meanjin

Supernova

Omar Musa

The telescope sat slightly apart from the clutter of the room – aloof, cool, shaded by a closed curtain. Azlan Muhammad ran a chubby hand down the length of its metallic form as he whistled a loud and tuneful melody. He paused to thumb the plastic toy rocket superglued to it before covering it carefully with a cloth. He belched, scratched an arse cheek, then traced a circuitous route through the stacks of books on the concrete floor, nimble for a man of his size. He had important things to do, after all.

Coffee first, though. He made it strong, sweetened by condensed milk, making sure not a drop spilled down the side of the cup. He hated that. 'Coffee first, and the rest'll fall into place' – he could hear his old boss's thick Aussie accent, even now. Azlan turned on the radio, his eyes still trained on the telescope. A serious voice was commenting on the imminent election. The lead-up had been full of skullduggery and intrigue, and there was a sense of excitement that after more than fifty years in power, the government looked to be in its death throes and the opposition was gaining traction. Today was election day.

Azlan cared little about the messiness of his house, but the surface of his body was sacrosanct. He showered and brushed his teeth fastidiously. Drops of water shone on his hair and big belly before rolling down to the concrete floor. He had once prided himself on a full, Samson-like head of black waves, but he'd taken to cropping it short as it receded slowly to the back of his head.

He swore the receding had started around the time his daughter, Rozana, had been born, and he'd tried his best to cover it up by combing his remaining hair forward. But there comes a time, he had told Rozana, where you just have to give in. She was only eight, but the way she had thrown back her head and laughed with such gusto had already seemed so mature and defiant.

Azlan looked at the clothes he'd laid out for himself on the single bed: a traditional Malay outfit – the *baju Melayu.* He struggled into the matching dark red, long-sleeved shirt and trousers, doing up the imitation diamond studs at the chest. The long-sleeved *baju* strained at the belly, but how proud and striking it looked. He admired himself in his mirror. He'd hardly ever been able to wear his national dress during his life in Australia, other than to that awful work function where he had been cajoled to wear it, to show 'diversity', of course. He tied the *kain songket* carefully around his waist like a short sarong, its pattern of gold threads shimmering and bending in the light. Last of all came the jet-black *songkok,* tipped jauntily on his head.

*

Election Day, yes, but food first. Even on an important mission, like today's, Azlan could never stop thinking of it. After spritzing on some cologne Rozana had sent him from Australia, he hurried, puffing slightly, outside into the humidity and headed straight for the restaurant next to his family home. He ordered three plates of *kueh teow goreng* and sat watching the clientele. All Malays. Was it true, as he had read somewhere, that 90 per cent of Malaysians had never dined with someone of another race? Multiculturalism – bah! Malaysia had moved on, his family kept telling him, it had become advanced, but they told him this while sitting in front of that damned television, awash in wave after wave of advertisements and dirty politics, the young ones staring into their mobile phones, letting the bullshit and religious rhetoric wash over them without listening. And they never read books! He seethed at the moral policing and juvenile displays of public piety but, nevertheless, he still went to Friday prayers where he recited Arabic he didn't understand and knew only by rote, thinking of the stars and constellations in the privacy of his own head. He'd never considered himself a political man but today was his chance to make a difference. By voting.

His plates of noodles arrived, steaming, and he picked up a marble-sized lime to squeeze juice on to them.

'Hey, Azlan!'

He looked up, surprised. Two men were grinning at him from the street, leaning on their mopeds as they watched the restaurant TV and smoked. Imran and Amir – he recognised them from high school. They had hardly changed since then. How classless they looked in their grubby football jerseys and thongs, particularly compared to his magnificent *baju Melayu.*

'Hey Azlan,' called out Imran, 'Did you see *anything* last night?'

'I saw *something,*' he called back good-naturedly, 'but who knows whether it was *anything* important.'

'Remember, Azlan, *anything* is possible with a good attitude!' yelled Amir. The two men laughed again, before ashing their cigarettes simultaneously and turning back to the Liverpool game playing on the flickering screen.

They had been making fun of him, he knew that. The 'anything' they were referring to was something he'd let slip in a conversation they had once all had over tandoori chicken. As Azlan had crunched the chicken down with red onions and spear-sliced pieces of cucumber, he'd mentioned that with his prized telescope, he hoped one day to take a photograph of paranormal phenomena – a spaceship, maybe, something unnatural against the stars, something not seen before, anything. The two of them had caught each other's eye and roared with laughter. They thought he was pretentious, he knew they thought he felt himself above his station because of all his years working as an engineer in Australia, so they had relished finding something to mock him with. And of course that gossip had inflated and distorted his words, so the story got out around town that Azlan was using his telescope to look for aliens. He looked down and realised he'd devoured two of the plates of *kueh teow* and was about to tip more chilli sauce onto the third. With a sigh he squeezed the last bit of lime juice on to them and forked them up, smacking his lips. When he stood to pay, he inspected the front of his red shirt carefully for spots. Still immaculate, he noted proudly, reaching for some money.

*

The bus was relatively empty. He was only going a few stops, and when he was young and fit he would have walked, but now he thought it would be unnecessarily tiring and, in any case, he didn't want to get his trousers dirty. He sat next to the window and watched the drifts of dust boiling up then dissipating to reveal houses speeding past. While the rest of Malaysia developed at the rate of knots, this place was still sleepy, still resembled his childhood memories. This was his village, his *kampung*, arranged along the banks of a broad brown river that led to the sea. It was in this river that Azlan had first found the plastic toy rocket. At the age of six, he had been swimming in the waters of the river when he saw something bobbing in the murk. 'Don't swim too far out,' his mother called, 'there are crocodiles out there.' He didn't believe her, but he didn't want to get in trouble, so he held on to a supporting pole with one arm while he tried to figure how to get the toy. For her part, his mother, squatting on a wooden platform some distance away, observed silently and spat betel nut as he held on to the supporting pole with his legs, fashioned the end of a length of rattan into a loop and managed to guide the toy towards him. She looked up and squinted down the river at Japanese fishing ships, which sat flat on the horizon against an oily orange sky.

Dripping and laughing, Azlan climbed up on to the platform and showed his mother the toy rocket, this gift of the water. She dried it on her sarong and handed it back, grinning. He asked her whether a Malaysian had ever flown a rocket into space. She screwed up her nose, thought hard and then replied that she didn't think so. Despite the fact that most of the paint had chipped off, he looked at the rocket with wonder. It was the first toy he had ever owned. That night, there was a clear sky and he could see a magnificent shawl of stars through a chink in the wall as he ran his delicate fingers and thumbs over the cheap plastic edges and curves of his new toy. One day, he vowed that night, he would become the first Malaysian astronaut.

No one told him until high school, of course, that only a few countries in the world have space programs, that the chances of winning a place in one was as unlikely as winning the lottery, and that growing up in a *kampung* in Malaysia made it about as possible as actually learning to fly.

*

For a while, he imagined growing up in Russia or the US, but it didn't feel right – Russia seemed cold, and America was full of cowboys. He remained interested in science and had a knack for it, consistently gaining top marks in his class. Over the years, as life went on, he tried to keep up with advancements in international space travel, and calls for more equity between rich and poor countries in this field. But by the time the Malaysian government announced a plan to send a Malaysian into space for the first time, Azlan Muhammad had already lived twenty years in Australia. He had a beautiful, rebellious daughter and a hairline so far back if he was asked to salute he would have to do so from the top of his head.

*

The palm oil plantation passed by now, a hypnotic pattern of green on green. The salary for an engineer was good in Australia, and he was proud at how far he had come from the days in the *kampung*. Yet his mind, always, remained in the stars. At the age of forty, he saved up and invested in a telescope and camera gear that would allow him to take detailed photos of the stars. He loved fiddling with his gear, experimenting, setting long exposures, identifying comets, seeing stars turned into white-hot lines and satellites into dot points when printed up. He would pin his photos all over the house and his office. The really good ones, he got blown up and framed. Even Rozana, who generally thought everything he did was uncool as could be, had to admit how impressive they were.

The school where he would cast his ballot was coming up and the bus shuddered to a halt. Azlan tried to squeeze down the aisle as delicately as he could, but he kept bumping into people's shoulders as he passed, to their great annoyance. He stood on the roadside in his *baju Melayu*, sweating already, somehow still unused to the humidity. The school was freshly painted white, with rich green lawns and a fruit tree out the front. It was the school he had attended as a child.

When his wife Janet had passed away and Rozana was off at art school, the idea of moving back to Malaysia had begun to obsess him. The family house was there, just as it had been for years since his parents died, the garden overgrown and no one was living in it besides a family of monkeys that neighbours kept shooing out. Azlan thought perhaps he could contribute something to a country suffering from brain drain. Also, he had always harboured the unsettling feeling that he never truly fit in in Australia. It was not the type of dislocation some of his Middle Eastern friends from the mosque felt, or Rozana, who railed against the 'system' with a fury that took him aback, but a kind of benign discomfort. So to Malaysia it was.

Azlan stood in the line to cast his ballot, thinking about the opposition. Change was better than staying the same, anything had to be, but the opposition seemed a gallimaufry of different elements and he did not trust the ageing leader, so slick, so wily. But fifty years! He remembered how proud he had been of his nation in the early years, how optimistic they had all been. As time had gone on, he'd observed from a distance, and it had gradually seemed more and more disillusioning.

A young man in front of him was fidgeting and sighing loudly, as if voting was a chore. And dressed so casually! Azlan shook his head in disapproval and ran a hand over his scalp. He was casting a vote for the first time in over twenty years, since becoming an Australian resident. *Resident*, not citizen. He loved Australia, and his daughter was most definitely Australian, but he was Malaysian. Especially today.

He was near the front of the line now. He stood straighter and readied himself for the voting procedure. First, he would have to present his identification card, and they would check his name against the electoral roll. Then they would get his thumbprint and strike a line through his name using a ruler. Then he would wait until his name was announced and move on to another group of officials who would give him the voting slip. Then, then, finally, he could go into a booth behind a curtain, draw a cross next to the name of the candidate he wanted to vote for, then fold up the slip and put it in the ballot box. Vote.

When he finally got to the front of the line, he whipped out his identification card immediately. The official sitting at a desk in front of him was skinny, moustachioed and middle-aged, in good shape. He was an official and looked, well, officious. There was a younger official standing behind him. The older man stared at Azlan's belly and *baju Melayu* before taking the identification card and looking down at the electoral roll. As the man flicked through the pages, Azlan noticed how carefully pressed his shirt was, but how cheap the material looked. The younger man had a pair of imitation designer sunglasses tucked in his belt, and thumbed the fake Gucci logo absent-mindedly. His own thumb, its whorls shaped like the spirals of a distant galaxy, would soon be covered in ink.

'Excuse me, *pak*,' said the officious-looking official. Azlan looked up sharply.

'Yes?'

'There was no need to come a second time!' The man smiled haughtily and the younger official smiled too.

'What do you mean?'

'Well, you have already voted.'

Azlan's mouth became dry. 'No, I haven't. I'm here to vote now.'

The man sighed. 'Just look at this. Your name has been crossed off. You have already voted.' He turned the page so that Azlan could see. There was finality in his voice and he was looking beyond Azlan in the line. Azlan stooped to look. Yes, he could see his name there, and it had been struck out. But he had not voted.

He stood open-mouthed. No words would come. If Rozana was here, she would stamp her feet, shake her dyed-blue hair and cause a ruckus at such a blatant injustice. But he could not. He did not have that same rebellious instinct. He looked back at the line and felt suddenly self-conscious in his *baju Melayu*. No one else was wearing one. He looked down at his un-inked thumb and at his identification card, which was grubby around the edges. A younger, skinnier man with a full head of hair stared back at him.

'I went to this school,' he blurted suddenly. 'Then I became an engineer in Australia.'

The two officials looked at each other and smiled again. Azlan stared, unable to move his feet. Soon the officials got back to business and gestured impatiently for the next in line to step forward.

*

The bus ride back was cramped, but he managed to find a seat all to himself. He opened his wallet and slid his identification card back inside, then took out the folded newspaper clipping and looked at it for a long time. A young, handsome Malay man smiled out at him, dressed in an astronaut's uniform with a helmet under his arm. This was the first Malaysian astronaut, Sheikh Muszaphar Shukor. Azlan felt foolish for carrying it around, and knew there had been controversy about whether the man even qualified as a true astronaut or a 'spaceflight participant', but he'd always kept it nevertheless. Beneath the photo was part of the speech the minister had given at the launch of the space program: 'It is not merely a project to send a Malaysian into space. After fifty years of independence, we need a new shift and a new advantage to be more successful as a nation.'

Not long to go now, to home and a comforting meal. He absently smoothed the *songket* fabric that reached halfway down his thigh, the intricate designs in gold thread, woven through the dark blue cotton weft. Once upon a time, everyone knew, the great weavers had heated real gold to liquid, coated the thread and woven the fabric for kings. The symmetrical patterns had to do with nature, but after so many years Azlan had forgotten what centre of weaving they had come from. To him, they looked like the stars, like comets and asteroids, soundlessly exploding in distant space, far beyond the dominion of him or any man. Like supernovae, with brightness enough to outshine an entire galaxy momentarily, emitting more radiance than a sun or an ordinary star does over its whole lifetime, but long spent by the time their light reaches us.

He closed his eyes. Tonight was going to be cool and clear, perfect for stargazing. He would point his telescope out of his window and the stars would be glowing without interference, close enough to press his face to. There would be a blur on the side of his vision, a pulse, a strange dot of a colour neither he nor anyone would have seen before. He would not be able to name it, or class it, or tell another soul about it, because it could be anything.

Griffith REVIEW

Alphabet

Ryan O'Neill

Q

The way you might get dressed in the morning and notice for the first time a bruise on your arm, and wonder how it got there. This was how he had come to think of his marriage.

W

The last time they had gone out together was two years earlier. They hired a babysitter, and went to a party at a friend's house. He didn't know many of the people there. When someone asked him what he did, he said he was a teacher.

'Don't be modest,' his wife said. 'He's a writer.'

'Oh, really?' a woman asked. 'What sort of things do you write about?'

'Oh, well,' he said. 'Language. Words. Teaching. They say you should write about what you know.'

'That's why he doesn't write about sex,' his wife said, and everyone laughed.

R

'You can't even tell your own daughter a story? Don't you think that's taking writer's block a little far?'

T

He lay beside her on the bed, eyes closed. She was reading a biography of Hemingway. On the front cover was a photograph of the American, sitting in front of a typewriter.

'Did you know that Hemingway's wife once lost everything he had written?' his wife asked him. 'She left her suitcase on a train when she was going to see him in Switzerland. All his stories were in it, and the carbon copies.'

'That's appalling,' he said.

'But he forgave her,' she said. She put the book down. 'If I lost everything you wrote, would you forgive me?'

'Of course.' He opened his eyes and looked at her. 'Of course I'd forgive you. Of course I would.'

Y

He knew he wasn't easy to live with. If he were a character in a story, his every line of dialogue would be followed by 'he said, irritably'.

U

During her pregnancy, she would spend hours looking at the ultrasound photographs of the baby, but all he could see were whorls and swirls like a satellite image of an approaching cyclone.

I

Their daughter woke up every three hours during the night until she was four. She slept in their bed. He slept on the couch. He and his wife were exhausted much of the time. They spent their days arguing in low voices while their daughter played on the floor. They spelt out swear words so she wouldn't understand them.

'You manipulative bee eye tee see aitch,' he said, irritably.

'Eff you see kay you!' she said.

When their daughter started school and learnt to spell, they had to stop doing this. Once, though, he found his wife had scrawled 'Bastard!' in his notebook. He didn't cross it out. For the past three years it had remained the only word written there.

P

They used to have a good sex life. He liked to lie with his face between her opened legs, slowly spelling out the alphabet on her clitoris with his tongue. By the time he reached V she would pull him up and inside her. Or they would take turns to read each other Anaïs Nin's short stories, or excerpts from Victorian erotica, and then they'd make love. Sometimes, she asked him to make up stories with themselves as the main characters, and so he searched his memory for all the Penthouse letters he had read when he was a teenager. The situations were clichéd: cheerleader and football player, college lecturer and student, delivery man and housewife. But she didn't seem to mind. He would whisper the story in her ear as she touched herself. He felt proud if he could time the climax of the story to his wife's.

A few months into her pregnancy, she asked him again to tell her a story. He started off with a maid cleaning a hotel room, and a man, himself, watching her. But after the man pulled off the maid's lacy underwear, he couldn't think of how to go on.

'What happens next?' his wife breathed, hand trembling under the sheets. 'Tell me, quick!'

'I don't know,' he said.

She opened her eyes and looked at him. Then she turned away and switched off the light.

A

Every morning at nine o'clock, he went into the spare room and sat at his desk. Sometimes he would look at the keyboard and say the letters out loud. Sometimes he would look out the window. Sometimes he would look at the walls, which were covered in cheap framed prints of pine forests and mountain lakes and deserts, hung at odd heights and intervals. His wife had put them up to hide the holes he had punched there.

At 11 o'clock he would stand up and leave the room.

S

'People don't want to read stories about writers,' she said.

D

One day, he noticed she wasn't wearing her wedding ring. He asked her where it was.

'I have a wart I've been getting treated. See?' And she held up her finger to show him. 'I haven't worn the ring in months.'

The one review of his last book had praised his acute powers of observation.

F

They never spoke about his writing now. Before meeting him, she had worked as an editor at a publishing company. Her name was in the acknowledgements of several award-winning novels. Until they slept together, he had welcomed her comments on his stories. He knew her judgements were astute, and had helped his work, especially when he was blocked. But when he became involved with her, he could no longer accept her criticism. Once, they didn't speak for a week; it was over a semicolon.

G

'Can't you even give the female character a name? Don't you think it's demeaning that she's just known as 'his wife'?'

H

He enjoyed driving his daughter places: to the park, the swimming pool, her friends' houses. They lived outside town, so almost anywhere was at least a half-hour drive away. He would pass the time by telling her stories. Sometimes he took two characters from different fairy tales and had them run off on an adventure together. Tom Thumb and Puss in Boots, or the Snow Queen and the Little Mermaid. But his daughter liked it best when he made up the characters and the plots himself. Over time he created, with prompts from his daughter, a long and complex tale about 'the smellephant', an elephant who had lost his sense of smell.

'And that's when the smellephant realised that the treasure was gone!' he said, as he drove her to a ballet lesson. 'Who could have taken it? he thought.'

'Daddy,' his daughter asked, 'is that the complication?'

'The complication? Who told you that word?'

'My teacher says every story has an orientation, a complication and a resolution. Is that the complication?'

'I don't know. Yes. I suppose so. The complication. Anyway, we're here. I'll finish the story tomorrow.'

But he didn't.

J

'You shouldn't keep reminding the reader that a story, especially a love story, isn't real,' his wife said.

'But none of them are,' he replied.

K

All their arguments ended with her screaming, 'And no! You can't use this in your book!'

Z

On their fifth wedding anniversary he gave her a silver necklace and a dictionary. When she flipped the book open, she saw her own picture glued beside the word 'Patience' and she laughed. A year later he went to look up something, and the picture was gone.

X

He won a short-story competition with an old story he had reworked. The local newspaper took pictures of him holding his book in front of a bookshop. When the article appeared two months later he looked awkward and uncomfortable. Still, he bought a copy to show his wife. She kissed him, and sat down to read it.

After a moment, she said, 'In the interview, you say you can revise stories at any time, but you only write new ones when you're happy.'

'That's right,' he smiled.

'But you haven't written anything in three years.'

C

For the past six months or so, she had read only biographies of writers. Alice Munro, Saki, Chekhov, O. Henry. He didn't know why. Heavy hardbacks always littered her bedside table, and on top of them, always, was a copy of his book. It caught his eye as he sat on the bed, waiting for her to come home. He hadn't opened it since it was published, but he did now. There was no dedication. He hadn't known anyone then to dedicate it to.

Carefully, he wrote under the title, 'For my wife.' Then he put the book back where he had found it.

B

He first came to know her when she sent him a rejection letter saying she regretted that the company was unable to publish his short-story collection. This was a reflection on the current literary market, she wrote, not his talent. Though he had been disappointed, he kept the handwritten note. The curve of her 'y' reminded him of the small of a woman's back, and he had found, to his shame and his puzzlement, that the note physically aroused him. He met her a year later, at a book launch, and she remembered him straight away. She had fought for his collection, she explained, and was pleased that another publisher had taken it on. He told her he had kept her rejection, and she was surprised. 'I didn't think of you as one of those writers who filed their rejection slips,' she said.

He knew that one day soon he would return from the library, or the university, or the shop, and find his wife and daughter gone, and there would be a handwritten note. He would read the note, and stand there alone, in an empty house, with an erection.

N

He wondered when his marriage had become full of complications. When his wife left her job? When his daughter was born? When he stopped writing?

M

He sits, staring at the letters on the keyboard, as he has for the last hour. Then he feels his wife's breath, softly, on his neck. Her arms reach around him. With the forefinger of her left hand, her finger pecks at the keyboard. First, the farthest letter to the right on the middle row, then the one above it, then down to the middle letter of the fourth row, and finally, as he watches, her finger trails to the second row and the third letter from the left.

He places his hands over hers, and asks if he can tell her story.

The Monthly

Into the Woods

Sarah Klenbort

Some kind of pain, Jolene says as they hand her a baby still bloody and wet. Then, *Perfect.* A bit of blood marks Baby's chin, or is it a beauty spot? Even that is perfect. Must be the hormones, Jolene thinks; she hasn't felt this high since high school – cocaine in a closet in Pasadena with her best friend, Tulah.

I am a mom, she says aloud and wonders if her baby will call her *Mum.* She counts: ten miniature fingers, ten tiny toes. She gazes: smooth translucent skin, white-blond hair, soft like the girls in fairytales. Then the baby – *Georgette* – closes her blue eyes, opens a toothless mouth and screams until a nurse instructs Jolene to stuff a red nipple between tiny lips. Silence.

Jolene spends a restless night lying next to the new life; she rises to feed and change her in a blissful daze. The next day doctors puff air into Georgette's ears and declare a sensorineural hearing loss of more than 85 decibels. *Meaning?* Jolene whispers. And then, *fuck, fuck, fuck, fuck, fuck, fuck, fuck.* She takes the sleeping baby from the nurse, stares at doll's ears. Was it the three glasses of wine she had on her birthday? The coffee? The virus in the second trimester? Ecstasy she did at twenty-two, before Georgette was even a notion?

The doctor tells her about hearing aids and cochlear implants, speech therapists, support groups, early intervention.

Right. And I'll have to learn sign language.

He looks up, bushy eyebrows scrunched low. *They don't really do that anymore.* He goes, leaving the memory of a white coat and black eyebrows. Jolene feels tired, emptied out. She looks down at her broken baby, takes a deep breath. *It's okay*, she says in a soothing tone. And then she remembers the baby can't hear.

Nurses bark in the hallway. The mother on the other side of the curtain sings to her baby. Jolene strokes Georgette's hair. She wants out – out from under stiff hospital sheets, out from the midwife's prodding fingers, out of the glare of fluorescent lights that turn Georgette's skin a greenish yellow.

A nurse takes her blood pressure. *And shall we be expecting a father?*

She considers lying, shakes her head. He's gone – fucked off back to America. They came to Sydney three years ago for his job and he got fired, she got pregnant; he went home, she couldn't refuse the free health care.

Women from the office visit the hospital. They coo and smile their lipstick smiles and present a plush yellow duck that quacks when you squeeze it. When told the baby can't hear, the women flinch, as if deafness was a visible affliction.

Is it permanent?

Are they sure?

Isn't there something they can do?

*

Jolene brings Georgette home to a pink bassinet in her unit in Waterfall. Mary from next door pops over and holds the baby. *Sit*, Mary says and Jolene perches gingerly on the edge of the sofa. Everything still hurts.

Mary rocks the baby with a natural grace that makes Jolene wonder why she doesn't have kids herself.

Well, Mary says with her Scottish accent, *Least you don't have to worry about blasting Bob Marley all hours.*

Jolene laughs for the first time since the Demoral wore off.

Lie back, Mary says, placing a sleeping baby on Jolene's chest. The baby rises and falls with the breath of her mother and Jolene pretends for a moment that everything's okay.

*

A year later and Georgette's filling up Jolene's lap in the waiting room of the ENT. Jolene reads a Disney version of *Hansel and Gretel,* shouts it into her left hearing aid – does she hear? *They dropped crumbs along the path into the woods so they could find their way home.* Georgette fidgets, rips a page. Jolene closes the book, kisses the top of her baby's blond head. She still falls asleep at night with the baby on her chest, the feel of her warm weight rising and falling. Jolene's never known such tenderness.

When it's finally their turn, the doctor shows Jolene a coloured illustration that takes up the page, a cross-section with an ear on one side connected to those familiar squiggles to the brain.

This is a picture of the inner ear, the doctor says.

No, I thought it was my right big toe.

Georgette bangs a chair.

I'd appreciate your focus, Mum, the doctor says. *We'll drill through the skull.*

Jolene closes her eyes. Does he even know her name? She looks at him looking at his watch. In her dreams the drill is a roadworks jackhammer and the first doctor's there, the one with the bushy eyebrows.

Mum leaves the doctor's office quiet and composed, pushing a sleeping Georgette. She enters a disabled toilet, lifts the seat and throws up. Then she puts the seat down, flushes, sits and stares at Georgette. The baby looks angelic. She doesn't look deaf. But she will with the clunky ear piece and circular transmitter on the side of her head. Jolene wonders what mean things the other children will say – cruel taunts that only groups of girls can think up.

Crying brings relief and Jolene might even feel good if the bathroom didn't smell like puke and used tampons, if she had a glass of wine.

*

Three and implanted and talking, Georgette runs naked round the table, doll in hand, yelling, *Mummy have boobies! Georgette no have boobies!*

Jolene stuffs a bite of chicken into the moving target. There are charts on the walls, the Ling test is posted on the fridge, the calendar is full of appointments.

Jolene is sick of waiting rooms with their worn-out toys and missing puzzle pieces; she's tired of speech therapy sessions with the pretty young woman singing in a high pitched voice every five minutes and throughout the hour, *Listening, listening now! Listening!* Sitting on her hands so she won't point or use gestures that may impede Georgette's language development. But all this is working; Georgette's talking. One day her daughter will look back and thank her.

More chicken? She holds a forkful.

Georgette takes it. *Fork,* she says.

Fork, yes! Jolene replies as she's been instructed to reply: *And what do we use a fork for?*

The toddler looks up at her mother, down at the fork. She stabs the doll and growls.

*

Jolene rushes down the sidewalk to pick up her daughter up from school.

How was your day?

Fine.

What did you do?

Nothing.

Jolene tries to hold her hand, but Georgette shakes it off.

Georgette stops at a tree in full bloom and they look up at purple flowers against a blue sky. *Jacaranda,* Georgette says and it sounds good, better than the other hearing-impaired kid at school.

Next week there will be a carpet of purple on the ground, a mirror to the flowers still left on the branches. The week after, they'll all be dead. Jolene and her daughter walk on.

*

By the time she's nine, Georgette puts her own cochlear in and changes the batteries herself. Her mum says it's special but Georgette knows it's not. She hasn't heard exactly what the other kids say, but she's read their faces and stopped asking, *What did you say?* Because eventually people stop telling you.

Some days, she turns it off and watches the teacher's lips move, imagines her saying, Georgette, you're too clever for all this. We've arranged to send you to America, back to your father, America, where the best and brightest live in huge mansions with swimming pools. And then the teacher isn't moving her lips; she's waving her arms, motioning for Georgette to switch on, switch back to the humid Australian classroom where the other kids stare. Georgette feels hot in the face. She looks down at a blank page. Never mind. Soon the itinerant teacher will come and give her all the answers.

What people don't get is that just because she can talk doesn't mean she can hear. She has 22 electrodes trying to make up for 30,000 hair follicles and if it's quiet, if she can see the person's lips, Georgette can usually make out what they're saying, but it's exhausting. And school is anything but quiet. Mostly her world is full of loud white noise. She hangs out for the end of the day, when she can switch off and lie in silence with Harry Potter.

That night Georgette dreams she's in the middle of a circle and all around her people are angry and shouting; she tries to hear what they're saying, but they interrupt each other, and she can't move her eyes quick enough from one set of lips to the next. Georgette wakes and goes to the kitchen. Her mother's back is turned at the sink. Georgette thinks of telling her mum about the dream, but then she'd have to put her cochlear back in. Instead she stands still and watches her mother doing dishes. Georgette sees a wine glass hit the tap – her mother still calls it a faucet – and shatter silently in the sink. She sneaks back to bed and lies in the dark, remembering when she was little and wanted to be just like her mum: jeans and high heels, earrings that swing. She remembers thinking her mother was so clever, just because she could hear.

*

At thirteen, school's all noise. Georgette slips out at lunch, walks home to an empty house. She grabs her bike and crosses the street to the Royal National Park. She's riding, wind blowing her blond hair back so you can see the transmitting coil on her head, the speech processor over her ear. She wants to take it off, but she's not allowed to ride a bike without her cochlear, and she's breaking enough rules for one day. The park's empty and the heaviness she feels in school, the weight of what rests on her ear and in her skull, the strain of trying to hear lifts as she coasts downhill into the forest. At first there's a bike path under the gums, where she's been before with her Mum on sunny days in winter. When the path ends, something compels her to get off her bike and walk into the bush. The woods, she thinks. But neither word is right.

She hears a kookaburra in a tree, not as most people hear it – her cochlear picks up forty of four hundred frequencies – but she hears it all the same. Georgette keeps going, further from her bike, from the path. The bush thickens. She thinks of turning back, and then she sees it: a clearing in the wood, a group of children laughing, not talking.

Georgette rubs her eyes. Teenagers moving their hands stand in a circle. Georgette freezes, hoping they won't see her, then hoping they will. A boy points in her direction and Georgette feels her face go hot. He gestures for her to come forward.

Georgette opens her mouth. The kids smile, laugh, pull her into the circle, hands on her shoulders. She feels a strange sensation go through her body. They're moving their hands so fast, eyes wide and then narrow. She's seen this before on a bus, in a train station; she watched it on YouTube. She has no idea what they're saying.

The boy's built like a rugby player, tall, with brown eyes. He's good-looking; he knows it. He approaches Georgette, makes a circular clapping motion, smiles big. *Happy*, she thinks and copies him. She giggles, nervous. He nods, then frowns, puts a hand under his chin, moves it forward. *Sad.* He places his hands on hers, showing her how to make the sign; her skin tingles with his touch. He puts a hand to the device on her head, gently removes the magnet, lifts it off so her world is silent like theirs. She's frightened; and then she's not.

Georgette feels a drop of rain, remembers Mum, dinner, home. She stands abruptly, points in the direction from which she came. The boy takes both her hands in his and Georgette lingers. He takes a pen and writes his number on the skin of her palm. Then he looks her in the eyes, points to her beauty spot and to his chin where the spot would be on him. He shows the others – they point to their chins and then to her, they nod. She doesn't understand, not yet.

Walking back to the bike, cochlear in her pocket, she sees giant ferns bouncing in the rain, notices the extreme green of a bed of moss. A bird flits by. All the world is quiet, the way it is in the bath or in the morning, before she feels her mother shake her awake.

Georgette doesn't put her cochlear back on for dinner. She sees her mother's pleading lips and she can read a bit of what they're saying, but she doesn't feel like hearing. Her mother doesn't know what the world sounds like to Georgette. It sounds like the skin of her knee feels on the road when she comes off her bike. Georgette takes a bite of peas, remembers the press of the pen on her hand, though she's washed away the ink. Her mum smiles; Georgette feels a sudden anger rise inside. She can't eat. Georgette stands, goes to her room, texts the boy, *Remember me?*

She waits.

When the phone vibrates, she jumps. *What's your name?*

Georgia, she replies.

John.

That night she falls asleep with the phone on her chest and her hands in the air, trying to remember the signs.

*

Jolene stands at the kitchen sink doing dishes, late for the M-HICS meeting. Mothers of Hearing Impaired Children. These days, her daughter won't look her in the eyes. Jolene can't remember when it got this bad, just that it's been bad a long time. Glued to her iPhone, messaging someone on the other side of the world, or the other side of the room, Georgette bears no relation to the fat toddler that threw her arms around her mother's neck and told her she loved her to the North Pole and back. She's even changed her name: Georgia, of all things. That redneck state. Georgia texted this new information to her mother last month because she no longer speaks.

Jolene reaches for a frying pan that's been soaking. She should go to the meeting. The other mothers are always so sympathetic, especially when it comes to teenagers. She could tell them how Georgette's become *proud* of her disability. Everyone's proud these days – gay and proud! Transgendered and proud! Indigenous and proud! And that's fine, really it's fine, but deaf and proud? Jolene scrubs at burnt egg.

She finishes the dishes, checks the mirror for any food in her teeth, writes a note to Georgia that she's going to M-HICS and puts it in front of her daughter's phone. Georgia takes the paper and gives her mother a half-wave without looking up. Jolene steps into the hall, pauses. She knocks at Mary's door instead.

In you get.

Georgette – Georgia. Fuck. Jolene closes her eyes and tries not to cry.

In you come. Mary says and Jolene lets herself be pulled passed the threshold.

He came over earlier today, John, and, I mean, besides the fact that my teenage daughter can get a boyfriend and I can't . . .

Is that what you want?

I want to be normal. They were signing and I know they were talking about me. I could feel it.

Teenage girls talk about their mums. Beer?

Tea. Mint tea, please.

Don't they drink in America? You could learn to sign.

She should've gone to the meeting. *Mary, you don't get it. All those appointments, all the waiting rooms with toys that smelled like vomit and books with half the pages missing, all that fucking speech therapy? It would negate everything.*

Would it?

She wants to go to a deaf school. Do you know the rates of literacy among the deaf?

Georgia can read.

I know she can read. I taught her to read. When did she get this angry at her own daughter? Jolene takes a deep breath, sinks to the floor.

Mary joins her on the blue carpet. She holds Jolene's face with one hand, and draws a finger slowly down the centre of her forehead, her nose, her mouth, stops at her chin. You're a good mum, she says. Let's not talk.

*

At fifteen Georgia comes home with purple hair and black nails. They sit at the dinner table. Some things are still normal: dinner at 6.30, *Modern Family* on the TV at seven. Jolene stares. She hates the hair, loves that distant creature on the other side of the table. Jolene reaches out and places a hand on top of her daughter's, and, to her surprise, her daughter doesn't pull away. Georgia looks her in the eyes, and then out the window at the streaky April sunset. She points.

Jolene doesn't turn to see pink clouds. She stares at Georgia, clings to her hand, which is soft, still a child's. Jolene would like to hold her hand all evening, all night and all of the next day; she would like to lift her teenage girl and put her on her lap and tuck her head – purple hair and all – under her chin, and rock her back and forth. Georgia pulls away, writes on a bit of paper, *I'm moving out.*

Jolene blinks.

John's family – they're all deaf, she writes. *I feel at home there.*

Jolene tells herself not to panic. *You're not deaf,* she hears herself say, but even as she says the words she knows she's wrong. *Do you know how small the Deaf community is?*

That's my decision, Georgia scrawls and then stands.

What happens next is a haze for Jolene. Georgia puts on a bulky backpack, hugs her mother and walks out the door. Jolene feels her stomach leap. She yells her child's name. But Georgia doesn't turn.

Overland

Something Wild

Jo Case

He is handsome, in the way men are at his age when there's nothing really wrong with them. His dark hair is not thinning, or even grey. His stomach doesn't push against his faded black t-shirt. He may be a dad, but he doesn't yet remind her of hers. Worth noticing, in this company.

'I guess we're sitting with you,' he says, pulling out the chair beside her.

'I guess you are,' she says. 'I'm Kristen.'

'Steve.' He flashes off-white teeth. 'I like your t-shirt.'

It's a pop-art cartoon of a black-bobbed woman declaring she's hitting the road after killing her parents. Kristen bought it at a concert, and the stitching has dissolved at the collar. She wore it every weekend when she was nineteen, but these days she wears it to bed. She's washed it for the first time in a fortnight, especially for tonight's dress-ups. She'd forgotten, when she put it on, that the whole point of being here is to present herself as a fellow grown-up, to get along with the others. She realises now – too late – that dressing in her teenage cast-offs was a bad idea.

'Me too,' she says. 'I like *my* t-shirt, I mean. My son Ethan likes Green Day, so I suppose he'd like yours.' Like her, he's dressed all wrong. Though maybe it doesn't matter so much for a man. The two men at the bookshop where she works dress just like him every day, right down to the Converse sneakers; if the women wear jeans, they're paired with a silky shirt or fitted top. She didn't notice the distinction until the day she wore Ethan's Batman t-shirt to work, for a laugh: loose on him, it fit her perfectly, though it pulled tight under the arms and strained across her chest. Her boss pointedly asked her to work in the back room all day, pricing stock.

Steve laughs, in a way that signals he's less charmed by her joke than by her short skirt. Kristen recrosses her fishnet legs, hooking a Doc Marten boot on the outside of the table leg. The woman beside Steve touches his shoulder and leaves her hand there, as if by accident. Like most of the women in the room, she's wearing a grown-up interpretation of tonight's theme: Something Wild. Black-lace dress, leopard-print heels, crimson lipstick. 'This is my beautiful wife, Meredith,' Steve says, leaning in to the woman. 'My *better half*.' It is an offering, an apology. He laughs again. His wife's mouth bends in a smile, but her kohl-rimmed eyes refuse to be charmed or placated. She is not, in fact, beautiful, though she is trying. Careful make-up fails to hide the wrinkles like quotation marks at the corners of her eyes. Kristen is comforted by details like these, collects them as armour against the daily indifference that is, to her surprise, wearing her down.

*

She almost admires the woman's hostility. She knows she deserves it. After all, she is flirting with her husband – partly because she's bored, but mostly to hold his attention. Ethan's been in Prep nine months now, and, apart from Cathy, this is the most interested another parent has been in her. Kristen doesn't care about decluttering, or different ways you can use lemons, or bulk-buying groceries at Aldi. It means nothing to her that the house across the road from the back entrance of the school sold for almost $70,000 more than the listed price at last week's auction. The rented apartment she lives in with Ethan is full of clutter: her clothes and books, Ethan's toys, pieces of paper covered in drawings or shopping lists. She does her grocery shopping on her bike, while Ethan's at school, cramming what she can into the baskets and her backpack. And her savings range, over the year, from $500 to nothing. She will never, in her whole life, afford a house in this neighbourhood. (She'll probably never afford a house at all.) She has no interest in these conversations, as well as nothing to say. Yet she still feels excluded from them.

*

'Steve, darling, let's get a drink,' says the woman, smoothing her dress towards her knees as she stands.

'Would you like us to get you a drink?' He dips his chin at Kristen.

She thinks about saying yes, just to see how his wife reacts. But instead, she shakes her head and watches as they blend into the dim light of the bar.

*

Her cheek is crushed in a lipstick kiss; she looks up from her phone.

'You must *hate* me,' says Cathy, taking the empty chair at her left, the one without Steve's jacket on it. A black bra strap escapes from one sequinned cap sleeve. Her hair hangs into her eyes and down her back, dark roots bleeding into blonde. Cathy is always like this: parts of herself trailing, as if catching up to the rest. Her house is the same. Dirty plates and glasses in a conga line to the sink; the couch a mosaic of abandoned clothes, Lego pieces and half-read magazines streaked with nail polish. Cathy's chaos makes her own seem organised. More importantly, Cathy shares the language of exasperating exes and shared custody – from school jumpers that always seem to be at the wrong house, to weekends confronting eerily silent bedrooms. Kristen erases the text she's halfway through – the one where she threatens to go home within the next ten minutes. She reaches up and tucks her friend's bra strap back under her sleeve.

'Don't be dumb,' she says. 'I'm just glad you're here.' She doesn't say that forty minutes late is a new record.

*

'Having a good night?' Cathy asks her. She doesn't want to know the answer; she wants reassurance. She knows Kristen didn't want to come in the first place. And she knows how she feels about this crowd. Kristen opens her mouth to reply, then closes it again. Meredith is back. She stands behind her chair, one hand resting on the steel arch of its back: poised for flight. Between Kristen and his wife, Steve anchors himself at the table. Kristen watches his denim legs disappear under the tablecloth.

'She's not drinking, so I doubt it,' he says, answering for Kristen. He extends a hand as Cathy hitches her handbag up her shoulder. 'I'm Steve, and this is my wife Meredith.'

'Oh, hey, nice to meet you. Haven't seen you around school before, are you new?'

'I don't get into the school much,' says Meredith. 'Steve does the pick-ups most days. From after-care.'

'Lucky you to have someone so helpful.' Cathy picks up Steve's wineglass. 'My ex is always busy, you know. Work comes first. Always has.' She tips the glass to her lips.

'Hey. You know that's my drink?' Steve says. Kristen stifles a laugh. Last Monday, at the bakery after drop-off, she ordered a coffee and Cathy drank it. She didn't say anything, she even paid for it.

'I am *so* sorry.' Burgundy liquid spills on the table as Cathy shoves it back at him, leaving a stain like an inkblot. 'I wasn't thinking.'

'Keep it,' he shrugs. 'We should get a bottle for the table to share anyway.' He looks at Kristen. 'Are you in?'

'Sure,' she says. Meredith looks at them all with dismay; sharing a bottle changes them from strangers who happen to be seated together to an active group. Kristen wonders if Steve is deliberately trying to annoy his wife, doesn't realise he is annoying her, or doesn't care. She is deciding, too: does she feel sorry for her?

*

Kristen wouldn't be at this primary-school fundraiser if not for Cathy, who went through mother's group and kindergarten with the others. Cathy understands comparisons with kindergarten teachers and can empathise about rising interest rates. Her kitchen may be messy, but she has a mortgage on it and can talk about tiles with some authority. She's regularly invited to Friday coffees at the bakery down the road from the school, even if she's no longer included in the dinner parties where the guests arrive in pairs. She says the dinner parties don't bother her, but says it so regularly that Kristen can tell it does.

*

'They don't hate you,' Cathy said, over red wine at her dining room table last week, while their sons played Lego under it. 'They don't *know* you.' It made a kind of sense at the time. Of course she should make an effort! Of course she was imagining things! Of course she would come to the fundraiser! But after forty minutes where no one would meet her eye when she looked at them, forty minutes spent playing with her phone in an effort to seem busy, she knows that they really do hate her. At best, she's invisible. Maybe it's because she's ten years younger than the rest of them. Maybe it's because she and Ethan's father are divorced (okay, never married and separated – but she says divorced because it seems more respectable). Maybe they think it's catching. Or is there something else about her – something indefinably wrong – that they can all sense, and know to avoid?

*

Cathy talks and Meredith endures it, responding with pursed lips and repeated 'hmm's. Kristen wonders sometimes if her friend overplays her absentmindedness: if behind her seeming incomprehension, she's just doing what she feels like and pretending not to notice the response. She watches the teacher's table across the room. She's heard that the teachers are planning a surprise group performance from *Cabaret* later in the night, and their costumes back up the rumour: the deputy principal, who doubles as the school's drama teacher, is wearing a corset trimmed with red ribbon, black hotpants and fishnet stockings. She seems as comfortable in her outfit as if it were her pyjamas. Ethan's teacher, one of the few men on staff, is wearing a suit and suspenders, with a trilby. (Is he supposed to be a gangster?) He sits stiff-backed next to his boss in her underwear.

*

'You can't go past a good schnitzel, can you?' Steve heaps cauliflower and potato in lumpy cheese sauce next to the glistening breaded chicken on his plate. Kristen lifts the lid of the casserole dish nearest her, leaking steam and revealing peas, green beans, sliced carrot and broccoli. This is what she gets for her $70 ticket? She craves leftover chilli con carne – or even grilled cheese on toast – in front of the television. The playlist shifts to the Spice Girls. *So, I'll tell you what I want, what I really, really want . . .*

'Oh, this is classic,' laughs Steve. He sings a line before forking chicken into his mouth. 'Don't you love it?'

'Yes!' says Cathy. She squeals and sings a line. *If you want my future, forget my past . . .* Meredith shrugs.

'Classic rubbish,' mutters Kristen. She's never heard a man enthuse about the Spice Girls before, at least not about their music. Ethan's father was a fan of Ginger Spice. And of Charlie from *Hi-5*. And, in a long-cherished childhood crush, of Noni from *Play School*. She's noticed that men – at least the men she knows – compulsively comment on the hotness of children's program presenters, as if reminding themselves of their masculinity. It's the same with girl bands.

'How can you say that?' asks Steve, clutching his chest. 'The Spice Girls were *hot*. Especially Baby Spice.'

'If you're into the little-girl thing,' says Kristen. She gulps from her wine. 'They're all awful, but the hot one was Ginger, surely?' She repeats what she's heard her ex say a million times before. 'The Union Jack corset, the Wonder Woman boots.'

Meredith cuts her schnitzel into tiny triangle wedges, her eyes on her plate. Cathy sings.

'Okay, you've convinced me,' says Steve. He picks up the bottle and refills Kristen's empty glass.

*

She rests her chin on her hand and leans in to laugh at his stupid jokes, feeling in control for the first time all year. Is this how Ethan feels when he acts up at school, telling jokes that make his class laugh and his teacher angry? He's found it almost as hard to fit in here as she has. 'He's not a bad kid,' the deputy principal told her, the last time she was called into the school office. 'But he needs to learn the word *no*. He needs to know when to stop.' Seeing herself through the teacher's eyes – young single mother with unbrushed hair and retail job – she was too embarrassed to defend herself, to explain that Ethan hears *no* (and obeys it) all the time at home. He doesn't listen to the teachers because he doesn't like or trust them like he does her. What can she do about that?

'I loved the Spice Girls when I was at uni,' says Cathy. 'I always wanted to be Posh Spice, because I liked her clothes.'

Meredith looks up from her mobile phone and puts it her handbag. She dabs a serviette at her mouth, erasing imaginary crumbs.

'If you'll all excuse us, we're being beckoned from across the room,' she says, hooking an arm into her husband's. 'Come on, *dear*.' She wields the word as a weapon.

'I'll be there in a sec,' says Steve, turning his smile on his wife.

'Come on,' she repeats.

'The *little woman* needs me,' he says to the table. And he gives his wife a purposeful pat on the arse as he stands to join her.

*

'Marriages like that that make me grateful I'm single,' whispers Kristen across the table, but Cathy doesn't laugh.

'What are you doing?' she says.

'What do you mean?'

Cathy looks at her for a long moment. 'Nothing,' she says eventually.

Kristen is glad she doesn't have to answer, because she doesn't know what she's doing. She doesn't even like Steve, though she is attracted to him: mostly because of the wine and the fact that it's been months since she's even kissed someone. She watches him across the room, deep in the fold of the other parents, and wonders what it would be like to have his mouth on hers, his hands under her clothes. She's been trying to do the right thing for so long: working amicably with Ethan's father to share custody, even though she hates him for leaving; working a job that bores her, because it gives her the flexibility to take Ethan to school and pick him up; even coming here tonight to try to make friends with people who look down on her. She'd forgotten the thrill of doing what she feels like, just to see what happens.

*

'He-LLO Footscray Primary!'

Rock Star Mum is at the microphone, leading a band of parents with varied experience – from touring the country and being in the Triple J's Hottest 100 (Rock Star Mum) to playing around on Friday nights in a friend's garage (most of the others). Kristen remembers watching Rock Star Mum perform with her band when they were both much younger, before Ethan was born. Looking up at the red-curtained stage of The Esplanade Hotel, part of a sweaty, drunk mass of bodies heaving to the music, her brother and best friend beside her. She misses being with people so familiar they don't have to talk; regrets that it's been replaced by boring conversations she has to work at. Conversations that miss the mark even when she tries, like there's a script everyone knows, except for her.

'Let's dance,' she says to Cathy, pushing her seat back.

'I don't think I'm drunk enough to dance.'

'Well, I am,' she says. 'Come on, bring your drink.'

*

Cathy dissolves into it, swaying her hips and snaking her arms as Rock Star Mum belts out 'I Love Rock'n'Roll'. Kristen squints deliberately at the stage, imagining herself back at The Espy, watching the same dyed-red hair and fire-engine lips. But Rock Star Mum's curves have seeped into stockiness; her leather pants replaced by a funky yet forgiving wrap dress. And Kristen can't forget that Rock Star Mum is no longer the lead singer of a band whose CDs she owns; she's now one of the popular girls at school who won't speak to her. In fact, if she's honest with herself, Rock Star Mum is one of the few who always smiles and says hello when she passes her at the school gate or sees her at the supermarket, even though her son is much older than Kristen's and she has no reason to talk to her. But Kristen's not in the mood to make distinctions. She tilts her head back and sways, trying to submerge her awareness that she is out of time, that her body can't locate the rhythm that has captured the crowd. And then she feels a body against hers; someone standing too close, standing still.

'Do you smoke?' asks Steve. She surprises herself by saying 'I do', even though she quit two years ago. Ethan would kill her if he knew.

*

They crouch on the footpath outside the hall. The cars and trucks of Whitehall Street roar through the darkness. Down the hill, the docks shine orange and white against the sky; cranes and scaffolding made beautiful, at least for now, by garlands of pinprick light. Kristen shivers in her t-shirt. She was almost too hot inside, where the heat had been turned up to accommodate short sleeves and bare skin. Out here, a biting wind blows her hair over her face and across her lips. She pushes it away so Steve can lean in to light her cigarette. He cups one hand around it as he flicks the lighter with the other.

'I have experience at this,' he says, concentrating on the uncertain flame. There is a familiar burn in her chest as she inhales, then a release as smoke curls into the night air, silvery under the streetlight. He settles beside her and lights his own cigarette. His knee touches hers, then rests against it. She doesn't move.

'I bet you do,' she says.

The Big Issue

Better Things

Balli Kaur Jaswal

'The house is made of red brick,' Rohan told his wife. The cheap connection to India gave his voice an echo. 'There is a yard and three bedrooms. And a secure fence around the area so it's very safe.'

'I can't wait to see it.' Prima sounded distant, which Rohan used to blame on the poor connection. But now he knew that she wasn't keen on coming to Australia. She'd heard that Melbourne and Sydney were dangerous cities, places where Indian students were being bashed by roaming youths. 'That's just the media exaggerating a few isolated incidents,' Rohan assured her. He neglected to mention that last week, returning from his first closing shift at Coles, he had run the entire way home, his black loafers thumping heavily on the shady paths of a local park. By the time he arrived home, he could not tell whether his chest was bursting with physical exertion or fear. The next morning, he asked Glen, his manager, if he could work only daytime hours. Glen shook his head slowly 'I can't have favourites. If I let you choose your hours, everyone will start coming to me with special requests. I can't have that, mate.'

The phone line crackled with static, breaking Prima's words. She told him about her day, what she planned to cook his parents for dinner tonight. For once there was no mention of her rivalry with his brother's wife, who also lived in the house, though she did say, 'It will be nice to have a place of our own.'

'Absolutely,' Rohan agreed. The word echoed in the receiver, sounding confident. He looked around his cramped room, relieved that Prima's visa had been delayed again, guilty for feeling relieved. Nothing he had told her about the house was true. They had saved and saved for his journey and first months in Australia, but most of the money had been swallowed by the unexpected costs of official documents, health checks, permissions and certificates. Once in the country, all he could afford was a shared floor space in a two-bedroom flat. He and five other tenants took turns sleeping on two beds. A sign-up roster for the shower and kitchen divided each tenant's life into ten-minute shifts.

Prima said something but the static noises overpowered her voice. 'I'll call you back tomorrow,' Rohan said.

'I can't hear you,' Prima said. Then the line went dead.

The next day Rohan invested in a superior calling card and phoned Prima at their usual time. He'd spent a few more dollars on it for the guarantee of a better connection. The shopkeeper, a stocky Italian man who sang along with the radio, had recommended it. 'It's worth paying a bit extra for better things,' he said. Rohan agreed. This time when he told Prima about the house, there was no echo, and he could describe the house without having to hear his lies repeated a moment later.

The following week, Prima told Rohan that she had located a distant cousin in Melbourne. 'Take down his number. I know you have people there but this is family,' Prima said. 'He will take care of you.'

Rohan insisted that he did not need anybody to take care of him. 'I'm fine,' he said, forcing a broad smile that he hoped she would be able to hear down the line. 'Besides, I've got double shifts every day.' He changed the subject before she could insist. 'How is Nidhi treating you?' he asked, knowing this would distract Prima

'She made a fuss about bills again today. She accused me of using more electricity than her and your brothers. Can you believe that? Just because she saw my light on in the night.'

'Are you having trouble sleeping?' Rohan pictured Prima's face whitewashed by the fluorescent bulb while the rest of the family dozed peacefully.

'I'm reading in the evenings,' Prima explained. 'Her real problem is that I'm reading English books and your sister-in-law thinks I'm rubbing the fact that I'll be going to Australia soon in her face. Do you know what she said the other day? In those countries, they speak so quickly that you won't be able to understand them, no matter how many books you read in their language. What would she know! She's never even left the village.'

'We won't need to be burdened by those problems here. No tension in our home. Just you and me,' Rohan said. Prima didn't respond and Rohan began to talk about the house again to fill the silence, adding ever more detail to the picture. There was a lavender bush in the front yard and when the breeze blew from the right direction, the air smelled fresher than soap. A two-seater outdoor wicker table setting, which had been generously donated by the landlord, sat in the back yard and in the evenings it was the perfect spot to watch the sky slowly darkening. By the time Rohan was finished, he could hear the smile in Prima's voice. 'I'll see you soon,' she said this time, instead of the usual goodbye. He felt a pinch in his gut. He ached to have her here in this room with him, but his lies had become too elaborate to unwind, and so he needed her to remain in India until he could provide the better things he was promising.

During work that afternoon, Rohan was assigned to a stock-take in aisle four. He was checking expiry dates on loaves of bread when a teenaged girl approached him and asked him where she could find a type of sauce.

'Sorry? Rohan asked. 'What is the name?'

The girl repeated herself but the brand sounded unfamiliar: Rooster-Shirt Sauce. He shook his head. 'I don't think we have this.'

'You do. My mum gets it from here all the time.' She sighed theatrically. 'Never mind, I'll just find it myself.'

'Sorry,' Rohan called out after her as she marched off. Moments later, the girl returned. 'Here,' she said, thrusting a bottle in his face.

Worchestershire sauce. Its spelling was different from the way she had pronounced it. Rohan apologised again. 'It's in aisle seven,' the girl said. 'You have, like, four different brands of it.'

On the bus home, Rohan took out the slip of paper where he had reluctantly written Prima's cousin's phone number. The encounter with the girl had made him feel acutely foreign. The bus rolled slowly through the silent suburban streets. The homes he passed had inspired some of Rohan's descriptions – neat rows of fences and bottlebrush trees, lavender bushes and bicycle paths. Maybe it wouldn't be such a bad idea to connect with some family in Australia. He typed a text message: *Hello Manu. This is Rohan, husband of Prima. Nice to meet you.* He was conscious of the formality of his English; he knew it was stilted and would probably make him seem stupid and obsequious. Surely this Manu would understand. He pressed the Send button and looked out the window, mentally recording details from the houses for his next conversation with Prima.

*

While he was eating lunch the next day, Rohan's phone rang. It was an unknown caller. 'Am I speaking with Rohan?'

'Yes, this is Rohan speaking,' he said.

'This is Manu.'

'Hello, Manu,' Rohan said. 'You can speak Punjabi?'

'Not much,' Manu replied cheerfully. 'A couple of phrases and some swear words.'

'I see,' Rohan said, hiding his disappointment with a laugh. 'So you are Prima's cousin. By which side?'

'Several times removed. It's a web of relatives, half of which I haven't even met but family's family I suppose?'

'Yes,' Rohan said, not knowing how to go on.

'You're living in Melbourne permanently now?'

'Yes, I am.' Rohan paused for a moment, 'Maybe we can meet?' He was intrigued by the casual manner of this man who sounded so Australian that Rohan would have to see him to believe they were somehow related.

'Sure. Are you free for drinks on Friday?'

'I am working on Friday night,' Rohan said, glancing at the calendar on the room wall where the scribbles of all the tenants' appointments and work shifts overlapped. 'I have Saturday free.'

'Right. Saturday then.' Manu gave a time and place and they made their brief goodbyes. As Rohan rushed to scrawl the details onto the calendar before they slipped out of his head, his flatmate Sarjeet walked by, buttoning up his uniform for his night shift for his security guard job. 'Lucky you,' Sarjeet muttered, 'Having a party on Saturday night I see.' He nodded in the direction of the calendar.

'It's Prima's cousin,' Rohan explained. He thought about the way Manu spoke and chuckled. 'The guy is Punjabi but can't speak the language.'

'Was he born here?'

Rohan nodded.

'I assure you, he can speak it just fine. These Australian-born Indians hate admitting that they're Indian. They think their Aussie friends will reject them if they associate with us. The girls are even worse. They laugh in your face and call you "Fresh off the Boat" if you try to talk to them.'

'He didn't sound stuck-up,' Rohan said. 'He was the one who called me.'

Sarjeet shrugged. 'I don't trust them. You think the whites here are racist? The Indians are worse.'

Rohan hoped this wasn't true. He did not know how Prima would cope with coming all the way here only to find that her own family didn't welcome her. Sarjeet put the kettle on and peeled the top off an instant noodle cup. He opened the cupboard door and asked, 'You're not using this?'

Rohan looked up to see the small square of empty shelf which had been cleared for him. He hadn't stored anything there; to do so would be to accept a permanent place in this flat. He thought about the sauce that was pronounced and spelled in two different ways. Rooster-Shirt. What did it taste like? He pictured the shelf filled with supermarket condiments that he had not heard of: herbs packed in plastic green-topped bottles, seeds that looked familiar but smelled entirely different from anything he had ever eaten before. He saw himself cooking with Rooster-shirt sauce in a spacious kitchen with a window that looked out onto a garden where the branches of a flowering myrtle tree reached brazenly for the sky. Prima materialised at his side in this fantasy. She stood by the counter and watched him casually picking the sauce bottle off the shelf and squeezing some into a saucepan.

'No,' Rohan told Sarjeet. 'You can have that space if you need it.'

*

At the start of Rohan's Friday night shift, Glen asked him to fill for another colleague the following Saturday morning, on top of his usual afternoon shift. Rohan agreed immediately. He always took on extra shifts. It dawned on him afterwards that he would have to cut through the park tonight if he wanted to get home at a reasonable hour. Otherwise he'd never get enough sleep to back here early tomorrow morning. At the end of his shift he walked briskly to the park and looked over both shoulders before breaking into a light jog. The path stretched out into the shadows, as if there was no end to it. He speed up into a sprint, ignoring the sharp bite in his toes as they dug into his loafers. His chest began to pound and his calves stiffened. 'Keep going,' he whispered to himself, imagining that if he stopped, somebody would pounce on him from the bushes and attack him just for being here.

Rohan didn't notice the steep dip in the path until he fell. The ground was dark and wet. He stood up and a bolt of pain shot through his ankle. He sat back down again, feeling the wet ground seep into the seat of his pants. Sucking in his breath, he stood again, placing all his weight on one side of his body, and he limped the rest of the way home.

In the morning, Rohan's ankle was swollen but he could not miss his two shifts. He winced as he stood up and stepped over the other tenants. At work, he swapped his strenuous duties with another worker, a high school boy who liked to do the heavy lifting in front of the teenage girls who worked there. By the end of both shifts, Rohan had trained himself to dismiss the pain. He took the bus home and showered before heading out again to the bar in the city that Manu had chosen.

Stepping off the tram, Rohan spotted an Indian man crossing the road to the bar. This had to be Manu – he had the loose, casual walk of someone who belonged here. Rohan's ankle prevented him from catching up so he walked several paces behind him.

Manu reached the entrance and turned around. Noticing Rohan, he smiled and they introduced themselves. 'Good timing,' Manu said. Rohan nodded politely.

Rohan followed Manu to the back of the bar where a spiral staircase led to rooftop seating. Climbing the stairs put pressure on both his feet, and as he reached the top, he had to grab the wall momentarily to brace himself from the dizzying pain which had returned to his left ankle. Manu was busy chattering away, telling him that the bar was owned by an ex-colleague of his who had left the corporate world to follow his dream. 'There's a great view up here as well,' Manu said. He turned around. 'You alright?'

Rohan smiled weakly. 'Just something in my shoe,' he said.

It was a relief to sit down and drink a cold beer. Manu asked Rohan lots of questions, to which Rohan could only give short responses. Seconds after each reply, he would realise that he knew perfectly well the English words and phrases to use but somehow he was too tongue-tied to get them out. He became aware that Manu was starting to speak more slowly and loudly to him.

'When will Prima come to join you?'

'Her visa is not yet,' Rohan said. 'No visa yet,' he corrected himself. 'She like to do some schooling here. Get a degree.'

'That's good,' Manu said. He looked past Rohan's shoulders. Rohan knew they would not become friends. This drink was an obligation for Manu – somewhere, a mutual relative had urged him to make Rohan feel welcome in Australia, but this would be it. Afterwards, they could return to their separate realities.

'You like Melbourne?' Rohan asked.

'It's the only home I've known,' Manu said. 'Most liveable city in the world. The quality of life here is excellent.' Rohan knew better than to argue but he did not think Manu would want to hear about his living situation, his quality of life.

'You go to India often?'

'I've been twice,' Manu said. 'When I was young. After my grandparents died, there wasn't any reason to go.'

'But it's your home,' Rohan said.

'Not really,' Manu shrugged. 'I'm Australian.'

'No,' Rohan said. He did not know why he felt so insistent but he could not let Manu get away with dismissing India like this. He had toffee-coloured skin and hair on his knuckles. He looked like an uncle of Rohan's from one angle, and from another he almost looked like Rohan himself. 'You are from India,' he insisted. 'I am from India. This country . . . we are borrowing it.'

There was confusion in Manu's smile and then he conceded. 'Okay,' he said. 'I guess I will go to India again one day.' Rohan knew he was being patronised. He spent the rest of the night giving one-word answers to Manu and watched his patience drain away. 'Let's call it a night then,' Manu said finally after a jug of beer. It was only nine-thirty but Rohan was happy to end this encounter. He swung his legs over the side of the barstool and bore his full weight on his ankles to stand before a shock of pain jolted through his body. His legs gave way and he collapsed to the floor.

'Whoa,' Manu said, helping him up. 'It was only two beers,' he joked. The couple at the next table laughed as well. Rohan felt humiliation burning in his face. He struggled to get up. Manu's face was lined with worry. 'Are you alright?'

'I am fine,' Rohan said. He stood again, remembering to put all his weight on his right leg. He gestured for Manu to walk ahead of him and then he limped painfully down the stairs. Outside the bar, Manu flagged down a taxi and insisted on giving Rohan a lift.

'Looks like you injured yourself,' Manu said as Rohan gingerly sat in the backseat and pulled his legs away from the curb. Rohan didn't reply. He was thinking of where to ask Manu to drop him off. His own suburb was miles away from the city, at the end of a train line, and he had a vague sense that they were traveling in the opposite direction. He wanted Manu to see his house. Not the apartment where he squeezed past other bodies while cooking dinner, where he had to stand in line for over twenty minutes just to brush his teeth on some mornings. The house that he had described to Prima.

'Take a left here,' he commanded the driver. 'Right there.' They wove into a suburb where tall hedges guarded the properties from view. Rohan would never hide a luxurious house this way. It would be on full display for everybody to see.

He noticed Manu looking closely at him. 'Look,' Manu said gently. 'It seems you're a bit lost. Shall we go out to the main road and start again? What's your address? Which suburb?'

A house came into view. It was shrouded by shadows but Rohan could see the brick exterior, the white fence bordering a neatly-trimmed lawn. 'Right here,' Rohan said triumphantly. 'I live here.'

Manu peered out the window and glanced at Rohan. 'You're sure?'

'I live here,' Rohan repeated, opening the door.

'Right. Okay,' Manu said. 'Well have a good night, and do call me if you need anything. That was a nasty fall you had back there – if your leg's still hurting, go see a doctor.'

'Thank you. Very nice to meet you,' Rohan said. He left the taxi and lingered on the curb, pretending to check his phone until the cab shot off down the street. The pain in his ankle persisted, and a dull ache had begun to spread through his leg, lodging in his hip. He walked close enough to the house without seeming suspicious and looked at the brick facade, the fence. How much would a house like this cost? He had no idea. He did not know which suburb he was in. There had to be a station nearby where he could catch a train home and walk to his apartment. He began walking in the direction of the main road. His ankle slowed him down, forcing him to notice the details of the other houses in this neighbourhood. There were more tall hedges and landscaped gardens. There were paved driveways and trampolines. Through most windows, a warm amber light glowed, as if the people within these houses only needed enough light to see the soft shapes of one another. He reached the main road and chose to go left but after fifteen minutes of walking, he seemed no closer to a train station than before, and his eyes had begun to fill with tears. Everything was closed. He sat on the front stoop of a milk bar and watched the occasional car pass by, wondering if they would stop if he stood in the street and waved his arms.

The phone buzzed in Rohan' pocket. Prima's name flashed across the screen. He picked up the call reluctantly, feeling the truth rise like a lump in his throat. 'There's no house,' he blurted out. Instantly he regretted saying it. Why disappoint Prima with the truth? Now she would never come to Melbourne.

'Hello?' Prima asked. 'Hello?' It always took a few seconds for the connection to become clear when she called from India. There were mismatched *hello*s and *how are you*s until the line settled. 'Hello, Rohan?'

'Prima,' he said, grateful for his confession to be swallowed by static. 'I am just out at the moment. Can I call you back?'

'There was a long pause. 'Rohan, can you hear me?' she asked.

'Yes,' he said. 'I will call you back.'

'What's wrong?'

'Nothing,' he said.

'Something is wrong,' she replied. 'You don't sound like yourself.'

He was surprised that Prima could distinguish the nuances of his tone over this cheap connection, where everything sounded tinny and faded. 'I've hurt myself,' Rohan said. 'I fell and twisted my ankle.'

'Have you seen a doctor?'

'Not yet. I didn't think it was serious.'

'Book an appointment to see one right away.'

'Prima, doctors are expensive.'

'But it's your leg. How will you do anything if you can't walk?'

'I'm sure it's just a bit sore for now – ' he said, but Prima was talking over him.

'How will you work? How will you do your grocery shopping? Or take your clothes to the laundromat?'

'The laundromat?'

'That's what people do there, isn't it? I was reading about student life in Australia on the internet and they said that taking clothes in the laundromat is a cost-effective alternative to buying a washing machine.'

'It is,' Rohan said. 'There's no washing machine in the house yet.' It occurred to him that he had rarely described what was inside his home in these conversations. 'You know what else? There is an electric stove, but it's old and the oven takes a long time to heat up. There are two sinks in the kitchen but there's a leak in one of them. I'm trying to figure out how to repair it.' These were truthful admissions, and as he listed more details, he gained the courage to speak another truth.

'I want us to have the best life,' he said, 'a life filled with nice things and only small worries.' There was silence on Prima's end. Rohan told himself it was just the connection's delay but he was nervous. None of the other men in his situation, all trying to make something from nothing, none of them had dared voice this wish. Because what would happen if it did not come true? Enough disappointment hovered in the cramped spaces of his flat; hope was a private, precious thing.

'I do too,' Prima said. Rohan smiled, feeling the rich warmth of her voice filling him with calm. After the call ended, he watched the passing traffic – cars gliding to their destinations and the occasional cyclist whose back lights flashed urgently to other vehicles: see me, please see me. A light breeze made dancers of the thin tree branches. He stayed on the milk bar stoop and waited till he was ready to stand up again.

Meanjin

Aokigahara

Jennifer Down

I phoned my father when I arrived.

He said 'Your mum's just round at Aunty El's' in such a way that I knew she wasn't; that she'd left the room with her hand to her mouth when he'd first said *hullo, love*, and I felt so sorry for us all.

The hotel room was cool and masculine. I drew back the curtains and looked out. The cityscape glittered through two big windows, like a part of some vast computer. My fingertips tingled if I stood too close to the glass. I wanted to sleep and slipped between the starchy sheets. I couldn't hear the city below, but all night I kept waking up and going over to the wide glass panes. I don't know what I expected.

In the morning the view was different and I could see it all as more than a billion lit squares. There was a sprawling park down below. Far off, the symmetrical peak of Mount Fuji. I sat in front of the window, naked, with the glossy map they'd given me in the lobby. I tried to work out where I was.

I met an American woman in the elevator. She was here for work, she said; she visited twice a year. Her husband had long since stopped coming with her.

'He thinks it's exhausting. The sort of place you visit once or twice in your life. He's from Montana.' She gave an apologetic smile. She took out a palm-sized mirror and inspected her mouth. 'Are you here on business?'

'I'm visiting my brother,' I said without thinking. A small mercy: her mobile phone rang, and we smiled at each other as the elevator doors opened into the lobby. I walked away with blood buzzing in my arms. I thought I'd better get my story straight.

In the house I shared with him and Sigrid we'd lain on the living room carpet in an oxy dream. I was too fucked to lift my arms. Tom and Sigrid kissed in a slow, decadent way, faces turned towards each other, but not for long. I dozed there on the floor in a thick shaft of sunlight, my face pressed to the carpet. When a knock came at the door, the three of us were paralysed: Tom gave an indulgent laugh, but nobody moved.

It was all summertime and glory that year: pikelets, braided hair, and blood oranges; television, speed, flower crowns, silver dreams, tricks of the light. Long walks home from the city after a night that ended in tears and new jokes and pissing on someone's front lawn, me and Sig giggling with our skirts up around our hips. Power-pedalling up the big hill at night, foreheads spangled with sweat.

We had a poster of the Milky Way tacked up on the wall opposite the toilet, and another poster of constellations beneath it. I learnt the names of stars and the pictures they made.

I had no friends – only Tommy and Sig. I was the spectator, the sister; the joyful witness to their Great Passion. The three of us loved one another very hard.

Eri called to say she was running late. I drank a beer and read my book in the greyish light. When she arrived she said *hisashiburi* and gave me a quick, tight hug. Her hair was cut to her ears. I liked how small and tough she looked.

'I was late at work,' she said. '*Osokunatte sumimasen.*' She inclined her head in a parody of her own culture and shrugged out of her coat.

I explained what I wanted. Eri might have known. She looked at me levelly while I spoke. A cigarette burned low between her knuckles.

'I can't go with you,' she said. I was the one who looked away. 'But my friend Yui – her father will take you. He's a doctor, but he volunteers there sometimes. You can take a bus to Kawaguchiko station.' Eri stubbed out the cigarette and took up a pen. She said she'd organise it for me. She wrote down her friend's name and phone number on a square of paper, and passed it to me with both hands. I never knew when to be humble, when to be reverent. I remembered the set phrases from high school, but not the feel of them in my mouth.

'Thank you,' I said again and again. '*Osewa ni narimasu. Yoroshiku onegaishimasu.*' Thank you for caring for me. Sorry to be a burden. It's the thing you say. We did it all back to front: first there was hardness; afterwards, decorum. We stayed there until after midnight. We talked about our jobs, about our families. Eri lied and said my Japanese was still very good. She was engaged to a schoolteacher. She hoped I'd come back for the wedding. I lied and said I would. She reached into her handbag and pulled out a blue envelope. Tucked inside was a photo – Eri, Tom and me on Phillip Island, smiling grimly into the wind. Eri wore the pained expression of the exchange student; Tommy grinned from under a ridiculous knitted beanie. He looked healthy, indefatigable, victorious. I was blinking.

Eri leant on my shoulder, so close that I felt her hair against mine. She looked down at our pale adolescent faces. 'I thought that I had taken more pictures that day, but I could only find this,' she said.

I had the spins at Koenji station. I sobered up on the train back to the hotel. In my room I called Sigrid; lovely Sig who'd stayed with him all that time, who'd weathered his shit when the rest of us no longer could.

'It's all sorted. I'm going the day after tomorrow,' I said. I realised I was going to sob.

'Come home. You don't need to do this for anyone else. You're only doing it for you,' Sigrid said.

'I'm sorry,' I said. 'I'm sorry.'

'What's it like there? Is it cold?'

'You know Buddhists get a new name when they die?' I told her. 'To move away from one world and into the next – the afterlife, or whatever, a dead person gets a new name. So they don't look back.'

'Like Lot's wife.'

I wanted to stick my head into the night, to run around a cricket oval until I was ragged in the lungs. I was aching with a mad, violent energy, but all I could do was curl up like a child in the cool bed. When we were kids walking home from school, Mum wouldn't let me cut across the oval without Tom. *It's not good for a little girl to walk there by herself,* she said. I did it anyway, but with a thrumming heart and quick legs, thinking of strange men and bodies in paddocks. It was a much shorter way of getting home. Whenever I banged through the screen door out of breath, schoolbag thumping against the small of my back, Tommy laughed. He'd say, 'What are you *scared* of, Cammy? Worst thing you're gunna see is Jade Pitrowski getting fingered in the tunnel.' He never told Mum. Mostly we walked together.

Dad and I found him once living in a shack up near Marysville. He'd been gone from home a few days. Detective games and phone calls to his friends led us nowhere: we had to wait for Tommy to contact us. He did at last, and we went to retrieve him. We left Mum standing in the driveway at dusk, telling us to 'drive safe'. I was still in my school uniform. Everyone was frightened of what we'd find that time; of what fool's gold lay at the end of the treasure-hunt instructions he'd made Dad scribble down over the phone. In the end, it was a monstrous Tommy, huddled like a dog in his windbreaker and filthy jeans in some abandoned shed. We couldn't go home, he said; we couldn't leave yet. And so we stayed with him in that wormy wood shack. It was not far from the town. Dad drove in on the second morning and bought food and polar-fleece blankets and we tried to make an adventure of it. I was impatient. When it got dark I lit all the candles and sat at the wooden table with my textbooks, highlighting the words someone else had coloured before me. I learnt nothing. I did it only to say, *Look, you selfish shit, it's not always about you. See what you're doing.* I copied notes into my exercise books with their ruled margins, and did every revision question surrounded by my lumps of molten wax. I remembered nothing.

Dad and Tom went for walks that lasted for hours. It was never that I was not invited. Once I looked out the window and saw them standing twenty yards apart, knee-deep in grass. Tommy was bellowing something and they were too far away for me to hear at all, but I could see the strain in his neck, his Adam's apple tight and tired, and I imagined him hoarse-voiced. He flung out an arm in a posture of desperation. Dad waited for him to finish.

We stayed there for three days. On the fourth day we drove home, all of us grimy and sour-breathed in our greasy wool jumpers and boots. Me, the learner driver up front of the station wagon, easing the car around hairpin bends. Tommy in the back with his headphones, snarling at me to *fucken' step on it, will ya.* Dad beside me mouthing to his Buffalo Springfield tape and looking over the sharp, ferny ledges when I wished he'd keep his eyes on the road, or tell me I was taking the corners too fast, because I was afraid. And the asphalt unfurling impossibly before us, canopied by the thickest forest I'd ever seen.

I slept beside a man I'd met in a bar. He was Dutch, an architect, thirty-two, here for a conference. I didn't care. We fucked twice, and afterwards we rolled away from each other and I told him everything. He tried to put his arms around me.

'He was your older brother?'

'Sixteen months older.'

'Almost like twins,' he said. 'I've heard about it, the *jukai.* Sea of trees.'

'I don't know what it will be like,' I said. I felt the grief rising in weak spasms. I got up and went to the bathroom, drank a glass of water from the tap.

'In some ways it's almost a pilgrimage that you're making,' he said pleasantly. His accent made everything sound silly. I wished he'd stop talking. Above the bedhead was a mirrored pane. I could see my own body reflected in it, the shadow of pubic hair, the faint tan lines from a summer ago. White breasts, glass of water in my hand, flesh settled on my hips. There was a smudged handprint on the mirror, not left by either of us. We'd fucked efficiently, neatly.

I thought I should leave, but he said I should stay. I got back into bed beside him and he reached for me again. He had his arms around me for a long time. One of those blokes who hated silence and loved touching. I wondered if he had a wife or a girlfriend. We must have slept, because I dreamed lightly of flooded fields. I was seeing them from above; I was seeing the water-damaged crops.

We said goodbye in the morning. I got lost trying to find my way back to my hotel. I ended up on the wrong train, then another. I stood on a train platform I didn't recognise, looking at the map with its complicated coloured lines. I might have started to cry, but one of the white-gloved station employees approached. He had a badge of the British flag on his lapel. He asked if I needed help.

'This is Yamanote line,' he said. His fingers traced the map. He showed me where my hotel was, where Tokyo Tower was, where Ginza was, where Akihabara was, smiling the whole time. I kept saying thank you. I felt as helpless as an animal by a roadside. 'Since you are here in Ikebukuro,' the man went on, 'why don't you try the *bōsai-kan*?'

'*Bōsai-kan*,' I repeated dumbly.

'It is a special and interesting earthquake museum. You can experience an earthquake. To feel the feeling.' He held out both gloved hands, fingers splayed, and bent his knees as if bracing himself. '*Wa-a-a-a-a!*' He laughed. 'Actually, there is information on various type of emergency situations. It is a good attraction. The entry is free of charge. I recommend this place.'

He'd been so helpful that I didn't know how to refuse him. I couldn't simply get back on a train and head off in the right direction. I thanked him over and over again. He gave me a fold-out map, the one I already had three copies of. Marked the route to the museum with a series of neat dashes; warned me it was easy to miss. I kept saying thank you. I wanted to wash the sex off my thighs.

I walked all over the city. I wandered around the streets as if in a hallucination. I was scared that if I went back to my hotel I'd fall asleep there in my cool, clean coffin room. I took photos in the fish markets; I bought a small bunch of peonies and carried them around all afternoon like a fool. I walked through the park I kept seeing from my hotel window. In a quiet suburb full of trees I sat in a tiny café styled like a French pâtisserie. Charles Bradley was playing over the speakers. The coffee was pale and sweet. Ordinarily I would have hated it, but I ordered another and a cake the size of my palm topped with gelatinous fruits and read my book for an hour by the window. It was late afternoon. The light was swimming-pool green. I caught another train, met Eri again for dinner. She brought her boyfriend. I wasn't hungry. I was beginning to get nervous. Afterwards the two of them headed off to sing karaoke with some friends. I turned down their invitation. I had to get up early the next morning.

I sat on the end of the bed to call Dad again. The bed was neatly made from the day before. I told him about the earthquake museum.

'The Life Safety Learning Centre,' he repeated, and laughed. 'But how did you bloody end up there?' He laughed harder when I told him about the man at the station, uniformed and well-intentioned, and how I'd gone out of politeness. I told him about the earthquake simulator.

'It was frightening,' I said. 'It went on for longer than I expected. I was surprised.'

He asked if I wanted to speak to Mum. I said I had to get up early the next morning.

There was a car accident. It wasn't me driving round the Black Spur, it was Tommy dozing off in the car on Swan Street, me in the passenger seat reaching over to grab at the wheel. He ruptured his spleen and in hospital he got high on pethidine. He had a vision – colour and dreams in his arms– and all I got was to sit by his chair. He went off the antidepressants after that. We learnt about them when I did my psych rotation, their uses and side effects. Of course that doesn't happen to everyone. Of course if you feel drowsy or otherwise affected, you shouldn't drive. Of course. He went cold turkey, like you're not supposed to.

'What does it feel like?' I'd heard Sigrid ask him once. One of the afternoons when we'd cycled round the Merri Creek trail with bottles of Mercury tinkling in our crates, sprawled out in the sun, read to one another, done the quiz in the paper. We had so much time.

'Dizzy,' Tommy had said, 'these sort of – *electric*-feeling brain zaps. Like shivers in your head that roll through.' He'd pressed his hands to her hair, scrunched his fingers, raked them down her skull to her neck, but tenderly. Sig's shoulders had tensed. They'd thought I was asleep. I realised it was too late to let them know I was listening. 'Like looking through fog. I just feel out of it.'

'Must be dreadful,' she'd said.

'Gunna be good when it's over,' he'd said. My brother with his silly, lovely grin, withdrawing from the good pills. That was May. He went to Japan in September. We'd all waved goodbye to him at the airport. He'd swaggered off singing 'The Internationale' for reasons I've long forgotten, waving his windcheater at us until he disappeared through the silver doors. The security guard had laughed and Dad had laughed and Sig laughed, too, but she'd been crying. Her eyes were leaking and her breathing was ragged. I thought she was just getting ready to miss him. In a way she was. Maybe she knew something the rest of us didn't.

I'd brought a book to read on the bus but ended up with my face to the window the whole way. I slipped in and out of light sleep, tiny flickering dreams. A sign in a window I couldn't read; tunnels into the earth; my father with white smoke rising from his belly or chest, he was on fire and didn't realise. I woke with a start and looked around me. I wondered if I'd cried out. I kept my headphones on and looked out at the mountain drawing closer.

Mr Ukai met me at the bus stop. He was a small, slim man in a parka. He held out his hand for me to shake. In the car he played Bob Dylan.

'*Osewa ni narimasu*. Thank you for doing this,' I said.

'It's good to be able to help. I go there to help anyway.' His English was clear. His eyes did not move from the road.

'Even so. It's a big ask – it's a big favour. I'm grateful. *Yoroshiku onegai itashimasu*.'

'*Ii-i-e*. I think it is not so good for you to go there by yourself,' he said gently. 'I think, if you are not too tired, we will go to there now. We don't want to be in the forest after dusk. It is a dense place.'

'I've read a little bit about it,' I said. 'I read about that book. *Kanzen Jisatsu Manyuaru*.'

'*The Complete Manual of Suicide*.' He shook his head. 'I think it is maybe a hysteria. I think you cannot blame a book. This sadness is an epidemic. It did not come from bookstores. But,' – we slowed at a corner and he turned to look at me, one hand on the gearstick – 'I have not read this book, so maybe I don't know.'

The roads were wet. The trees were fat with the sort of haze I imagined would burn off later in the day. I felt as if I'd been awake for a long time, but it was still morning.

'Yui tells me you are medical student. Very good.'

'Well, I'm not very good. I'm just passing,' I said. 'And I still don't know if it's what I want to do.'

'I still don't know either. And I am a doctor for thirty years.' He laughed. 'What do you like most?'

'I want to be a diagnostician. I like solving puzzles,' I said. 'But I don't know if I work hard enough for that.'

We pulled in to a car park. We'd arrived suddenly. I hadn't been looking for signs. Mr Ukai sat for a moment after he cut the ignition, looking at something I couldn't see in the rear-view mirror. I thought he was going to ask me if I was ready, but he just reached into the back seat for his plastic water canteen.

From the car boot he took out a smaller women's rain jacket and handed it to me. He retrieved a backpack, a torch, and a length of fluorescent-yellow nylon cord, neatly coiled. That nearly brought me to my knees. I had a bad feeling in the guts. It smelt like new earth out here, petrichor; like bright air. I tried to think about that instead of the nylon cord.

Mr Ukai shut the boot gently. He slung the backpack over his shoulder, and his waterproof jacket gave out a rustle.

'*Ja, ikōka*?'

We started towards the entrance. The leaves were wet underfoot.

'People say it's a mystical place, they say, *nanka*, many kind of things, but it's just a forest,' he said. 'The mystery is why are so many people sad.'

It struck me as a distinctly un-Japanese thing to say. The woods were darker than I'd imagined. It was all electric green moss and untamed tree roots crawling over the forest floor. It felt prehistoric. We came to a length of yellow rope stretched across the path. There was a sign that said *No Entry*. Mr Ukai stepped right over it, then held it down so I could do the same.

'I think it is best, from here, if I walk first,' he said. He inclined his head. I nodded.

'Of course.'

'Cammy-san. If the experience becomes too heavy, *nanka, tsurai* – we will go back to my car. Please do not be troubled. Do – not – hesitate.'

He pronounced my name *kami*, like 'god'. I nodded again. I had my thumbs looped through the straps of my backpack. I felt like a child on an excursion.

We fell into step single file, me behind him. I wondered what he'd meant, exactly, with his polite, broken English. There was such a chasm between us. I thought about Eri saying *I can't go with you.*

I kept my eyes fixed on Mr Ukai's back, or on my own running shoes, caked with wet leaves. When he started humming to himself, I thought it must be safe to look up. There was tape everywhere, strung between trees. Some of the trunks had numbers spray-painted on them. Mr Ukai stepped off the main trail onto a smaller one. He looked back at me. He said, *daijōbu*? and I said *daijōbu*. I could feel sweat cooling on my neck.

It had been weeks before the funeral took place. There were complications bringing Tommy's body back. For a while the Japanese seemed to think there should be an autopsy, and that they should be the ones to undertake it, but that faded. I took half a valium before the service and another after I'd read my eulogy.

There was no word for *closure* in Japanese. I'd looked it up online in my hotel room the other night.

Mr Ukai had stopped humming. He was walking respectfully, if that were possible. Everything he did was gentle. He surveyed the forest calmly. His eyes went everywhere. I flinched at it.

There was human detritus everywhere. Plastic umbrellas, food wrappers, mittens, lengths of rope, a bicycle, a pair of scissors, a blue tarpaulin. The trees were so thick overhead, I wondered how they let any light through. I could see why Tommy would have loved it here.

Mr Ukai paused. He waited until I was beside him, then he pointed at the base of a tree a little way off the path. There was a marker at its base. Someone had left a bouquet of flowers, pink cellophane, and a tiny banquet of food, laid out on a piece of cloth.

'It is recent,' Mr Ukai said. 'Maybe someone else is making our same journey today.'

A few steps further I saw a skull turned green and a rotten shoe. There was a crop of tiny mushrooms growing by the heel of the shoe. Their stalks were young and firm. I squatted with one hand on a damp tree and vomited. Mr Ukai handed me a pocket pack of tissues. I wiped my mouth. I waited until I was sure I wasn't going to do it again, then I stepped past Mr Ukai. I zipped my water canteen back into my backpack. I apologised in a way that sounded too formal.

'Maybe a place near here would be good,' he suggested when we started walking again.

'It's beautiful, but there's no light.'

'Aokigahara is a very dense place. That's why it is *jukai*. Sea of trees.'

'I know,' I said. I felt rude. 'I just thought maybe we could find a clearing.'

We walked for a long time. I watched the soil under my feet. The trees closed over almost completely, so that I had to bend my head in parts, but we did come to a clearing. 'Here,' I said, 'I think this is a good place.'

'It is,' he agreed.

My mouth tasted like vomit. I took off my backpack and fished out the plastic bag.

'Cammy-san. If you wish, I can go somewhere else. So you can be discreet.'

I looked up at him. I shook my head. 'I don't need to be here long.'

I took the letters and the hammer out of the plastic bag. I chose a tree. I lined up the pieces of paper. They were neatly folded into four, no envelopes. I fixed them to the tree. The nails were probably too small, but they held. I nailed Eri's Phillip Island photo to the trunk, too, then the yellowed poster from our bathroom in the Yarraville house, the one with the constellations.

When I finished hammering I stood back to look at my shrine. Mr Ukai was on the other side of the clearing, sitting on the trunk of an enormous fallen tree. He was watching me with a placid face.

'Please take your time. Do not hurry,' he said.

'I think I'm done,' I said. I left the hammer by the tree. I had no further use for it.

Afterwards Mr Ukai took me back to his house. His wife served us green tea and small sweet cakes and mandarins with tough skins. We sat at a low table. Mr Ukai said it was all right not to kneel. Mrs Ukai looked at me the way you might look at an orphan. She asked gentle questions. We winced at each other. Once the sugar sadness in my mouth was almost too much, but I looked down at the table and it passed.

Their daughter Yui was my age. She arrived home from university and introduced herself.

'Yui has just been on student exchange. For one year. In Austin,' Mr Ukai said.

'Texas,' Yui said. She gave a little smile. Fathers and daughters were the same everywhere you went. Mrs Ukai insisted on cooking me dinner. She made yudofu, tsumire and daikon. I was surprised at how hungry I was.

'Yudofu is my favourite,' Mr Ukai said. 'I have tried to cook yudofu myself, but I am not so good as my wife.' He laughed pleasantly. His wife did not speak English. She smiled at me through the steam rising from her bowl.

After dinner Yui and I stood in the dark outside on the wooden verandah and smoked a joint. She spoke with an American accent so convincing she even had a slight drawl.

'I'm sorry about your brother.'

'It's okay. I don't think there's anything we could have done to stop him.' My arms were feeling warm on the inside. I had the sudden urge to stand close to Yui, to let our arms touch, to see if hers were hot, too, but some part of me realised I was high.

'Why did he come here to do it?' she asked.

'I don't know. He did a student exchange here when he was in high school. He never knew what he wanted to do. I'd never heard him talk about Aokigahara before.

But now I've seen it, it makes sense to me.'

'It's a beautiful place,' Yui said. I wanted my mother.

The last bus to Tokyo left at 8.10 p.m. Mr Ukai drove me back to Kawaguchiko station. As we approached the station I began to thank him again, clumsily. We parked beneath a floodlight.

'There is a Japanese saying: *nodo mo to sugireba atsusa o wasureru*. Do you understand?' Mr Ukai asked. I shook my head. 'It means, *one forgets the heat once it has passed down the throat*.'

My backpack was heavy on my lap. I went on thanking him. He got out and waited until I was on the bus. I waved at him from the window. He was still standing there when the bus pulled away. I waved until I couldn't see him anymore.

I felt as if I'd been gone for days when I got back to the city. I couldn't bear the trains and the streets. I couldn't bear this country.

I felt filthy. In my hotel room I took off my muddy running shoes and threw them straight into the wastepaper bin. I started to undress to get in the shower, and then I thought I'd better phone my dad if I was going to do it at all.

'I went. I saw it.'

'Oh, Cammy,' he said. 'Are you alright?'

I sat on the edge of the bed. 'Do you remember that time we went to get Tommy from the mountains, and we drove home through the Black Spur? The trees were thicker than that.'

He began to cry. I heard him sucking in air through his teeth.

Australian Book Review

The Same Weight as a Human Heart

Nick Couldwell

Harry's up ahead ducking and weaving between the seaweed and bluebottles washed up at the high tide mark. He keeps his eyes on the dirty horizon, huffing through his nose when he throws his jab. *Hfff, hfff.* He's slower than he used to be, arms as stiff as a 4x4, but you can see he still has it in the way he shifts his feet, bobs his head. He circles the debris left at the shoreline, his t-shirt billowing in the northerly like a raised flag. *Hfff, hfff, hfff.*

It's September 22nd, the same date Jack Dempsey lost the heavyweight championship of the world to Gene Tunney. He was Harry's favourite boxer after Grandpa played an old black-and-white tape of his most famous fight, dubbed the Long Count. Even asked Mum to cut his hair with a side part. We never heard the end of it. I'd catch him in front of the mirror in Mum's room with his mitts up, toilet paper around his knuckles and he'd say, 'Tall men come down to my height when I hit 'em in the body,' and he'd see me in the reflection and wink like he was three gins deep.

When his cheekbones glisten and his shoulders brew with lactic acid, he stops, and ambles back towards me with his arms swinging like oars. He bursts bluebottles with the callused part of his heel and sometimes little pieces of tentacle hits me in the leg and sting like nettles in a cow paddock. As we drift towards the edge of the dunes where the softer sand is, the bluebottles thin out and he has to run down to the tideline to find more.

We pass sandbars and deep gullies perfect for bream and flathead but we keep walking and I don't mention it. I don't really want to fish. Couldn't be stuffed. But I have to try, at least for Harry's sake.

'Where do you want to go?' I ask him.

He shrugs his shoulders and toes crab holes in the sand. His finger traces a line down the front of his shirt like he's pulling down an invisible zipper. When he sees me watching, he rips his hand back to his side.

His scars have always been tender. The first week home after the operation he woke the whole house trying to tear his chest open because it felt like ants were trying to get between the stitches. When I walked into his room, Mum had a paper bag to his mouth while Dad trimmed his fingernails on the bed. The paper bag was brown like the ones we use to hold our school lunches. It expanded and crumpled with every breath and if you shut your eyes it sounded like waves lapping the shore. When he finally gave in and fell asleep, I looked at his limp hands resting on his chest, the nubs of his fingers tender and bloody.

Dad was waiting for me beneath the skylight in the hall. I couldn't bring myself to look at him so I stared at a crack in the tile next to my big toe. He grabbed me by my chin and brought my eyes to his face.

'Give me your hand,' he said.

He took my fingers in his fist and ripped down the collar of his shirt.

'Watch.'

He squeezed my fingers, pulled them to his bare chest and dragged my nails down right through his skin.

He gripped my chin again.

'You see?'

Beneath the strange glow of the skylight, even through the tears, my father's blood looked blue under my fingernails.

I keep an eye out for rips and currents. I search for floating debris and darker water like Dad taught us. I remember him walking us up to the river mouth where the waters boil like blood and dredge out past the waves. He dangled me over the sweeping current until my feet were skimming across the highway of water, just so we could see how fast it was, how dangerous the sea could be. Then Mum slapped him in the face and walked ahead, sobbing into her sarong. Dad stood behind us with his broad hands on each of our shoulders and he talked about what's best for me, what's best for all of us.

We continue heading down the beach, the northerly wind at our backs. Harry looks back at the asbestos shacks bunched at the end of the bay.

'No-one can see us,' I say.

I drop the tackle bag in the sand and check my line and trace. Nothing is tangled.

'Dad's been better,' I tell him. 'Now that he's working again.'

Harry doesn't listen. I begin to rig Dad's beach rod. I put the line in my mouth and moisten the knot, just how he showed us.

'He's different now, ever since—'

Harry brings his eyes from the sand. I can't help but stare at the scar line poking above his shirt collar like a pink beach worm. He runs a finger across it, shiny and smooth like weathered glass.

When the rod is ready, I wade into the shallows and leave him at the shore with the tackle bag full of discarded tobacco packets and beer cans; mementos of our father and the long nights he'd spend casting his line below the lighthouse. I swing the heavy rod over my shoulder and leave it there for a moment, the lure dangling close to Harry's face. He inspects it closely, counts the tiny painted gills before I haul it above the shore break.

He stands close. I can almost feel him there, feel his awkward lope; that stance that would put you off for the first two rounds before you worked out it was unintentional. He has the same look on his face he had in his first fight. He was scared then, but he shouldn't have been. It was his right hook you had to look out for. It left a constant dent in the side of the heavy bag. I'd see it swinging silently from the corner of my eye when I went into the garage. It reminded me of what he could do if he ever decided to really let 'em fly.

I survey his lips and they flinch like he's going to say something but the mosquito buzz of my reel and the waves rushing around my legs are the only sounds between us. When my lure takes a hit I act like I don't give a shit. I just wind in slowly and throw him a glance when the time is right, but I know that deep down in his bones he knows I'm shaking like a kicked mutt.

'Not much happening,' I say after a while.

Harry trudges back in to our stuff. I try to stay out there but my calves burn like I've just done six rounds on the rope. I finally give in and slump next to Harry in defeat and watch the green waves rearing up at the shore.

'It's not ya fault, Harry,' I say. 'You know, with Dad and everything.'

He toys with the sand and regards the sea.

'Harry?'

Just the sight of his hands trembling in the afternoon light is enough to keep us both quiet. He eventually pulls his eyes from the horizon and I follow the sun etching itself into the lines of his white face. It makes him look old, too damn old for his age. The lagoon tinge beneath his eyes makes him seem weaker than he is. I'm tempted to drag him out of the light. He's tougher than that. The flowers at his bedside always seemed so out of place. I've seen him on the cliff edge of giving in and even then he could send you packing with a single glance.

I start to shape a ball of wet sand with the rough parts of my hands. I bury it like a turtle egg and wait until it's cooked, hard and ready.

'Mum reckons it's complicated.'

I don't know why but I reach out to graze his now fragile fingers, just to stop them from sifting the earth between his legs. Dad said Harry had all the potential in the world when he was younger; long arms, lean. Said they'd never see him coming if he stuck at it. Said he could see he was a southpaw from the way Harry threw his jab. That was before they found out his heart wall was too thick on one side. Dad would always ruffle his hair and say it was just a bung ticker. Harry never laughed though. He'd say he was tired and the nurse would usher us into the hall. Then Mum would clip Dad across the ear with a rolled up magazine and tell him to go make her a coffee. Black and mean, she'd say, like Sonny Liston.

I brace myself for the now unfamiliar touch of his skin, the fridge door feel of his nails. I remember his knuckles wrapped in tea towels from the kitchen bottom drawer. He was only a kid but he opened me up, big time, and wanted to stop when he saw the claret. I made him keep going until the tea towels were flecked with busted brows and I held out until he was so exhausted I won by default.

They're big knuckles for a kid, bony, gravel-shaped. I wonder how many teeth they would have dislodged if he stuck at it like Dad said. They'd never see it comin'.

He must feel my gaze, see my creeping mitts because suddenly he's up, bounding for the bush behind the dune walls. I scramble after him, the sand ball bouncing in the sagging belly of my shirt. He stops on the ridge between the land and the sea and looks down at a flock of seagulls huddled against the wind. I climb the dune and stand beside him. He eyes the birds with devout concentration, a closeness that would perk a teacher's ears up. He brings his hand towards his chest, an unknowing reflex since the first operation, and presses his sternum with his fingers. The gulls shiver the sand from their wings and my brother's fingers dig into his shirt fabric until the cotton leaks blood. I tell him to stop. I tell him what he wants to hear, that Dad's an old bastard, too old-fashioned. I tell him I should have tried harder, we all should have. His eyes burn like a fever and the birds watch us perched on the dune like we're something more than bickering kids.

I take the sand ball out from the bottom of my shirt. Harry keeps prodding his chest like it's made of canvas. Before I throw it, I see his grin; the same one he had when he was drawn to fight another out-of-towner in his first bout. I remember it being so sharp it could cut your soul in two. Dad and I watched from his corner as the bell rang. We knew it wasn't going to last very long. We knew how Harry moved. Like a younger, leaner Sugar Robinson, the old man said. We held onto the ropes and got ready for an early ride home with the radio as loud as it could go. We were drunk with confidence, you'd almost call it cockiness but you had to be there.

Harry examines the blood between his fingertips. He never really had the guts for the ring. Couldn't go for the throat when he needed to. He could run a mile in six minutes but it's not a substitute for the nerves.

I take one last look at him; his shaking hands, that same smile that got him knocked cold, got him tasting the dirty canvas with his lips, and I lob the ball over my head. The dune grass whips at our ankles as we watch it falling through the sky like a giant sinker. We hold our breaths, tense our guts as the gulls lift in a cloud of scurrying wings until they're just a mad white blur. Harry begins to laugh. I'm laughing too, cackling like a toddler and I don't really know why.

Then we notice one left squabbling, its weight dragging in circles through the sand. My mouth feels like it's full of shattered glass. I taste the fighter's blood behind my teeth, the glove sweat stink coming from our skin. I leave Harry and sprint down to the harder sand where the bird shakes and squawks on its buckled wing. I pick it up and hold it under my shirt, hold it against my skin. I feel its silky feathers and the soft flurry and rhythm of heart and blood.

On the way home after the fight, we stopped by the local butcher and bought a hunk of wet meat for Harry's eye. Dad talked in proverbs from the driver's seat, about having heart, saving face. When I looked back at Harry, I knew that was it, I knew his gloves would be hung on the hook by the back door and never laced up again.

The swell is up, breaking unevenly and sending cold spray shoreward. I wade through the waves with the limp bird in the pit of my shirt. I stop at the edge of the sandbank where the water is dark and the land falls away. Where the world ends. I want to say something, to scream at god for everything, to tell him I'm sorry, we all are, but the words are stuck like shells between my toes. My hands tremble and the bird just stares. Dad never believed in god, because of Harry and the war and all that stuff, so I hold the bird and wait.

The tide starts to come in. The current drags around my knees. The waves begin to hit me in the belly and chest but I don't move. The bird hovers above the rising water, quivering in my hand. The sea starts to creep up and around my neck like one of Grandma's knitted sweaters. She always knitted us jumpers while Harry was in the hospital. Just a bung ticker, my Dad would always say. It's funny; the bird in my fist would be the same weight as a human heart. A heart drained of life and blood. A heart clogged with seawater. And now I'm under, my feet kicking free from the world below and it's like he could still be here, Harry, dancing across the dunes, bobbing and weaving behind his household-famous jab.

Westerly

Vital Signs

Nicola Redhouse

Imminent death came to Alice in an unexpected place: the freezer section of the supermarket, with a twelve-pack of toilet rolls pinioned to her shoulder and an alfoil tray clutched under her left arm.

It came in the form of the return of a headache that she now realised had been there for two weeks – since the last time she had been in the freezer section. It radiated a pain that filled her cranium and sharpened when she lay down, felt as though there was something inside her head trying to move everything else out of the way. She should probably see the doctor.

The toilet rolls were slipping. She wasn't prone to hypochondria, but it seemed, there in front of the party pies, like a storm was drawing in around her. The bags of peas and cartons of ice-cream took on a grey pallor in the fluorescent light.

And then, at once, the headache dulled. Perhaps it wasn't fatal after all, she thought. She dumped everything into a trolley and pushed on to the confectionary aisle. Liquorice Allsorts were down, two bags for a dollar.

*

Dr Kline shone a light. 'Follow the beam,' he said.

The headache pulsed along with her heartbeat. 'It's better today,' she told him, fearful suddenly that the source of the pain knew it was in the presence of a doctor and would withdraw.

He was not a talker. She imagined he could see her thought like a tiny pinball rattling around her head.

The doctor felt her neck, took her blood pressure, prodded around her ears, taking a look inside each. He palpated her cheeks and forehead.

'Does this hurt?' he asked. He was breathing through his nose.

She felt she should say yes.

'No.'

It seemed an interminable wait while he took apart the otoscope, washed his hands and returned to his desk.

'I can't find anything,' he announced. 'But I'd like you to have an MRI, just as a precaution.'

The clock ticked as he wrote out a referral.

*

It was quiet in the car park, nothing but leaves whipping around into whirligigs. The headache had lifted again and she absorbed the peace left in its wake. She was aware, too, of the pendulous nature of her mind; that she could swing it towards rapidly unfolding tragedy – a tumour, hospice, the selection of music for her funeral – or towards a clear scan.

And, ridiculously, she was bothered by the inconvenience of it all – having to leave work early again; becoming embroiled in a discussion about illness with her boss, Janice. She'd wanted to avoid mentioning the headaches.

She sat in the car and phoned Frank, who seemed to take the doctor's non-verdict as good news. 'You just need a good sleep.' Twenty years out of France and he still pronounced it *slip*.

The irritable feeling expanded, prickled her skin; she felt it like a burr underfoot. She phoned the hospital and booked the scan, then sat back and closed her eyes.

*

She became conscious of the thing with colour later that week: a tint settled over her vision, as though she was looking through a sheet of cellophane, and dissolved as quickly as it came.

The first time, down the side of the house while she took the bins out, she thought it must be the evening light – a gentle blue, almost opalescent. But then it happened again at her desk, citron this time, and she saw that the colour did not behave as though it came from a light source. It was dense. Consistent.

She made another appointment with Dr Kline.

This time, he didn't bother with the physical examination.

'Are you feeling anything when you see this colour? Are you smelling anything? Eating?' he asked. There was a hint of excitement to his tone, Alice noted.

She gave the questions close consideration. 'With the blue, I was in a rush – I'd left a curry on the stove,' she paused. 'The yellow . . . I was eating a chicken sandwich.'

She pondered the memory further. 'My shoes were hurting me.'

'A chicken sandwich.' he repeated. He was on the edge of his chair. His leg was jiggling up and down.

'It was delicious,' she ventured.

He looked up at her over the edge of his bifocals.

'It had dill in it, too.' She felt a little like she was giving a police statement, both hopeful and idiotic.

'And you weren't eating when the blue colour came?'

She tried to recall. Dr Kline had the air of a tortoise about him. In anticipation of her answer she saw his face had become more human. Still, her answer was no. She had not been eating.

He scribbled in his notebook for some minutes, and when he finally looked up she saw he was his ancient reptilian self again. 'Come and see me after the MRI, and call if you notice anything else.'

Something about having disappointed Dr Kline made her feel peculiarly edgy and, driving on the freeway towards home, agitation bloomed – she ground her teeth, tried to loosen her jaw, tasted something like metal. She turned the corner off Brunswick Street, and it dawned on her that their cream weatherboard was slightly green. That everything was green.

*

She decided not to tell Frank, who had been out in the garage all morning sanding down a bureau he'd bought on eBay. He'd have too much to say about the psychology of it all; probably tell her she needed to see a shrink again. She wanted to turn this idea around on her own for a while.

She turned on the computer and opened a spreadsheet, typed date in the first column, sensation in the second, and emotion in the third.

The empty document, its promise of filling up, of accumulating to an answer, excited her. She knew this sensation – it was the pleasure of deliberate reflection; a luxurious curating of the self. It had come to her in her twenties when she had kept a diary. She had been religious about it, amassed a boxful of youthful optimism.

It had petered off, the record-keeping, the two years they tried to have a baby, and stopped altogether the day they had at last been told it would never happen. Not in her womb, in any case.

It was better to engage, she had decided. Better to appreciate each moment as it happened, than to feel, while it was happening, that it was going to become inscribed, immutable.

The room had become a deep mauve. The colour moved through her like the low bass note of a cello.

She entered her first record of data.

*

Frank pushed through the front door, holding his key-ring between his teeth, hands laden with Indian takeaway.

The whole car would smell tomorrow, she thought. She had become so attuned to her feelings since she'd started the spreadsheet; it was like having a detective inside her mind.

They settled down in front of the television – a documentary about Iceland – and ate, a habit she often worried was a sign of stagnancy in their relationship. But, this night, with the rain streaming down the windows, and the strange lilting narration, she felt a love for Frank so powerful it had the vulnerability of a wound. She feared if she moved she would open up entirely.

Frank was her home. They had made it through childlessness, which she'd seen destroy other couples, and had determined a new future for themselves. It was a future without school plays and tree houses – or chickenpox and unidentifiable rashes, for that matter. But it had, she felt, comparatively unconstrained time. There were only their own slow years to pass by; no lives counted in weeks, months, words, teeth, height, report cards or shoe size, graduations, the chaos of it all sending the days into freefall.

A clear white light had spilled in to the room, from the glaciers on TV, or from her mind – for once she didn't care to know. She took his hand.

*

The scan was less frightening than she had anticipated. There was her initial claustrophobia – she had been unable to shake a memory of Janice, years ago, likening it to being buried alive. And for a while she felt slightly queasy, imagining radio frequencies invisibly searching out her body, the thought of what they might come upon.

But then she seemed to give way, to find the limitations of the capsule comforting. The blankets and the padding, the cocoon of white plastic that both contained her vision and offered an endless horizon. Only the intermittent buzzing and strange knocks filtering through the earplugs offered a distant reminder of the context of her reverie.

Lying in that strange empty space, she tried to remember back to when she had met Frank. She was three years in to a law degree and had taken a semester out to travel, feeling increasingly certain that she did not want to be a lawyer.

Her choice of study had been born of a romantic notion that the law was a high form of the arts – a realm of the classics in which she would be most deeply engaged with stories, tragedies. But she had found it to be deviously mathematical. Logic minus hope: a world in which intention was flawlessly calculable.

She spent hours in the library, lost in the detail of tort cases: the story of the men who had lured their victim to a hut, gotten him drunk and knocked him unconscious, then thrown him off a cliff, believing him dead – What had they drunk? What had they talked about? She'd wondered. But in the end all the tutor had wanted was the precise principal on which the case was decided. *Ratio decidendi*: the Latin turned the events into an object. It was an alchemy of joylessness, a puzzle whose un-coding reminded her of the childhood feeling of trying to discern if her father's temper was connected to her.

She had much preferred her Arts classes: analysing literature, feeling that she had the power as a reader to make a story what she wished. It was a philosophy class that had nudged her over the edge about the law degree, made her see that it was ludicrous, punitive even, to ask for a single narrative truth from anything.

And it had been in Dahab, smoking shisha and drinking a lot of fresh pawpaw juice, that she found herself thinking about these things, and then discussing them, upon a swathe of pillows overlooking the sea, with a young Frenchman: François, as he called himself then.

*

Alice lay still and, at last, from far away, came a long beep, and then the sounds of the technician clomping around the room.

She dressed quickly in the small change cubicle, leaving her singlet straps twisted and not bothering to pin up her hair or put her rings back on, eager to get out into fresh air and away from the antiseptic smell of the room, which had begun to transmute into an uncomfortable sensation on her skin.

She walked down to the river, enjoying the wash of orange that had settled over the late-afternoon bay – tasting it at the back of her throat. She felt light, as though something had been excised from her; but she knew it was nothing more than the weight of waiting that had lifted, the familiar relief of an exam being over. The question of whether she would pass still remained.

*

When Dr Kline's receptionist phoned she was in the supermarket again. She waited on hold for him while a tinny strain of James Taylor fought its way through the earpiece, a song she had loved as a child. It came to her then that time was capable of containing infinitely disparate experiences. This whole event – from her initial symptoms until this moment of diagnosis – had unfolded in precisely the lifespan of a twelve-pack of double-ply toilet paper.

The music cut off and she heard Dr Kline clear his throat. For the moment of silence that followed she wondered if he had forgotten she was on the other end of the line, but then she realised the pause bore an indefinable gravity.

'Alice. I've got your scans,' he began. Then a sound like laminate being shook out, a wobble board, the clang of metal.

'Sorry, I'm trying to look at them as we speak,' he continued. 'There's an area of concern. It makes sense, in terms of your symptoms – '

She saw her hands on the trolley, the fine movement of her metatarsals slipping up and down under her skin like thread in a loom.

*

It was a growth. Shadow-grey, smaller than a pearl, burrowed in between her occipital and temporal lobes. They would need to do a biopsy, Dr Kline explained. He had booked her in with a neurologist for the next day.

She clung to those words, occipital, temporal, anchors to lower with assurance into this unseeable internal terrain. She had made her way into adulthood with a constant sense of unease, fuelled by stuff only of the imagination: impossibly slippery cliffs, aeroplanes that fell to earth like stones. Never death by illness; a tumour. In her wildest nightmares she would never have anticipated such a plausible ending for herself.

She asked Frank that night, 'Do you think one day they will be able to send tiny drones in to the body to retrieve cells, through your ear or your mouth?' She had begun to imagine her brain as the moon. And wasn't it as treacherous, she decided, hanging brashly in its vast space, but all the while unknowable.

'Non,' Frank replied, sleepily. He squeezed her arm tightly where it lay beside him, the two of them staring into the thick black night of their bedroom. They lay like that for hours, the steady beat of Alice's now certainly fatal headache carrying her out onto a plateau of half-sleep from which she felt herself wade into memories long discarded: Frank, smooth and pale and somehow exotic in his European swimming trunks, so different to the men in Australia in their fluoro boardies, salt-stung and red from the heat. In Toulouse when they went back to meet his family; at his university, his friends talking fast and raucously through wine-stained teeth at the student bar about their PhDs. They had smoked a few joints and she'd retreated happily into a stoned state of observation, making what she wished of their words even if she didn't know their language. Their very difference, their Frenchness, excited her.

But François was Frank now, spoke almost like her, watched the footy and went for the Bombers, and, just as she dipped into sleep, she felt this realisation as a physical pain.

*

'I'll take you through it slowly.' The neurologist had bright eyes, neatly clipped nails.

Alice's scan hung, like a world map, behind her desk, and the doctor used a white pointer to direct her to the relevant anatomical areas.

'The growth is a tumour,' she explained, 'but we don't know if it is malignant. If it's benign, it could well be left alone. There are other scans we can do to try to ascertain this, but a biopsy would tell us. The procedure, though, is tricky in your case.'

She drew two shapes resting on each other like a yin and yang, and then circled their shared curve.

'The growth is located between two of the brain lobes. Those in-between areas are like computer cables. If they are damaged, we're risking cognitive impairment. It's a small risk, but we're talking potential damage to your vision, to your capacity for emotion and memory.'

They left the hospital with a bag full of brochures, infrared brain images blooming like bouquets across shiny pages, medical insurance forms, staid and official in dull green. Alice noted colour all the time now; it was a code of sorts, she was sure.

*

They decided to go away for a few weeks. It was impulsive. Frank wanted to head to the Peninsula. She had always found the ocean soothing, but the water's expanse, the illusion of its glinting surface – it was too symbolic. She insisted they drive inland, towards the mountains, find a town with a pub, a bed and breakfast.

She had scrapped the spreadsheet. Words couldn't seem to touch on the depth of how she had begun to experience things. Feelings had become multidimensional, with texture, taste: shock was an ice shard of lime water in her mouth; deep sadness she felt as a slightly nervy tickle along a scar she had on her left arm.

The endless drive to Canberra, her wonder at the new trees budding from black where bushfire had swept through, a tinge of melancholy when a song came over the radio – she felt these things as a collage of senses, fluid and connected.

They stayed in a cabin one night, with a log fire and a bath out on a deck, then a caravan by a lake, waking to the caw caw of galahs. They were travellers again, thrifty and vulnerable to the world.

*

In the second week on the road, Alice woke up and it was not Frank with her in the bed. It looked like him, but she knew it wasn't him. It was the body of Frank but another person inside. She saw his hands – yes, there was the small scar on his thumb from a fishhook – his arm, resting along his side, the fine sandy hairs. But when he turned and asked if she wanted her coffee yet she saw something of the essence of him was missing. It was like he was an avatar.

At first she was alarmed. He, whoever this man was, had roused her with the noise of his knuckles cracking. Frank did this too: stretched and limbered when waking.

She lay quietly with her eyes half closed, panic setting in, watching him move about, embody Frank's habits: heat the milk for the coffee, flump back into bed, bend his book over at the spine, breath noisily through his nose.

Why would he do this? If anything about this replica gave away Frank, it was in the impeccable set-up of this scenario. He was nothing if not an auteur when it came to his work: always devising impossible research projects; always talking about his frustrations with the limitations of existing studies in identity, how we couldn't study the mind because observing it could only be done from within. That had to be it: this was a body-double, some elaborate experiment. It didn't seem ethical. Or perhaps it was: could it be designed to help her come to a decision? She couldn't imagine how, but it was possible. Either way, it would be necessary, she realised, to not let on what she knew; she'd play along.

*

The next week was inevitably difficult for her. They made their way inland, back towards National Parkland, through towns small and barren, on roads so straight and new that it felt the car wasn't moving at all.

A few times, not-Frank asked her if she was alright. 'You seem – quiet,' he said, and she smiled at how, just like Frank, he assumed her silence was anxiety.

They stopped for a day and a night at a camping area near the Snowy River, where she watched as not-Frank set up their tent and started a fire with the wood they had gathered earlier on their way through Jindabyne. This man insisted on placing a large tarp over the tent for extra measure. She marvelled at the pointillist detail of his imposturing, at the same time wondering where real Frank was by now – he must have had a lift waiting to take him back home; or perhaps he was still back at the hut where she had woken to find him replaced.

It was impossible not to be self-conscious; she was both aware of being with a stranger yet determined not to reveal what she knew. And it was a challenge to be intimate with this man, though strangely exciting, too: the knowledge that she was permitted to be with someone else.

And all the while her mind was ticking over and over, trying to work out what the purpose of this not-Frank was, and how he would help her know what to do.

*

On the last evening of their time away, they sat on the verandah of a homestead they had come upon, sharing a bottle of wine. She was reading the newspaper – an article about a court case that was raging over two young children whose Australian mother had taken them from their father in Spain. It was hard to choose sides; both parents were bereft. But the law would find a certain path, fall where it must.

And it was then that it came to her. It was not for Dr Kline or the neurologist or Frank – via not-Frank – to show her the way. Equations or risk-calculations would be of no help, nor would there be compensation delegated for the parts of her that were changing. And there could be no injunction on what was to come. What would happen to her was happening to her already.

Not-Frank shook wattle pollen from his deck chair, beat the underside of the fabric, unaware that the particles were flying into his wine glass. He would begin sneezing soon, Alice was certain, and she smiled now at the nuance of his act. She breathed in the sweet evening air, heard it as a call, a joyous bell-tinkle, felt the bristle of the sunset on her tongue.

She had to think about the real Frank in all this, of course. She would play it cool, wait till she was home and he had swapped places again with his double and collected his data and resolved whatever crazy hypothesis he had now gotten her involved in. There would probably be a questionnaire, no doubt a waiver; universities were so careful these days.

The important thing was that she didn't want him to worry. She would tell him the doctors had reviewed the scans and deemed it benign. She might even say it had gone altogether. Shrunk.

Twenty Dollars

Annette Trevitt

Carnival

A distant starter-gun fired, followed by the boom of a false start. Another delay. I didn't think I could take much more. Everything – the sky, the track, the day – was over-bright and baking hot. It all felt endless.

'Attention,' Lyn shouted into the megaphone. 'Attention. Under-13 boys 100 metres to the call room. Under-13 boys.'

'Lane five, what're you doing?'

Lane five, I'm lane five.

I looked up. Lyn had the megaphone detached from the mouthpiece and pointed at the boy's shorts where I was pinning on a six instead of a five.

'Sorry. Sorry, Lyn.'

Lyn Beale had been a call-room manager for athletics carnivals for years. She ran her cordoned-off section of ground as if Sergeant Major to a useless platoon.

My phone rang as I pinned a five onto the shorts.

'I have to get this, it's my sister.'

'Can you make it quick ... and why haven't you got your vest on?'

Because, I'm not putting on that fluoro piece of nylon shit for anyone.

I walked to the furthest corner, next to a sapling wilting in the dirt. Its pencil-thin shadow fell over my sandals.

'Hi, Bettina.'

'How's it all going?' my sister asked.

'I'm ready to test the new synthetic track under a blowtorch,' I said, squinting against the glare.

'How's Ned doing?'

'He's through to the final of the 200.'

'Terrific,' she said.

I kicked at some stones. When she used that word, Bettina sounded a generation – not three years – older.

'The race is at five,' I said. 'We've been here since seven-thirty, it's furnace-hot, no shade and I've been stuck behind marshalling tape for three hours with a psycho.'

I looked over as Lyn marched boys into lanes.

'We'll have to stay the night somewhere on the way,' I said to Bettina. 'It'll be too late to drive all the way through.'

'Stay in Taree. George's cousin, Ron, is the chef at the Criterion. Anyway, Camille, guess who I just spoke to?'

'Don't make me guess in this heat.'

'Frank Walsh,' she said.

'Frank Walsh?'

'Don't pretend. He was in the year between us, led the school band, always up the back of the bus. You had a huge crush on h—'

'Frank Willis,' I said instantly.

'Ha, I knew you'd be pleased,' Bettina said. 'And all this time he's been in Sydney. He's coming to tune our piano on Thursday. I won't be home, but I told him you'll be here. When he heard my name, he wanted to know if I was from Walcha and had a younger sister, Camille. He wanted to know *all* about you.'

'What did you say?'

'He couldn't believe you stayed in Walcha after your divorce.'

'You told him I was divorced?'

'He is too. No kids,' said Bettina. 'He sounds keen.'

Lyn glared at me over a group of girls entering the marshalling area. I signalled I was on my way back and smiled. She didn't.

'Better go, Bet.'

'Wish Ned luck and hey, thanks to you, Frank gave us a twenty-dollar deal. A discount. I tell you, he's keen.'

'Lanes four to eight,' Lyn said as I walked past her.

I nodded. All of a sudden the carnival felt bearable.

Service Station

The old woman in front came up to my shoulder. She was shaky on her feet and her head bobbed as she moved to the counter and reached up to hand over her card to the attendant.

'Pump five,' she said.

He held the eftpos machine over the counter and looked away as she pressed in her PIN numbers. He tore off the receipt from the machine and gave her card back. The woman didn't move.

'Do you want a copy?'

'Yes,' she said. 'Yes ... I knew I was waiting for something.'

He printed one out and handed it to her.

'Waiting for my life to take off,' she said, shoving it into her over-stuffed purse.

Road to Sydney

We pulled out onto the road south to Sydney, heading to my sister's for the first week of the school holidays. We were looking after her house and pool while she flew to Singapore to meet her husband on his way back from Japan, and have a holiday. They had met in their first year at university and married after their graduation. They were successful. They were high flyers. The family always said Bettina had the gumption, as if she'd taken the family's quota.

My son put his feet on the dash.

'Ned, your toes. They're the toes of a man.'

They looked absurd on a lanky nine-year old.

'They've got to be the first thing to stop growing,' I said.

He had come fifth in the final race. He was happy. I was happy the athletics season was over. I was happy, too, that I'd got a laugh out of Lyn, even if it had been at the expense of a couple who had been sent to help her. They hadn't realised their holiday in Bali was over. Their hair fell in tiny, beaded braids, each toe had a toe ring and they had their sarongs tied like nappies. They looked ridiculous.

I dropped gears to climb the mountain. We overtook a truck. As we pulled back into the slow lane, I noticed what I had on.

'Ned, why didn't you tell me?'

We looked at the vest.

'I thought you liked wearing it,' he said.

'Why did you think that?'

'You look important,' he said.

I overtook another truck.

'Then maybe it will come in handy in the city,' I said. 'I can redirect traffic, stop construction, climb power poles.'

'Yeah right,' he said.

'Rewire telephone cables, enter manholes.'

'You don't look that important.'

We slipped into silence as we drove over the mountains.

By the time the road levelled out and begun to ribbon through a forest of tallowwood, the sky was flame-pink and shadows had merged. It was a relief to be off the steep mountains, and to have hairpin turns behind us. My thoughts drifted back to my sister's call and to Frank up the back of school bus, where we had smoked cigarettes the driver had left behind after his naps. He napped on the backseat. Frank and I sat close to avoid his smelly, oily hair patches on the vinyl. We didn't talk, not even when we fell against each other on sharp bends and sudden turns.

Frank had left town in Year Eleven. Mid-year. He left one weekend with his mother and two sisters. I hadn't seen him since. I thought I had once, on the main street, two years out of school. It wasn't him, but my heart kept double-skipping beats long after the stranger had gone.

I wondered how it will be to see Frank again.

*

We had come out onto open river flats and were driving past major road-widening construction. I had no idea how long we had been on the flats. I could no longer tell what colour anything was. I turned on the headlights. A sign came up on the left telling us Taree was ten kilometres away.

'We're nearly there, Neddy,' I said.

'I'm so hungry,' he said.

'Me too.'

The sun had nearly gone. The road was empty. I flicked the headlights to high beam and the sign lit up.

'Stop,' Ned said, pointing at it. 'STOP.'

I registered the pup only when we were alongside it. I braked too fast and skidded on the crumbly shoulder. The pup stayed under the sign watching us, waiting. Ned got out and called for it. It ran to him. Back in the car it clamoured all over him. It was skinny, grubby and collarless. They looked at each other. It licked Ned's face. Ned looked over, beaming, already in love.

Bistro

Ned flipped over his pizza. It landed with the thud of a plastic lid.

'I can't eat it,' he said.

I pushed my roast lamb away.

'Me either,' I said. 'So salty.'

'Mine smells like a dirty sink.'

'Maybe Bettina got the pub wrong,' I said, as a bell rang and the waitress got up from behind the counter.

She approached us, carrying a plate of yellow nuggets.

'On the house,' she said.

We were in the right pub. I had stupidly sent a text to my sister, after we had ordered and paid, to say we had arrived. She must have contacted George's cousin.

'The chef wants to meet you after you've finished,' said the waitress.

She walked back to behind the counter and resumed her heavy-lidded stare. I looked at Ned.

'"Chef"?'

In one swoop, Ned looked at her, the nuggets, then me.

'This is uncomfortable,' he said.

I picked up a nugget. It collapsed in my fingers.

Ned poked one with a fork as if it were a dead mouse.

'What's in it?'

'Don't know,' I said.

I pushed the plate towards him.

'No way.'

'Come on, give it – '

I stopped. I didn't want to argue over a nugget. We were the only customers except for an old couple behind a fake palm in a corner. They looked local yet lost. I looked towards the kitchen and back at the meat and gravy on my plate.

'That sure redefines the word "cooking",' I said. 'Don't these people watch TV?'

'Who?'

'For God's sake, with all those cooking shows, have they learnt nothing?'

'You hate those shows.'

'I don't charge people to eat my food.'

Ned broke open a chip. It smelt of chicken fat and petrol.

I leant across the table so the waitress didn't see me wrap the nuggets in a serviette and put them in my bag. My phone pinged a message. Ned grabbed it.

'It's Bettina,' he said. 'How's dinner. Delicious?'

'Write, "it was the worst food ever served on a plate in a public place",' I said.

Another message pinged through. Ned read it out.

'Chef wants to meet you. Recently separated.'

My God.

'What does that mean?'

I took the phone from Ned.

'We're out of here. That's what it means.'

A family of five walked in. They stood checking out the blackboard menu above the counter. Two more couples came in.

'Quick,' I said.

We wrapped up more of the food, shoved it in my bag and, on our way out, waved to the flustered waitress. I pushed open the glass door and, in my reflection, saw the fluoro-yellow vest.

Motel Room

The motel room was stifling, as if wrapped in cling-wrap. The air-con, stuck on low, gave out next to no cool air. No air moved through the window. Ned was asleep, starfish, on the other bed and the pup – who Ned had called Sparkie – had curled up next to my head. He knew he was staying. We had snuck him in. I didn't want him barking and shitting in my car all night. The airless heat and dread of Sparkie peeing on the pillow made sleep impossible.

I picked up the novel I'd been trying to finish for weeks. After ten pages I put it down. The author, Caroline Finch, was well known. She had moved to Walcha, to a house three doors down from us. Not that that helped her to remember my name. She was in her fifties and divorced. She got around in red, egg-shaped glasses and over-sized, asymmetrical dresses. She was hard to miss and that's how she liked it. Caroline loved publicity. She loved a mic. She loved any chance to promote her books. Sometimes I wondered if people put up with her out of gratitude she'd chosen us, our country town, over any other town.

Her novel was about a woman getting on with her life after the death of her husband, but it felt wrong. It couldn't be right. The tone was smart-alecy and distant. All I could think, as I read it, was how Caroline's divorce must have crushed her heart to powder.

*

I must have fallen asleep because I woke to a different light in the room and to the sound of the pup scratching at the door. Once outside I saw the light was from the moon – a big, white, misshapen moon as bright as the motel's neon. Sparkie zigzagged through the grass, his nose to the ground. Trucks worked their gears, out of sight, on the mountains. A hot, lonely gust of wind sent dust and dirt swirling around my legs and into my eyes. I tried to picture Frank again, wanting to slip into the comfort of the earlier day-dream, but instead I remembered the service station attendant and the old woman who was waiting for her life to take off.

Pool

'Something's wrong with that dog,' my sister said.

She lifted a jug of cordial, glasses and some snacks from a tray and put them on the table next to the pool. I had been dozing. I couldn't recall what had been running through my mind, but it left me relaxed, almost swept away.

Sparkie was going crazy, running up and down the side of the pool and barking at Ned in the water.

'No wonder someone dumped it,' said Bettina.

'Maybe that's why it's like it is,' I said.

'What, mad and clingy,' she said. 'Have you checked it for worms, fleas, parasites?'

We had arrived the day before and already I was glad her flight was tomorrow morning.

'Ned, get out for a while and let the dog calm down,' I said.

Ned climbed out and Sparkie stopped barking. I heard

squeaking next door. Over the paling fence, a woman bounced up and down on a trampoline. She faced us. She had on a snorkel and mask. I laughed.

'It's not funny,' Bettina said with quiet urgency. 'She always does it. She gets her kid in on the act too.'

'Why don't you invite them over?'

'Are you serious? My God, once you let someone like that in, who knows what will follow.'

I looked at my sister. She looked at me.

'You know what I mean,' she said. '*You* don't carry on like that.'

She handed over a bowl of roasted chickpeas.

'Here. You don't want to be a woman with cholesterol,' she said.

The squeaking went on.

'My God, who behaves like that?'

'A woman who wants a swim on a 40-degree day,' I said.

A woman who had nothing to lose, I wanted to add.

The rhythm of the squeaking changed and a boy's head appeared. He looked Ned's age. He had on goggles, zinc across his nose and a towel over his shoulders.

I smiled.

'Camille, don't even think about it.'

Bettina stood up and grabbed a handful of chickpeas.

'I've got to get ready.'

She had gym, and then a hair appointment. Ned jumped back in the pool, and Sparkie started up again.

'If that dog refuses to listen, you'll need to get rid of it,' she said.

*

Fifteen minutes later, Bettina returned with a woman following her. They were dressed in pale, tight singlet-tops and black gym pants that stopped below the knee. She introduced Suzy to Ned and me. Suzy had her hair pulled back tightly into a high ponytail. She looked the sort of woman who loved to organise school reunions. I was surprised to watch Bettina tie her hair back the same way and look more like someone else than like me, or any one from our family for that matter.

'I'm across the road in the house with the Porsche,' said Suzy. 'Come over if you need anything. The gate is behind the Porsche. You'll need to press the buzzer.'

'Thank you,' I said, knowing I never will.

'I've left the $180 on the kitchen bench for Frank,' Bettina said. 'Remember he's coming at two.'

'I know, Bet,' I said.

'Just want you to be ready,' she said.

A sentence like that was enough to make me pack my bags and head home. Suzy came closer. I had to move the banana chair and shade my eyes to see her against the sun.

'I understand he's an old flame. That's exciting for you,' she said.

Jesus Christ.

'We just went to school together,' I said.

'Can't be like that about it,' said Suzy. 'He gave Bet a special deal because of you.'

I looked at her.

'You need to get back on the dating circuit,' she said.

Dating circuit? I looked at Bettina, but she had turned to walk back inside.

'Have a fun afternoon,' said Suzy, twirling car keys on her finger. 'Call in sometime for a wine in the spa. If the Porsche is there, so am I.'

They left. I closed my eyes. The sun lit up my eyelids. I felt swollen and tangled inside. I knew that in the Porsche, Bettina will retell her take on my life and Suzy will nod, tutting as if I were her sister messing up.

I told myself I didn't care if Frank came this afternoon or not, but that was untrue.

'Mum, have you seen my flippers?'

Ned leant over the pool's edge kicking water over me.

'No, sure you packed them?'

'Yeah ... oh I know where,' he said. 'In the Corolla.'

We looked at each other and laughed.

Piano Room

Frank was late. Ned was with Sparkie in the lounge-room, watching a movie and eating popcorn to avoid the heat. I was in the front room punching cushions into shape when a van pulled up out the front. It was after three. My heart tightened. I let out my breath slowly. A heavyset man with big thighs got out. It wasn't Frank. He must have sent someone else. The disappointment was physical. I patted my pocket with the $180 in it. My hands hardly felt they were mine.

I had expected the doorbell, yet its ring startled me.

'Frank,' I said, still startled – mostly at his dyed orange hair.

'Hello Camille,' he said with a lift of his chin.

I moved aside. He came in, smelling of soap and cigarettes. I led him into the front room and stood pointing to the couch until I realised what I was doing. I had put the cushions along the couch in a neat row of diamonds. Never in my life had I placed cushions like that. Frank tipped his head towards the sheet music on top of the piano.

'Who plays?'

'George, Bettina's husband.'

He nodded. I stared at him and as I struggled to find words, I saw that he was doing the same. It had been fourteen years. Frank had been a lean, languid teenager. His limbs used to move like poured mercury. I could see how his unhurried manner had led to his changed buttery appearance, although it didn't explain his hair. That had to be a post-divorce decision. As he looked at me, I picked up a cushion and put it back the same way.

'You look different,' he said, and moved over to the piano.

He put down his toolbox and pulled off the piano lid. He's going to let a remark like that just hang between us? He had taken off the front panel and the fallboard and was bending over to get something from his toolbox. His t-shirt rode up over his jeans. *I* look different? He took his phone out of his back pocket and, after tapping some buttons, propped it on the keys. He played some notes, a loose tune, as he asked how long I was staying in Sydney.

'A week, maybe two,' I said.

A lie. I had to get back to work in the second week.

'Do you ever go back to Walcha?'

He went on playing as if he hadn't heard. I pictured the row of abandoned shops on the first bend into Walcha and felt embarrassed I had asked.

'Would you like a cup of tea?'

He heard that. I went into the kitchen, turned on the kettle and ducked into the bathroom to see what he saw. I wished I hadn't.

As I made the tea I listened to him test notes. I thought of the drive here and of how the daydreaming had taken me so easily and effortlessly from the back of the school bus to here, to now.

*

Frank took a sip of tea and as he put the cup on the coffee table, he told me about the free tuner app on his iPhone – how it was as good as the $2000 machine in his van. He went on playing and adjusting notes and discussing the app. I listened, irritated he chose not to use the expensive machine. He hammered more pegs.

'It's in pretty poor shape,' he said, tapping and tightening another stubborn peg.

'I thought it sounded ok.'

'There's been a lot of hidden wear and tear on the keys,' he said.

He looked at me.

'It's seen better days.'

I smiled, trying not to take these comments to heart. His phone pinged. He read the message and texted back. He stopped to run his hand through his hair.

'I'm too busy. I'm looking for a girl to help with repairs in the shop,' he said.

A girl?

'I want to concentrate on getting the band back together.'

'What sort of music?'

'Jazz-rock,' he said, texting.

I had no idea what that was and felt no inclination to ask.

'You should come to a gig,' he said.

Something about that word grated. He looked over. I nodded, as I had with Suzy. I was still nodding when the front gate clicked and two young men in ill-fitting, old-fashioned suits came into the front yard.

'Jehovah's Witnesses. God, in this heat,' I said, and headed to the door before the bell rang.

*

When I came back into the room, Frank was texting. He finished the text and put the phone back on the keys.

'That was quick,' he said.

It wasn't. The two men had a tall glass of cordial each and one had a second glass while the other held up what looked like a very old copy of *Watchtower* in his sweaty, beefy hand and heaved his way through a rave about the perils of modern stress.

'Jehovah's Witnesses lack an understanding of the part,' I said.

'The what?'

'They don't understand how to part their hair. The parts are too straight and never in the right place, the low angle makes the men look – '

'I forgot that about you,' he said.

He went back to hitting a B flat.

'Your sister said you've been on your own since your divorce,' he said.

My face grew hot.

'I have my son. And dog,' I said, but I knew how that sounded.

'So you haven't met anyone at all, in three years?'

Frank looked at me. His look was hard to gauge. I looked away, out the window, and drank my tea hardly feeling the cup in my hand. I stayed silent. My voice would've given away the sudden stampede of memories, memories of wanting too much and of desertion. A leaf blower started up nearby and set a flurry of birds across the sky. I turned around. Frank was oblivious. He was finishing his cup of tea. I wanted to tell him his hips were girlish and thanks to his shit hair, his nose stood out and he looked like Shrek.

He put his cup down.

'What about you?'

I was trying to gain ground, trying to gain something.

'You should move to Sydney,' he said.

'I've thought about it,' I said.

I hadn't. I had never felt a reason to leave Walcha. Ned was happy there. His father knew where to find him on birthdays and at Christmas. I felt at home there, too, although at times I wished it wasn't Walcha where I felt that way.

'Want another cup,' I said.
'Why not,' he said.

*

I took my time making the tea. I washed up, wiped the table and benches, took the rubbish out the back and made Ned a sandwich. All the time trying to feel as I did when I was at home.

*

My eyes smarted as I entered the room. I put Frank's cup on the coffee table. The room reeked of aftershave. I hadn't seen any in his toolbox and there wasn't any in the downstairs bathroom. The panels were back on the piano and he had packed his toolbox. He's finished so soon? He ran his hands up and down the piano, banging the thing with too many jazz chords.

'It sounds good,' he said. 'Came up better than I thought.'

I couldn't hear any difference.

'It surprised me,' he said, and broke into a smile that put me back on the school bus.

'Mum!'

'MUM!'

Ned ran in with Sparkie.

'Can I go in the pool?'

He looked around.

'What's that sm—'

'Ned, this is Frank,' I said, quickly grabbing Ned's shoulder. 'We went to school together. Frank, my son Ned.'

'Hi,' said Ned.

Frank had stopped playing and was looking at Ned. He went on looking at him. After a few beats, I steered Ned towards the door.

'Have an ice-cream,' I said.

He ran out followed by Sparkie. Frank looked back at the piano and got up. He picked up the cup, had a sip and another, and put the cup on top of the piano.

'Right, I'm off,' he said.

He pressed his lips together and waited. I handed him the

money. He unfolded it as if deciding whether to count it or not, then he thanked me and put it in his wallet. He walked into the hallway. I followed. He stopped and I bumped into him.

'You know,' he said, half-turning around. 'I charge $200.'

My heart thumped.

'Sorry?'

'I gave your sister a discount … I thought maybe … well, I don't know what I thought, but I will take the extra $20.'

I walked around him and into the guest room, feeling as if I were leaping from one canoe to another. I opened my handbag. Frank stood in the doorway staring at the fluoro-yellow vest hanging over the doorknob. I had two ten-dollar notes in my purse, but, as my heart pounded, I tipped the contents of my handbag onto the bed and took my time to rummage around for loose change to make twenty.

Pool

Bettina walked out. She had had a spray tan and her hair cut and coloured for the holiday. I wondered if Susy had done the same. Ned was in the pool. The dog tore up and down the side, biting at the water, and I was in the banana chair trying to give Caroline Finch's novel another go.

'How was it?'

'The piano sounds good,' I said.

'How was Frank?'

'Ok,' I said and looked back at my book.

The glare on the page hurt my eyes.

'He had on Lynx,' said Ned as he got out of the pool. 'Heaps of it, didn't he Mum?'

'Really,' said Bettina.

She smiled knowingly.

'Told you,' she said to me. 'When are you seeing him again?'

'Mum said he's lazy,' said Ned. 'She reckons she could do a better job.'

I smiled at my sister.

'He used a free iPhone tuning app,' I said. 'It didn't look—'

'How do you expect anything to change if you don't make an effort?'

Ned did a bomb. Sparkie went berserk.

'That dog *is* impossible,' Bettina said.

She went inside, slid the glass-door shut and disappeared. As Ned climbed out of the pool, I heard Bettina bang around in the kitchen. I thought of her insistence for change. Whenever I thought of change, it was hard not to feel sideswiped.

I took a long drink of warm cordial. Frank had changed. I saw so little of his teenage self in him. But neither of us were kids anymore. I finished the drink, recalling how I had felt when he got out of the van, then I had a flash of the way he had looked at Ned.

I reached over and put the glass on the table and stayed there, holding the glass, my arm outstretched. I had got it wrong. Daydreams were daydreams, making the impossible possible, I knew that, but it was the wrong daydream. Where was Ned in it?

The thought made me sit up.

Ned emerged from another bomb. I called out to him. He kicked through the water and came up at the side. Sparkie joined him, twitching with excitement.

'Ned, if anything happens to me and I can't talk anymore or move my arms, don't let Bettina do my hair.'

'Can *I*?'

'You can,' I said.

'Mum, can I get Lynx. Lynx Africa.'

Someone was on the trampoline next door. I didn't look over. My book had fallen onto wet tiles and begun to curl and swell. I watched it warp, and then I picked it up. Who can blame Caroline Finch for choosing to write about death over divorce? Who'd want it to be public knowledge that someone had chosen to leave you.

I moved over to the edge of the pool. The trampoline's squeaking went on. I slid into the pool and underwater. It was bracing below the warm surface. I kicked off the side towards Ned. I heard Sparkie's muted barks, but not the trampoline squeaks. I thought of the neighbour next door and wondered what she'd make of Frank. What did she imagine he thought the twenty dollars would get him? I couldn't wait to find out.

Manyuk

Mark Smith

Monica wakes to him pushing inside her again, his morning breath hot on the back of her neck and his hands kneading her breasts. As she feels her milk begin to seep onto the sheets, she focuses on the curtain print – sailing boats on an aqua sea. He finishes with a muffled groan, rolls away and stands up, still catching his breath. In the half-light his grey shape pulls a singlet over his head and walks to the bathroom. She hears the heavy stream of piss hitting the water. When she rolls over he's standing at the foot of the bed, cupping his balls in one hand.

'I love ya babe. Ya know that, don't ya?' he says.

'Mmm, love you too Frankie.'

He disappears into the kitchen, his weight on the creaking floorboards near the sink, the tap turning on and off, the click of the kettle. Fluorescent light floods the hallway and the baby stirs. Frankie pads through to the front door in his bare feet and she waits to hear the low rumble of the diesel that will need to warm up before he leaves. The engine kicks and the walls of the flat vibrate in time. The aqua sea shivers.

There'll be weeks without him now, doing the run down to Adelaide, then over to Perth if he can get a load. Weeks of damp quiet in the build up to the wet. Her milk has saturated the front of her t-shirt so she swings herself to the side of the bed, her hands resting on the damp sheets. They'll need washing again.

As she sits on the toilet and pisses him out of her, she can feel the dull ache where the stitches were, an ache that becomes a sharp pain when she tries to stand up.

The doctor had said, 'She's young. She'll heal quickly.'

'How quick?' her husband had asked.

*

In the kitchen he sits and pulls his work boots over newly darned socks, his stomach stretching the hi-vis shirt, his head sinking into his shoulders. Monica stands in the doorway and watches him, her arms folded tightly across her breasts.

'Be a good trip this one, babe. Coupla grand clear if I get a Perth run. Maybe more. We'll go out for a real good dinner when I get back. You could wear that nice blue dress I brought ya back from Broken Hill.' As he talks he looks past her to the flat-screen TV mounted on the lounge room wall.

The blue dress fitted her last year, before the baby, but she doubts she could get into it now.

'That'd be great Frankie,' she says.

The baby cries, woken by the voices and the scent of her mother's milk.

'She got some lungs on 'er, our Layla, eh?' he says, buttering two pieces of toast and smothering them in jam. 'Ya better give 'er some brekky.'

As he squeezes past he kisses the top of her head. She runs her hand up under his shirt and across his chest to the sweat already gathering in his armpits.

She picks the baby up and brings her to the door. As he opens it, the heat pushes in.

'You got some money for me before you go?' she asks.

He stops and makes a show of opening his wallet and pulling out a fifty.

'A pineapple do ya?'

'You gone maybe two weeks Frankie. We gotta eat.'

The smile leaves his face as he pulls out another note.

'Jesus Mon, I'm not made of fuckin' money.'

He slaps the notes into her hand and jams his boot in the door.

'An' none of that blackfella nonsense while I'm away, ya hear. Her name's Layla, like the song,' he says.

She eases the door closed and his heavy frame recedes through the opaque glass. He was never that big, she thinks. He's put on weight since last year.

She returns to the kitchen, turns on the ceiling fan and listens to Frankie shift though the gears as he nurses the truck out towards the highway. The flat is losing its morning coolness. She sits down, eases a swollen breast out and the baby attaches herself and begins to suck. Monica strokes the soft down on the baby's cheek.

'Slow Manyuk,' she says. 'Don't be greedy now.'

Monica leans back in the chair and turns her face up to the fan. With her toes she traces the joins in the lino floor.

'Your Dad, he gone for a while. Coupla weeks. We gotta make do, you and me.'

The baby's hand is wrapped tightly around her finger. She pulls her little head away and Monica switches her to the other breast.

'You wanna hear a story, Manyuk? How your Dad and me met?'

She waits a few seconds, listening for the sound of the diesel above the hum of the morning traffic, but he is gone.

'He always bin a truck driver, Frankie. Long haul. Road train. An' he says he always lookin' forward to that Adelaide River stop. Not far from Darwin now he always says, when he's comin' up from down south. He like to freshen up, have a shower an' a bite to eat.'

Manyuk stops sucking, looks up at her mother, closes her eyes and starts to suck again.

*

'I was workin' there, just on the weekends and he starts comin' in an' humbuggin' me, you know, but he got that sweet smile. Says I'm pretty and one day he gonna take me up to Darwin with 'im. After coupla times he says he wants to take me out for dinner, real romantic like ya know. So we go in the bistro and everyone's lookin' cos I'm so young and with this white fella. But he don't care. He buys me this big meal, steak an' all. Tender. An' then he's talkin' serious 'bout me comin' with 'im soon, maybe nex' month. Then he gets me dessert too. Strawberry cheesecake. I still remember that cheesecake. So smooth an' sweet it was.'

*

She eases the baby on to her shoulder and pats her back, like she's seen her mother do with her little brothers and sisters. Manyuk's body is hot against her skin so she stands under the fan and gently rocks her.

When the baby settles she manoeuvres the pram into the kitchen and lays her down. Manyuk's arms are raised above her head, her palms open, her eyes closed. Monica opens the fridge. There's last night's leftover Thai takeaway, half a dozen stubbies and, in the crisper, a mottled lettuce. The milk has been left out overnight and has curdled. Frankie has eaten the last of the bread. She dips her finger into the jam jar and sucks the sweet stickiness into her mouth.

She returns to the bedroom, peels off her clothes and stands in front of the mirror. Her skin has lost its glow and her breasts still hurt. There is slack skin on her belly that had been stretched to envelop the baby. The postnatal nurse visited for the first two weeks but didn't come after that. She had explained the pelvic floor exercises but Monica was never sure if she was doing them properly. She turns around and looks at her back and legs. Even when she was pregnant her legs looked like stilts, too thin to support her swelling body. She likes them though. They remind her that she is only eighteen, that she can still run and dance if she wants to.

*

In the bathroom she runs the shower. Even with the cold tap on, the water is lukewarm. She leans against the tiles and allows the stream to wash over her. When she closes her eyes she sees the big banyan tree outside the one shop in the community. The women would be gathering there before the day gets too hot, sitting cross-legged on the grass and talking in circles. Someone would pull a deck of cards from their bag and the first game of the day would begin. It would be interrupted by a dozen conversations as people walked in and out of the shop.

'Hey, old man! You bin fishin' yesterday? You catch me some barra?'

The man would dismiss her with a grunt and a wave of his hand. She would laugh and return to the game.

Old Kitty Kamartama would shuffle through leaning heavily on her walking frame, stand above the card players and wait until someone asked, 'What you need from that shop today Aunty?' She would hand over a list, written on the torn side of a cigarette packet, and her Basics Card, and return to overseeing the game.

*

Monica opens her eyes and uses the soap hurriedly. She dislikes the film it leaves on her skin. Stepping out of the shower she stands for a few seconds allowing the air to cool her. She leans into the mirror and curls her wet hair into a bun. She thinks of her mother sitting behind her, drawing the brush through her long, dark hair. Her sisters had to have theirs cut short because her mother said they didn't look after it, but Monica was allowed to keep hers long.

'Pandella,' her mother would say, 'you my princess.'

*

By ten o'clock the flat is too hot to stay inside. She wheels the pram to the door and draws the netting over the top. It's a two-kilometre walk to the supermarket but she doesn't mind. It gets her out of the flat and eats up hours in the day while Frankie is away. And the heat reminds her of the community in the build up, the kids running in and out of the sprinkler on the oval while the young men in council shirts rake leaves backwards and forwards, trying to look busy.

Monica walks to the side of the pram, her bare feet sinking into the grass next to the footpath. At the end of the street, where she leaves the shade of the front gardens and pushes out onto the highway, she slips thongs onto her feet. As she crosses at the lights she looks up at a woman sitting in the cool of her four-wheel drive. The woman swings around to talk to the two children sitting in the back seat. They look at her for a moment then return their attention to the iPads in their laps. Monica drops her head and pushes a little faster but she can feel the woman's eyes following her.

The asphalt of the supermarket car park is hot enough to penetrate the soles of her thongs but at the automatic doors the cool of the air-conditioning envelops her. She leans over and pulls the netting from the pram. Manyuk is wide awake, her eyes blinking in the artificial light. Monica sits in a chair outside the Bakers Delight and looks around. Shoppers idle in the food court, middle-aged men in too-big shorts and floral shirts, their wives in loose, patterned dresses with perspiration stains under the arms. A couple of backpackers walk through, tall blonde girls not much older than her, their lean bodies wrapped in tiny shorts and singlet tops.

Monica rustles in her bag and extracts one of the fifty dollar notes Frankie has given her. She flattens it on the tabletop with the palm of her hand as though this will make it stretch further. She plots her way through the next two weeks – nappies, wipes, washing powder and food. She treats herself to a slurpee and returns to her seat, sipping slowly through the straw as she rocks the pusher back and forward.

'Hey,' a man in the Bakers Delight calls across the counter. 'Sorry luv, these seats are for customers only. You'll have ta move.'

Monica keeps her eyes down, waves and moves to the bench seat by the toilets entrance. Manyuk is restless and begins to cry. She shouldn't need feeding again but Monica doesn't want to draw attention so she drapes a thin blanket over her shoulder to cover herself and allows the baby to suckle her breast. She slips her thongs off and spreads her feet on the cool floor tiles.

She begins to talk softly to Manyuk.

'You know little one, this the best time for turtle hunting, out in your grandma's country, out there past Peppi Crossing. Chicken-hawk dreamin' country. She Ngan'giwumirri woman, like your Momma.'

She dips her finger into the slurpee and runs it across the back of her neck.

'We go out there one day, you and me and your grandma. She sing us into that country. Big waterfall there. Stone country up top and a big spring bringin' the water right outa the rocks. We go swimmin' there with that old hawk up above us, keepin' us safe.'

She repeats the words to herself. 'Keepin' us safe.'

*

A woman, skin dark against her bright yellow vest, walks towards the ladies toilets and places the *Closed for Cleaning* sign at the entrance. Pushing a trolley and a mop bucket ahead of her, she looks at Monica then disappears inside. A few minutes later she reappears and replaces the sign with a new one: *Caution, Slippery Surface.* She walks past Monica to the men's entrance, turns back and stands above her, one hand on the mop.

'I know you, girl. What your country?' she asks.

Monica looks up at her. Her voice seems familiar but before she can answer the woman says, 'You that Peppi mob. One of Gracie's girls. What your name?'

Monica looks at her carefully now but she can't place her.

'Monica.'

'What your real name?'

'Pandella. But we livin' in Darwin now. Husban' and me.'

The older woman leans forward on the mop. 'Las' time I seen you, you was swingin' on your Momma's clothes line, gigglin' and carryin' on with your sister.' She nods her head as though the memory is precious to her. 'That your little one there?'

Monica slides her hand down, detaches the baby from her nipple and quickly buttons her top. 'This Manyuk,' she says.

The woman's mouth softens into a half smile. 'Manyuk? Like your aunty.'

Monica lifts the baby onto her shoulder and begins to rub her back. The woman eases herself onto the seat and brings her hand up to touch Manyuk's face. 'She Ngan'giwumirri, this one,' she says.

The two women sit in silence listening to the baby's murmuring.

A minute passes before the older woman says, 'Your brother, that T-Bone, he in Berrimah now. Got six months, muckin' up down there. Your Momma, she on dialysis, two times a week. Your aunty, that Molly, she lookin' after her.' She doesn't look at Monica as she speaks.

The older woman struggles to her feet and pushes the bucket toward the mens. Without turning, she says, 'They needin' you, that mob.'

*

Monica watches as the woman disappears through the doorway. She quickly places Manyuk in the pram and pulls the netting over the top. When she turns the woman is standing there again, pulling the rubber gloves off her hands and rummaging in the large pocket of her apron. She pulls out a folded fifty dollar note and hands it to Monica.

'What this for, Aunty?'

'Bus fare,' she says and walks back into the toilet.

Monica slips the note under her bra strap and turns the pram toward the supermarket entrance. As she picks up a basket a man approaches her and touches her shoulder. He flashes a badge and says, 'Store security. I'll be watching you girl.' Monica nods and drops her head. He waves her through and returns to his post by the checkout.

*

Later that night, as she undresses, Monica unclips her bra and the folded note falls to the floor. She bends wearily to pick it up, feeling the sharp pain again where the stitches were. She opens the wardrobe and wedges the note into the little gap between the trim and the plaster.

The night air hangs heavily in the flat. She lies on the bed, still keeping to her side even without Frankie. There is a crusted patch where her milk has dried on the sheets and she reminds herself to wash them in the morning.

In her dreams she follows the highway south to Adelaide River, her face pressed against the glass, Manyuk asleep in her lap and the hollowness inside her gradually filling until she can hardly bear it anymore.

Review of Australian Fiction

Publication Details

Melissa Beit's 'The Three Treasures' appeared as 'The Uncarved Block' in the anthology *Still Life* (2015).

Jo Case's 'Something Wild' appeared in the *Big Issue*, no. 491, 14–27 August 2015.

Nick Couldwell's 'The Same Weight as a Human Heart' appeared in *Westerly*, vol. 60 (1), July 2015.

Jennifer Down's 'Aokigahara' was published in the *Australian Book Review*, no. 364, September 2014.

Goldie Goldbloom's 'The Pilgrim's Way' appeared in *Meanjin*, vol. 73 (4), 2014.

Balli Kaur Jaswal's 'Better Things' appeared in *Meanjin*, vol. 75 (1), 2015.

Cate Kennedy's 'Puppet Show' appeared in *Review of Australian Fiction*, vol. 13 (1), 2015.

Sarah Klenbort's 'Into the Woods' appeared in *Overland*, no. 216, 2014.

Julie Koh's 'The Level Playing Field' appeared in *Capital Misfits* (Spineless Wonders, 2015).

Jo Lennan's 'How Is Your Great Life?' appeared in *Meanjin*, vol. 73 (4), 2014.

Eleanor Limprecht's 'On Ice' appeared in *Kill Your Darlings*, October 2014.

Gay Lynch's 'The Abduction of Ganymede' appeared in *Breaking Beauty* (MidnightSun Publishing, 2015).

Colin Oehring's 'Little Toki' appeared in *Meanjin*, vol. 74 (2), 2015.

Ryan O'Neill's 'Alphabet' appeared in the *Monthly*, March 2015.

Omar Musa's 'Supernova' appeared in the *Griffith REVIEW*, 49.

John A. Scott's 'Picasso: A Shorter Life' appeared in *Southerly*, vol. 74 (3).

Mark Smith's 'Manyuk' appeared in *Review of Australian Fiction*, vol. 14 (3), 2015.

Notes on Contributors

The Editor

Amanda Lohrey is the author of the acclaimed novels *Camille's Bread, The Morality of Gentlemen, The Reading Group* and *The Philosopher's Doll,* as well as the novella *Vertigo* (2008) and the award-winning short story collection *Reading Madame Bovary* (2010). She has also written two Quarterly Essays: *Groundswell* and *Voting for Jesus.* In 2012 she was awarded the Patrick White Literary Award. Her latest novel is *A Short History of Richard Kline* (2014).

The Authors

Melissa Beit has had stories published in the *Big Issue, Southerly, Meanjin,* the *Sleepers Almanac,* the *Australian Women's Weekly* and various national and international anthologies including *New Australian Stories.* She lives in coastal New South Wales.

Jo Case is the author of *Boomer and Me: A Memoir of Motherhood, and Asperger's,* which was shortlisted for the 2015 Russell Prize for Humour Writing. She is Program Manager at the Melbourne Writers Festival, and a freelance writer and reviewer.

Claire Corbett has been published by *Griffith REVIEW, Spineless Wonders, Overland, Southerly* and *Antipodes.* Her first novel, *When*

We Have Wings, was shortlisted for the 2012 Barbara Jefferies Award and the 2012 Ned Kelly Award for Best First Fiction. She is currently completing her second novel.

Nick Couldwell has been published in *Visible Ink, Writing to the Edge, Seizure, Westerly, Northerly, Out of Place* and *Award Winning Australian Writing.* Nick has a Diploma of Professional Writing and Editing from RMIT and lives in Byron Bay with his partner and two daughters.

Jennifer Down is a writer and editor from Melbourne. Her work has appeared in the *Sydney Morning Herald,* the *Saturday Paper,* the *Lifted Brow* and *Overland.* Her first novel, *Our Magic Hour* will be published in 2016. 'Aokigahara' won the 2014 *ABR* Elizabeth Jolley Short Story Award.

Goldie Goldbloom's first novel, *The Paperbark Shoe,* was awarded the AWP Novel Award and IndieFab Novel of the Year. Her collections, *You Lose These* (2011) and *The Grief of the Body* (forthcoming) include many prize-winning stories. She has been granted NEA, Dora Maar and Rona Jaffe fellowships. Goldie teaches fiction at the University of Chicago.

Balli Kaur Jaswal was a high school teacher in Melbourne for five years. She has received fellowships from the University of East Anglia and Nanyang Technological University. In 2014, she was named Best Young Australian Novelist by the *Sydney Morning Herald* for her debut novel, *Inheritance.* She lives in Istanbul, Turkey.

Cate Kennedy writes fiction, poetry and non-fiction, and is currently working on a second novel. She has authored two collections of short stories, *Dark Roots* and *Like a House on Fire. Dark Roots* is currently on the Victorian VCE syllabus. She lives in regional Victoria.

Sarah Klenbort is a casual academic and writer based in Sydney. She is currently looking for a home for her novel. Next year Sarah will travel around Australia in a pop-up camper trailer with her Welsh husband and two girls, eight and four. Starting at the Deaf Games in Adelaide, they will then visit Deaf schools around the country, interviewing members of the Deaf community and writing about their language: Auslan.

Julie Koh (許瑩玲) studied politics and law at the University of Sydney, where she won the Hedley Bull Prize in International Politics. Her short stories have appeared in *Kyoto Journal*, the *Fish Anthology*, the *Sleepers Almanac*, the *Lifted Brow* and *Seizure Online*. Her first collection, *Capital Misfits*, was published in April 2015. UQP will publish her second collection in 2016.

Jo Lennan has published short stories in Australia and the United Kingdom. She studied in Sydney, Japan and Oxford, and has worked as a lawyer and journalist. Her reportage appears in *Time*, the *Economist*, *Intelligent Life* and the *Monthly*.

Eleanor Limprecht's first novel, *What Was Left*, was shortlisted for the ALS Gold Medal. Her second novel, *Long Bay*, was released in 2015. She also writes short stories, essays and book reviews. Eleanor was born the United States and raised in Germany, Pakistan and the US. She now lives in Sydney.

Gay Lynch is a writer, editor and teacher of English and creative writing at Flinders University. She has published *Apocryphal and Literary Influences on Galway Diasporic History* (2010), *Cleanskin* (2006), an adult psycho-fem-thriller, short stories, educational children's texts and academic papers. She is currently working on a historical novel.

Colin Oehring's fiction has appeared in the *Review of Australian Fiction*, *Island*, *Meanjin* and the *Australian Literary Review*. He lives in Melbourne.

Ryan O'Neill is a short story writer. His latest collection *The Weight of a Human Heart* is published by Black Inc.

Omar Musa is a Malaysian-Australian author, rapper and poet from Queanbeyan, Australia. His debut novel *Here Come the Dogs* was longlisted for the Miles Franklin Award and he was named one of the *Sydney Morning Herald*'s Young Novelists of the Year in 2015.

Nicola Redhouse is a writer and book editor. Her fiction has been published in *Best Australian Stories* (2014), *Meanjin, Kill Your Darlings, Wet Ink,* and *harvest,* and her non-fiction in the *Big Issue, Indigo* and *RealTime.*

John A. Scott's writing has been published internationally, twice shortlisted for the Miles Franklin, and received two Victorian Premier's Prizes. A major experimental novel, *N,* was published in 2014. He is currently working on a book-length series of poems, *Barbarous Sideshow,* which resurrects an abandoned project dating from 1967.

Mark Smith lives on Victoria's west coast. His writing has appeared in *Best Australian Stories* (2014), the *Big Issue* and *Review of Australian Fiction,* among others, and he has won a number of awards, including the 2015 Josephine Ulrick Literature Prize. His novel *The Road To Winter* will be released in July 2016.

Annette Trevitt grew up in northern New South Wales. Her short stories have been published in literary magazines and broadcast on ABC radio and by the BBC. She teaches short fiction and screenwriting in a professional writing and editing program. She lives in Melbourne with her son, Marlon.